W9-BZF-073

MORE CRITICAL ACCLAIM FOR
Birds of Paradise Lost

Grandma is in the freezer, there's Zoloft in the chicken curry, and a man is on fire in Washington D.C. The immigrant story will never be the same again now that it's gone through Andrew Lam's prose—razor-tongued, sophisticated, achingly aware of where it comes from but never imprisoned by its memory. Lam takes the traditional immigrant story and set it ablaze and then serenely rescues from its burning embers what had been there all along—the all-American story.
—**Sandip Roy**, commentator, *Morning Edition*, National Public Radio

These poignant, sometimes humorous, often heart-rending stories gift us with the voices and faces of the Vietnamese-American community: a community that has finally been able to express itself through the fiction of a new generation of writers such as Andrew Lam. Yet this is also fiction which in its universal and human truths pulls off the delicate trick of both including and transcending the ethnic genre and firmly situates Lam among the best writers of American—and world—literature.
—**Wayne Karlin**, author of *Wandering Souls: Journeys with the Dead and the Living in Viet Nam*

As a fellow Vietnamese American, I don't read Andrew Lam's stories; I experience them. There are very few writers who can achieve this for me; Andrew can.
—**Lac Su**, author of *I Love Yous Are for White People*

After reading *Birds of Paradise Lost*, it feels as if one has been to the opera. This is a work drenched in color and music, sorrow and beauty. The intensity of emotion conveyed in these pages is stunning. A bravura performance.
—**Lori Marie Carlson**, author of *The Sunday Tertulia*

Andrew Lam is one of a handful of writers who are truly necessary to the emotional and intellectual health of American culture today. Whether exploring the contemporary political ironies of the streets, the fates of individual victims of war, or the indefinable tenderness between lovers, his stories show us truth we may have turned away from or never recognized. Lam's stories go deep and stay with you a long time.

—**Frank Stewart**, Editor, *Manoa: A Pacific Journal of International Writing*

Loss, longing, the riotous, the incongruous: There is nothing predictable here. Lam revels in the unexpected and makes it his country.

—**Gish Jen**, author of *World and Town*

While Andrew Lam's characters share a broader history, each story is an entire world that Lam animates fully with remarkably spare strokes. What these stories have in common is the intelligence behind them, which is at once fierce, compassionate, and wonderfully perverse. Each story pleases and surprises, and the collection as a whole resonates long after the reading is done.

—**Elise Blackwell**, author of *Hunger*

Birds of Paradise Lost

stories by

Andrew Lam

 Red Hen Press | *Pasadena, CA*

Birds of Paradise Lost
Copyright © 2013 by Andrew Lam
All Rights Reserved

No part of this book may be used or reproduced in any manner whatso-
ever without the prior written permission of both the publisher and the
copyright owner.

Book design and layout by David Rose

Library of Congress Cataloging-in-Publication Data
Lam, Andrew.
  Birds of paradise lost : stories / by Andrew Lam.—1st ed.
    p. cm.
  ISBN 978-1-59709-268-5 (alk. paper)
  I. Title.
  PS3612.A54328B57 2013
  813'.6—dc23
                       2012023849

The National Endowment for the Arts, the Los Angeles County Arts
Commission, the Los Angeles Department of Cultural Affairs, the
Dwight Stuart Youth Fund, the Pasadena Arts & Culture Commission
and the City of Pasadena Cultural Affairs Division, Sony Pictures Enter-
tainment, and the Ahmanson Foundation partially support Red Hen
Press.

First Edition
Published by Red Hen Press
www.redhen.org

Acknowledgments

Thank you to the following publications where these works were first published:

PUBLICATIONS

Amerasia Journal, "Grandma's Tales"; *Arts and Letters,* "Everything Must Go"; *Asia Literary Review,* "Close to the Bone"; *Crab Orchard Review,* "Show & Tell"; *Glassworks Magazine,* "Slingshot"; *Manoa Journal,* "Birds of Paradise Lost" as "Fire," "Love Leather"; *Michigan Quarterly Review,* "Hunger"; *New Sudden Fiction: Short-Short Stories and Beyond,* "The Palmist"; *Writing on the Edge Literary Journal,* "Sister"; and *ZYZZYVA,* "Slingshot," "Yacht People."

ANTHOLOGIES

Bold Words: A Century of Asian American Writing, "Show & Tell"; *Growing Up Poor,* "Show & Tell"; *Language Lessons: Stories for Teaching and Learning English,* "Show & Tell"; *Legacies: Fiction, Poetry, Drama, Non-Fiction,* "The Palmist"; *Literature Without Borders: International Literature in English For Student Writers,* "Grandma's Tales"; *Novel Strategies: A Guide to Effective College Reading,* "The Palmist"; *Once Upon A Dream,* "Grandma's Tales," "Slingshot"; *The Perfume River: An Anthology of Writing from Vietnam,* "The Palmist"; *Selected Shorts: A Touch of Magic,* "The Palmist"; *Sudden Fiction International,* "Grandma's Tales"; *Watermark: Vietnamese-American Poetry and Prose,* "Grandma's Tales," "Show & Tell"; and *Where Are You From?: An Anthology of Asian American Writing (Volume 1),* "Yacht People."

SOUND RECORDINGS

Selected Shorts: A Touch of Magic, "The Palmist," performed by James Naughton, recorded on June 26, 2011, Symphony Space, October 1, 2009, Compact Disc.

I wish to express my deep gratitude to my friends Susan Palo and Eric Schroeder, who pored over the manuscript at the last minute, then, to top it off, fed me. I also owe a great debt of gratitude to Sandy Close, Richard Rodriguez, and the late Franz Schurmann, editors at Pacific News Service, who believed in my writing long before I did. I'd like to thank all my creative writing classmates at San Francisco State University all those years ago, and my creative writing professors—Michael Rubin, Molly Giles, Charlotte Painter, and Fenton Johnson—who encouraged me to continue writing. I cannot ask for a better writing teacher than Professor John L'Heureux at Stanford, who made me look at prose in a brand new way during my wonderful year as a Knight Journalism Fellow. I also wish to acknowledge the enthusiastic support of my friends— Kevin, Gioi, Steven, Tim, Ming, Don, Isabelle, Richard, Milbert, Robin, Scott, Shawn, David, Dennis, Randy—who make writing less lonely a task than it usually is.

Lastly and most importantly, I owe an enormous debt to my family and extended family and the Vietnamese American community. Their joy, sadness, and triumphs continue to nurture my life and my literary inspirations.

—Andrew Lam

For my mother, whose memories of the floating world are fading, but not her knack for spinning a yarn.

Contents

*Anything is bearable as long as you can
make a story out of it . . .*

—M. Scott Momaday

Love Leather

Mr. Le looked up one morning from mending a vest at the Love Leather and saw a very good-looking Asian kid, his oldest grandson's age, maybe, seventeen at the most, staring quizzically at him from the sidewalk. When their eyes met through the glass pane, the boy's ruddy cheeks turned a deeper shade of red and Mr. Le had to look away.

Behind him, Steven commented, "Ooh, a hotty! If he comes in—baby, hide the dildos! We'll have to shoo our twink for browsing too long." Then he offered his trademark baritone Lou Rawls guffaw, "Hahhahah, hahr, hahr." "Personally, Mr. Lee," Steven added, "I wouldn't touch him with a ten-inch pole, know what I'm saying? Not 'less I want to be somebody's bitch in the slammer in a hurry."

Mr. Le turned around. "Slammer? Shoe?" he asked, adjusting his glasses. "Sorry. I don't know this slammer and this shoe you say, Steven."

"Oh, honey, don't be. I'm sorry," Steven said, slower this time, and with mild exasperation. "Shoo—SHOO, as in, 'chase out

1

somebody.' As in 'shoo, you crazy sex pig, shoo, get off me!' Slammer is 'jail.' You know, 'prison,' like your re-ed camp? And a 'twink' is someone too young, underage, you know? Hairless, smooth, smells like milk? And 'being somebody's bitch in jail' means . . . oh, never you mind what it means."

An inveterate note taker, Mr. Le committed "slammer" and "shoo, SHOO," to his growing vocabulary, to be written down later in his spiral notebook during lunch break. When he looked back out the window, the twink was gone. He already knew "twink." And "dildos" he learned right away that first day when he asked Roger Briggs, the store owner, about them. In a controlled tone, and as he intermittently cleared his throat, Roger Briggs told Mr. Le about their usage, including those with batteries. When Roger left, Steven thanked Mr. Le profusely. "That was simply precious," he said, laughing, clasping his hands as if in prayer. "You made RB squirm."

Roger Briggs, a big, tall man, with most of his blond hair thinned out and a beer belly, once served in the 101st Airborne Division in Nam. He remembered enough Vietnamese to say "Let's love each other in the bathroom" and "How much for the entire night?" When Roger said the latter in Vietnamese, Mr. Le inevitably laughed, though why, exactly, he couldn't say. Most likely, it was because Roger said it in a toneless accent, and it sounded almost as if someone wanted to buy the night itself.

Still, whenever he listened to Roger Briggs talk of wartime Vietnam, Mr. Le would often get the feeling that another Saigon had gone on right under his nose. Were there many Vietnamese homosexuals? And were they finding one another in the dark alleys and behind tall, protective flame trees?

Roger—who was once very handsome and fit when he roamed the Saigon boulevards at night, and who read entire biographies from furtive glances in the moonlight—said yes. "There are many versions of any one city," he said, his eyes dreamy with memories. There was another Saigon that Mr. Le didn't know, a Vietnam of hurried, desperate sex, of bite marks, bruised lips, clawed backs, and salty sweaty nights and punch-in-the-mouth morning denials, and of unrequited love between fighting men that was just as painful as shrapnel wounds. Just as there was another version of San Francisco that Mr. Le couldn't possibly have imagined when he was reading his *English For Today!* textbooks years ago, dreaming of the majestic Golden Gate Bridge and the cling-clanging cable cars climbing up fabled hills.

Mr. Le's last name is pronounced Lay, but Steven liked Lee better, and somehow it stuck. If Roger Briggs corrected Steven half a dozen times since he hired Mr. Le, who had extensive experience working with leather, it was to no avail.

Steven was "poz," he told Mr. Le right away that first day at work, and his mind was out of control half the time because of some "cocktail." It made him "a chattypatty," and "so please, Mr. Lee, don't you mind my rambling roses." A few days later Steven mentioned AIDS again, but sounded oddly upbeat: "I'm kept alive by a drug cocktail! Imagine that, Honey Lee. Too many cocktails unsafed me. But now? Now, gotta have me three a day— that's three, to keep me a-go-goin'. Well, honey, make mine a cosmo, please!" Then he laughed his Lou Rawls laugh, "Hahhahhaaahhaah."

Were Mr. Le to run the place, it'd be very different. For one thing, Steven was bad at math and shouldn't be working the register but peddling leather goods to customers. He would have an assistant make some of the leather pieces at the Love Leather rather than order everything from a factory. He would offer wallets and purses as well, and not just chaps and harnesses. If there was one thing he knew besides working with leather, it was running a business. Back in Vietnam, during the war, Mr. Le was considered prosperous. A three-story villa in District 3, four servants, a Citroën, two shops— the main one in Saigon, on Rue Catina, no less, the other near the Hoa Binh market in the lovely hill town resort of Dalat—and a small factory making leather goods at the edge of town, employing over twenty workers. Not bad for a man in his late thirties. That was, of course, before he was deemed a member of the bourgeois class by the new regime and ended up spending close to four years in a re-education camp after the war ended.

When he got out, almost everything he owned was gone. The villa, the factory, the two stores—along with his beloved gray

Citroën—were replaced by two rusty bicycles and a small, one-room studio in a mold-infested building near Cho Lon, the old Chinatown section. His wife and three children peddled wonton noodles at a little stand, and the family worked tirelessly on the street to scrape together enough money to buy a seat on a fishing boat for their only son to escape. Vietnam had invaded Cambodia, and the boy was facing the draft. Older boys from the neighborhood were already coming back maimed or in coffins. Their son escaped and, three years and a few refugee camps later, managed to get to America. It took another dozen years after that for him to sponsor Mr. Le and his wife and one of their two daughters. The older, married with a family of her own in Vietnam, was ineligible to be sponsored by her brother.

If he could, even now at fifty-seven, Mr. Le would start his business again. He was saving money, taking notes, and talking to potential investors, including Mrs. Tu, their neighbor and landlord. Mrs. Tu was rich, the owner of the popular Cicada Pavilion restaurant on Geary and 7th and a five-story apartment building. If he had a successful business, he could send his two grandsons in Vietnam to college in America. He could even fly his eldest daughter over for visits.

But to start all over again—what a dream! He wasn't taking notes for nothing. It depended on the support of his family, especially Mrs. Le, and serious business backers. Alas, he was targeting a clientele with an income as disposable as their penchant for kinky sex. His dream would make anyone he knew, with perhaps the exception of Mrs. Tu, a widow who was targeting him, more than a little queasy.

At home, his wife said in Vietnamese: "*Minh a*, how are those *lai cai*? They're fondling you?" Then she laughed her girlish laugh. Her hair was almost half gray, but Mrs. Le's laughter always had a certain twang that would send Mr. Le reeling back to the past, to a happier time before the war, before they were married, teenagers too shy to touch. He sat at the kitchen table in their San Francisco apartment with the partial view of the Bank of America building, but he was also walking down the tamarind-tree-lined boulevard near the high school when they first met. That was in Can Tho, a sizable town in the Mekong Delta where he'd spent two years courting her. Back then there was no hand-holding, not even when you desperately wanted to. Mr. Le was extra shy. For about half a year he trailed a few meters behind her and her laughing girlfriends.

Then one day, opportunity knocked. She was alone. It had been raining, and the straw flower attached to the tip of her stylish purple umbrella fell off. She didn't see it and kept walking. Mr. Le picked it up from the mud, cleaned it with his handkerchief, and went to her. In a stammering voice, he offered to tie the flower back on. The future Mrs. Le blushed and nodded but couldn't manage a word. It didn't help very much that her first name is Hoa, which literally means "flower," and there he was holding one in his hand, hers to be exact. Under the pouring rain he stood trying to put the flower back on, shivering. They started walking side by side the next day, and, after months of courtship and enough bad love poetry to fill a small book, finally held hands.

"Why, what if they are? *Minh oi*, jealous?" Mr. Le teased as he looked at his wife, still thinking of her umbrella and that small straw flower that got them together. Then in a rather mischievous voice, he added: "So, what do you think, my little flower? Should I bring home one of those rubber things for you to play with?"

Mrs. Le shrieked and covered her mouth. She looked out the window to Mrs. Tu's apartment across the courtyard and drew the curtain. She had seen the rubber dildos from the shop, had in fact helped him with his work on the weekend when she could spare time from her garment factory job, but the idea of having a large rubber dildo in their apartment, even as a prank, was too hilarious and far too shocking to entertain. What if their son and his wife saw the thing in one of the drawers, say, by accident, when they visited from San Jose? What if their second daughter came home from college in Houston? What if their long dead ancestors who stared out from the faded black-and-white photographs on the altar could see the thing? And what if Mrs. Tu came over—uninvited as always?

When she calmed down, Mrs. Le deadpanned: *"Minh a*, it's called dildo. If you bring one back, I'll beat you with it." Mrs. Le found it liberating to slip in a few dirty words in English in the middle of her Vietnamese sentences. She could never swear in Vietnamese. Dirty words would not fall from her tongue. But since her husband started work at Love Leather, she'd learned many dirty words from his notebook, and the two, like giggly teenagers, had been using them with each other with gusto when alone.

One day, at the bottom of a page on the subject of sadomasochism, she found her husband's meditation on the Vietnamese word *minh*, which both she and Mr. Le were fond of using.

"Don't know why, but Steven's 'sadomasochism' reminds me of the word '*minh*.' It's a difficult word to explain. *"Minh oi"* literally means, 'oh body.' What it intends: 'my dear husband,' or 'my dear wife,' depending on who the speaker is. How to explain the usage of this word to Steven? The self, when loved, is shared, no longer singular, the self a bridge to another. '*Minh*' can be 'you,' '*minh*' can be 'me,' '*minh*' can be 'us,' all depending on the context— your body is mine is yours is ours, as long as we exist in an intimate circle. Also consider: '*Nha minh*': 'Our house,' or 'our family.' You and I, through love, and its consequences, are connected in a way that bonds beyond sex, beyond shared flesh—a communion of souls."

When she read this passage, Mrs. Le was moved to tears and resolved not to read Mr. Le's notebook again. America—what a shock to the system! This whole subculture, its obsession with sex and youth and physical attributes and—more curiously—the penis, was all very perverse to her. Until her arrival in America, she lived in a world where the genitals never hovered in the imagination beyond a curse word or a dirty joke. It seemed to her American culture forced one's eyes upon them, and now she, who couldn't resist flipping Mr. Le's new pages to find out what he'd been up to at the shop, had been slowly poisoned by it.

STEVEN FOUND OUT one day that the Asian kid's name was Douglas, Douglas Kim, and he was of legal age, barely. "He browsed and he browsed—and he browsed," Steven reported breathlessly. "In the end he bought some Liquid Silk. He's a talker, that one. He was afraid to talk before 'cuz you were around. Asked me if you were gay. I said, 'Pshaw, honey, Mr. Lee is as gay as Liberace is butch. But if you need him to fix your penis harness or chastity belt, well, he's your man.' "

"Liberty?" asked Mr. Le, reaching for his notebook. "Bush?"

"No. Liberace. And definitely not Bush. Butch. BUTCH. You know, macho, strong, like . . . I don't know . . . Barbara Stanwyck."

Mr. Le remembered Barbara Stanwyck. His favorite movie of hers was *Bitter Tea of General Yen*. In it she played a missionary captured by a powerful Chinese man and, despite her resentment and the horror of his cruelty, fell in love with him. He even remembered the TV show *The Big Valley* on the American television channel in Saigon during the war. Although dark-skinned, Steven had her air, and the same dramatic flair. "Steven," Mr. Le offered, "I think you're butch. You're too good teacher."

Steven waved his hand, pretending to be bashful. "Oh pshaw, Mr. Lee, I might be very, very beautiful, especially my Angie Dickinson legs, but I'm no teacher. And I'm certainly not butch. Just a burned-out queen sitting on the dock of the bay." Then he started humming and gyrating.

Mr. Le, befuddled, watched Steven perform behind the cash register and wondered if too much freedom could lead you astray. This had been unimaginable to him as he hustled and bled and scrimped for enough money to buy passage on that rickety boat for his son to escape, dreaming of another America. But back then the dream was vague and defined by what Vietnam was not. America was safe. America was hope. America was where you don't step on land mines or disappear in the dark of night. It certainly did not take the form of the wanton, unmitigated desires of Love Leather.

One afternoon a week later, Mr. Le turned around and saw Douglas Kim at the other end of the store, where the porn rags and dildos and leather toys were on display. Mr. Le could see the kid's hands in his jean pockets making fists as he leaned forward to study the dildos and magazine covers. The boy's clothing was so loose his blue boxer shorts were showing. And the way his pant legs draped over his tennis shoes seemed like an accident waiting to happen.

Meanwhile, from behind the cash register, Steven pointed conspiratorially at the kid's back and mouthed silently to Mr. Le, "Hide the dildos!" then giggled into his hand.

Douglas Kim turned. Their eyes met briefly. The boy looked away immediately. In a fraction of a second Mr. Le saw all at once resentment, shame, lust, and confusion in the boy's eyes, and perhaps something else, too: defiance.

The kid avoided looking in Mr. Le's direction after that, but Mr. Le intermittently glanced at his back. He imagined he could hear the boy's nervous breathing over Steven's palpitating music. He thought of his oldest grandson in Saigon and wondered if the boy was doing as well as he had boasted on the phone to him last week. He would, if he could, give Douglas Kim a scolding. No kid should come in a place like this. He contemplated talking to him, then Roger Briggs walked in and, instead of saying hello to his employees, immediately zeroed in on Douglas Kim. Mr. Le flipped through his notebook, trying to remember the words. As Roger's hand descended on the boy's small back, Mr. Le remembered the words. He stared at the boy's neck and whispered, "Shoo. Twink. Shoo."

IN HER LIVING ROOM one bright Sunday afternoon with the windows wide open, Mrs. Tu, whose satin peach pajamas matched her swaying curtains, popped the deal as she poured chrysanthemum tea for her neighbors and tenants. "Brother, sister, now listen. Mr. Ba in Salinas, who runs a little factory making leather bags and jackets, just told me he's very interested in helping out if we buy Love Leather. What do you think: I put in eighty and you come up with twenty? We'll split fifty-fifty, counting your skills and labors as the other thirty percent. With your skills, brother, and Mr. Ba's, we will sell those knickknacks for half what those leather stores are charging their customers—it's a winner. Of course, I can easily put in the hundred, that's not a problem. But I want you to have a stake in it, you understand, so that you're co-owners, not my workers. We're like family, after all."

Mrs. Le paused from drinking her tea and looked at Mrs. Tu for a full second. Xing-Xing, Mrs. Tu's white cat, had leapt onto his owner's lap and was now purring under attentive, stroking fingers. "Sister, you're serious? What you offer us sounds very generous, but you know where he works, who the customers are, don't you?" It was a rhetorical question. It was Mrs. Tu, after all, who had bragged to Roger Briggs, a regular at her restaurant, about Mr. Le's skills with leather.

Mrs. Tu was ready. "*Lai cai* clientele? Their money is as good as anybody else's. There are *lai cai* and *lai duc* couples in this building, some of the best tenants I ever had. *Lai duc, lai cai.* Makes no difference in business, as long as the business is *lai loi.*" Then she laughed at her own joke. *Lai duc* in Vietnamese is slang for "lesbian." *Lai loi,* on the other hand, means "making a profit"—Mrs. Tu's witty way of rhyming gays and lesbians with money.

Mr. Le started to laugh, too, but stopped short when Mrs. Le gave him a look that could have frozen the chrysanthemum in his cup. Mrs. Le gestured to the big mahogany cabinet, which was graced by photos of Mrs. Tu's grandparents, her parents, and her two husbands, the last one an aged American who had left her the building. A large bowl full of burnt incense sticks sat in front. "Sister, I know you are modern, but you are at heart traditional. If you invest in that place, wouldn't it mean you and I both having to help my husband on a regular basis to keep the business going?"

"I look forward to it." Mrs. Tu took pride in the fact that she came to America not as a refugee but as the wife of a midlevel Vietnamese diplomat during the war. "As for modernity, I'm Vietnamese, but I'm very modern. Must the two have to be contradictory? As you know, I studied French in Vietnam at Marie Curie and then Vietnamese literature at Saigon University. *Alors moi, je m'en fous totalement ce qu'ils font les homosexuels.*"

Mr. Le understood French but his wife's was at best rusty. He was about to explain to her what Mrs. Tu just said, but thought the better of it. He acted calm, but he could feel his heart beating wildly in his chest. If he was half-consciously currying Mrs. Tu's favor, he still hadn't expected this windfall of a proposal, this soon. Yet there it was, looming near the horizon, Love Leather, soon to be his. He could see it—money for the grandchildren, the entire family in one place. He could taste this dream in the bittersweet aftertaste of the tea.

"I'm not as modern as you, sister," Mrs. Le said presently in a cold, slightly sarcastic tone. "But I'm open-minded just the same. I'm not worried about *lai duc, lai cai* either. My husband and I love and trust each other. Why else would I agree to have him work with them when you told us about the job? If anyone can seduce my husband, let me tell you, that person must possess magic charms because our love—"

Mrs. Tu didn't let her finish. She clapped her hands once and Xing-Xing jerked his head up, eyes wide and alert. "Of course you are. Of course you're open-minded, sister. Why else would I propose it?" Mrs. Tu smiled as if everything had been agreed upon, the business settled. But the smile stayed a bit too long on her face, which now blushed brightly.

Mrs. Tu's face reminded Mr. Le of people who felt the exact opposite—hurt and embarrassed. He felt sorry for her and quickly looked down to study his empty teacup. When he did so, however, he incurred the wrath of his landlord. "Brother," Mrs. Tu said, looking at him, "I hear they have some kind of festival next month. We should all go and see what it's like, the lifestyle of our clients. I believe it's quite sexually liberating." She was still smiling. "And afterward, I would love to treat you both to a fancy dinner at the Pavilion."

"It's called Folsom Street Fair," he said weakly. Though he hadn't seen the festival himself, he'd seen the photo album Steven kept from the previous years. Images swam in his head of near naked women in leather bras and leather thongs and overweight men in leather chaps and harnesses, their butt cheeks showing. And then there were the photos of Steven, who had gone the year before as a Marilyn Monroe in a blond wig. "Not a good idea," he added.

"Oh? Why not?" Mrs. Tu feigned disappointment. She looked over to Mrs. Le as if they were chummy and Mr. Le was spoiling their fun. "If we are going to sell these knickknacks to them, we need to face these people sooner or later. They may be sex addicts, but they are sex addicts with disposable income. I've seen them. Harmless fun, that's all." Then she dropped the clincher. "Trust me, you two, if there's one thing I know well, it's making money. Roger Briggs is inept. That store, well managed with cheap supplies and with good advertising, could bring the rest of your family over in three years, guaranteed."

Mrs. Le, who knew nothing of the fair, but was familiar with business dealings, put her teacup and saucer down so they wouldn't rattle. Then, her dark, steely eyes slowly met Mrs. Tu's. "Eighty five-fifteen," she calmly announced.

"Goodness, sister, how marvelous! You never talked business to me before, but I can see, honestly, that you're good at it. But let's talk about details later, how we share," Mrs. Tu said and looked for a reaction from Mrs. Le. "In business, it's relationships that you've got to build. So first we should check out the clientele, *n'est-ce pas?*"

"*N'est-ce pas!*" harrumphed Mrs. Le, her face flushed with emotions. For some time now she had been staring at the well-mended tear in Mrs. Tu's fleshy leather couch, where the cat had caused much damage the month before, now barely visible. "It's a date," she said. Her voice was cold but her body trembled slightly. "It's not as if I haven't seen dildos and butt plugs and cock rings and dykes on bikes! My husband taught me everything." When she said "dykes on bikes," Mrs. Le's voice rang out despite her effort to hold herself in. Mr. Le supposed it was his wife's version of French, for it caused Mrs. Tu to involuntarily clutch at Xing-Xing's neck and pull his face backward to reveal an expression he'd never seen before on a cat: that of utter astonishment.

My wife, he decided, shaking his head slightly, feeling strangely amorous, is very, very butch.

A WEEK BEFORE the festival, however, Mr. Le fretted. He couldn't concentrate at work. The feud between the two women occupied him. He fretted about what his wife would see. Worse, he didn't know how to fend off Mrs. Tu, whose love seat, she told him, had a new tear that needed mending, and she was in need of his assistance.

When Steven asked Mr. Le if he had been in the army, he could barely hear him. "Bet you were a stud," Steven said. "Yeah, you in uniform. Hmm hmmhmm, I can see it now. All the girls in those pretty slit-up oriental dresses and some of the boys in theirs, all hot and bothered when you parade by."

"My brother and me were soldiers, yes. I was soldier for three years. I get shot in leg, they let me out." Mr. Le paused from putting a new zipper onto a pair of leather pants and pointed at his right thigh. Then he added, choking, "My brother, not so lucky."

There was a long, awkward silence between them.

"You know, Mr. Lee, I've been thinking. I'm a refugee, too," Steven said. Mr. Le looked at him, fixing his glasses.

"I'm serious now," Steven said. "I fled from my God-fearing old man's crazy Mississippi shit. It was not the beating; every kid I knew got whopped. Hell, I even fancied myself a preacher when I was young, if you can believe it. No, I ain't afraid of his belt, you know what I'm saying? Just that way he looked at me when he found me out and wished his faggot son was dead. So I ran. Then here, I made real good friends but lost half to AIDS, and they were more family to me than my family ever was. So I figured it's kind of like a war, too, you know, what I went through. I'm serious now."

Steven's voice was sad and low, but Mr. Le only nodded and said nothing. AIDS is not the same as war, he was thinking, not even close. People with AIDS at least knew carnal pleasure, which in the end was what killed many of them. People who died under bombs died right away or soon thereafter from their wounds. They don't dance behind cash registers to trance music talking up a storm. They die without saying goodbye to loved ones, in horror and screaming and in anguish. Bombs and bullets give you no time.

"My brother was very young. He was just a twink," Mr. Le offered.

Steven stifled a laugh, and Mr. Le looked at him sternly. He could tell when his coworker was thinking something naughty. It was there in the eyes. "Well, that's a shame!" Steven said. "But maybe some of his army buddies gave him a good time before the end."

Mr. Le slammed the pair of scissors he was holding onto the worktable. "Not everything in life is sex, Steven," he said evenly.

"No," Steven's voice rose to meet his. "But everyone's ruled by some kind of desire."

Mr. Le frowned. But Steven backed down quickly, his voice barely a whisper, "Hey, Mr. Lee, listen, I didn't mean anything by it. Mr. Lee, you can write down in your little notebook there that Steven is a royal jackass. That's JACK-ASS. Honey, write down that his sorry-ass libido runs amok."

Mr. Le didn't say anything. He took off his glasses and turned to look out the window. For some reason, he half expected to see Douglas Kim looking in. But all he saw was a sun-drenched street. That was when he felt Steven's hands on his shoulders, the warmth passing through his shirt. Up close, Steven had a distinctive smell, not unpleasant exactly, but powerful and salty. It vaguely reminded Mr. Le of freshly turned earth. "Libido. LIBIDO is sex drive, pure lust and desire; it's what makes someone a fool of his old self," Steven murmured quietly above Mr. Le. "I never had any control, Mr. Lee. I've always been a fool. Fool for love. And look where it gets me."

With his mind's eye, Mr. Le checked himself. No arousal, no sexual feelings, no fear, no quickening rhythm of the heart. Rather, the opposite: lethargy settled in. Steven's kneading was comforting; he felt tired all of a sudden. He opened and closed his fists, his fingers aching from the leatherwork. He wanted to laugh. He thought of how he struggled so hard all his life—of the horrors he'd seen, the war, the re-education camp where real whipping tore many a dissident's flesh and left horrid scars, and now he found himself in a childish, ridiculously genitalia-obsessed world, where whips rarely leave a mark but the pain and suffering are hyperbolized, become theatrics—yet, how odd that this was going to fulfill his hopes and dreams to reunite his family.

"Relax," cooed Steven. Mr. Le yawned and closed his eyes. "Relax." And Mr. Le saw that he'd somehow turned into a bird flying across a mysterious ocean, and there was no land in sight.

Ode To Flower

The poetry of the flower
Tis the hardest to write
Her admirer sits at the dawn hour
Beguiled by her beauty, fueled by her light

Months later, no matter where he is, Mr. Le remembers with absolute clarity the way he stood at the fair, in a white shirt with the sleeves rolled up at the elbows, his arms outstretched as if he were a traffic cop at an intersection. His glasses have disappeared in the scuffle. Behind him stands Roger Briggs in an opened black leather vest, stomach protruding, his cat-o'-nine-tails raised high in the air. In front of him stands Mrs. Le, pushing toward Briggs, her face enraged, her folded parasol also raised, ready to counter Roger's attack. To his left, a naked Douglas Kim lies bent over a sawhorse, wrists bound to ankles, his buttocks striped with red marks. He is turning sideways and looking up at Mr. Le.

Farther out, Mrs. Tu stands with the staring crowd, her mouth agape, her eyes wide with fear. Most striking to Mr. Le, however, is Steven. He is wearing a sort of adult diaper, holding a bow and arrow, a pair of strapped-on wings protruding from behind his bony shoulders. Steven is jumping up and down, and, in Mr. Le's memory, the tiny wings are flapping, as if they can somehow bear Steven, body and soul, toward the heavens.

Indeed, this riotous tableau seems to Mr. Le to have been tapped from some underground river of libidinous dreams, such that a part of him imagines, or rather wishes, that it were a modern pantomime of sorts—until reason and shame step in and clear the fog of denial and remind him that the image is, alas, too real.

MR. LE IS forced to search again and again for a way to tell the story of what happened. How, after all, to explain himself, a quiet, dignified Vietnamese man, a participant, albeit unwillingly, in a public S&M ritual?

If one has never seen, say, a rose or a chrysanthemum, can he imagine it in full bloom by looking only at the bud? No, no more than he could have imagined what would come at the fair. His mind repeats the scene until it turns, over time, into a sort of metaphysical flower in motion, each of its petals a different color, and they, in their complete ways, balance one another.

Nothing of that day belongs to the ordinary, and everything seemed to lose its original meaning thereafter. Take Mrs. Le's parasol, for example. On its silk fabric her husband had penned his "Ode to Flower," a gift to her on her fifty-fifth birthday. Mrs. Le, who had wept upon reading it, had brought the parasol to the fair for an entirely different purpose than protecting herself from the sun; it was to hold it over Mrs. Tu's head. Still, even in her wildest dream, how could she possibly foresee that it would end up repeatedly striking Roger's sunburned bald spot?

Take, for example, Folsom Street, transformed into a collective display of very private passions—a bazaar of flesh. Plenty of it, in fact, in various shapes and sizes, wrapped tightly or spilling out, all in a kind of casual sexual overture. Stalls lined the middle of the street like a makeshift hamlet whose denizens shared a penchant for leather.

Onlookers of all sorts came, too; there were even families with strollers, Japanese tourists with cameras. Eight blocks had been sectioned off, and the air, veiled in barbecue smoke, was festive and oddly communal.

TWO PETALS UNCOIL and turn.

Mr. Le sees again Mrs. Tu. She appears more "modern" than he's ever seen her, in matching black leather jacket and pants; on the street fair, a new personality emerges: vamp. She touches people's breasts when invited and slaps men's buttocks even when not, laughing gaily afterwards. More than once he catches her eying Mrs. Le, looking for a reaction.

In Mr. Le's memory, there is a sad and nervous quality to his own voice when he says "*Minh oi,* let's leave" to his wife, who shakes her head. Since entering the fair, Mrs. Le's face had turned pallid and her fingers now grip the parasol's handle the way she would the metal bar in a crowded bus, knuckles turning white. Mrs. Tu's laughing banter with a blond dominatrix in a pair of red leather boots and a red leather thong that barely covers her groin has somehow given Mrs. Le the grim resolve to brave on.

Nearly naked and sunburned Americans in leather harnesses and thongs moon them with their large behinds from every possible direction, and the few who recognize Mr. Le from the shop shake his hand or even hug him. Mr. Le trails slightly behind the women as they walk on, feeling miserable, trying to be invisible.

Then he hears his wife say in a surprisingly cheerful voice: "Sister Tu, mind holding my parasol for a minute?"

"Sure," answers Mrs. Tu as she takes the parasol. "What's a neighbor for?"

"Thank you. My husband made it, pretty but heavy. Must be his sappy poetry that weighs it down."

Mrs. Tu glances up. Mr. Le's "Ode to Flower" casts a faint shadow. She mumbles the words, and the parasol wobbles. Mr. Le looks down and pretends to study his dry, opened palms, but not before glimpsing an unusual look on his wife's face as she retrieves the parasol: triumph tinged with a modicum of guilt. He feels immense love for his wife then, not for the harsh act, but for what she is willing to do in order to protect what she has. In memory, his love is partially obfuscated by Mrs. Tu's face, however, for his landlord's face seems to have infinitely aged. Her grin has reappeared and she now wears it vacantly. It must be his imagination, but has the widow's hair somehow turned grayer under the harsh sunlight?

"Sister," Mrs. Tu finally musters, "you're a very lucky woman."

THEN—"HAH HAH hah hahhh," that Lou Rawls laugh—another petal unfolds.

There's Steven, unrecognizable at first to Mr. Le because he appears in a diaper and holds a bow and arrow. Steven laughs as he prances toward them. "I do declare, Scarlett, I just adore your parasol," he says to Mrs. Le, then to Mr. Le he adds, "I saw Douglas Kim stripping for some serious whipping at the Love Leather demonstration. You might want to check it out, Mr. Lee. Roger's doing a number on our twink."

"Our twink?"

Mr. Le does not see it at the moment, but in the recalling, he sees Steven in another light. Playful Steven of little self-control and three-a-day drug cocktails wants Mr. Le to save Douglas Kim. When Mr. Le shakes his head no, thinking it is too much for his wife to see, and turns, Steven places a hand on his shoulder and says in a slow, serious voice, "No, Mr. Lee, you didn't hear me. Our twink is this way."

Our twink. Perhaps the store could have been saved if Mr. Le had not responded. But Steven's hand would not leave Mr. Le's shoulder, and the trill in his voice moves Mr. Le's feet.

"You will want to see this," Steven says, his cupid arrow pointing toward a gathering crowd.

THREE PETALS UNFOLD and swell.

In the middle of a large crowd stands Roger Briggs, his face red from drinking, a cat-o'-nine-tails in his hand.

Roger Briggs's motto, "There's always a different version of the same city, different version of the same story," applies most aptly to himself that day. Roger, who once cried in front of Mr. Le at the memories of a fallen comrade, is a leather daddy who has found a tasty morsel in a newly inducted masochist willing to be humiliated in public in Douglas Kim—a demonstration of equipment all available at Love Leather. The easygoing man is gone, replaced by a drunkard.

Douglas Kim's alabaster skin glows under the sun. He is tied face down on a bondage rack. "Who's your daddy?" Roger demands in a loud, slurred voice above him. "Tell me. Tell your daddy you love him."

"Please," cries Douglas Kim. Despite his discomfort, he sports an erection. "Give it to me. I've been bad, sir. I deserve it."

The whip whirls in the air. Douglas Kim screeches. As the whip makes its impact, two things occur to Mr. Le: that Roger Briggs is not faking, and that this is the end of his dream of owning the store. Blood trickles from the welts on the boy's buttocks.

He is slow to react, but his wife is not. She steps in and, with precision, brings her folded parasol down on Roger's head.

Twack!

"What!" Roger Briggs exclaims. He dazedly turns to look at Mrs. Le and promptly receives yet another hard blow—twack!— on the side of his head, which forces him to drop the whip and, out of his daddy character now, to squeal, "Ow!"

"*Minh oi*," yells Mr. Le, but it is much too late. Mrs. Le can no longer hear him.

The crowd roars with laughter.

"You horrible! You cocksucker!" yells Mrs. Le, her voice more ferocious than Roger's had been. "You hit a boy."

Something in Mrs. Le's voice gives weight to her accusation. Roger looks stricken, as if she is about to take away his toy. He looks down at Douglas Kim's naked back. Then he gathers up his courage and cries through his stupor, "I hit a sex slave. Not a boy. My sex slave! He's mine! And he loves me."

Mrs. Le ignores him and fumbles at Douglas Kim's shackles. "Oh, God!" says Douglas Kim when he sees her face. He starts to cry. This is not the humiliation he'd bargained for. Beads of sweat and blood run down his back and buttocks, a strand of saliva drips from his lower lip. "Oh, God! I can't believe . . . ," he mutters and closes his eyes.

Roger meanwhile fumbles for his whip on the ground.

Mr. Le steps into center ring, arms outstretched.

THE FLOWER BLOOMS.

A *pas de six*.

Behind him Roger raises his cat-o'-nine-tails. Mr. Le can smell the faint alcohol wafting from his employer's breath.

Mrs. Le looks up, turns, and picks up her parasol once more. Then she rushes toward Roger as Mr. Le strengthens his arms to block her.

Farther out, Mrs. Tu turns partially away, her hand goes up to shield her eyes.

Next to Mrs. Tu, Steven jumps up and down, aiming his fake arrow at the center stage, wings flapping.

Douglas Kim looks up at Mr. Le and groans in pain. Mr. Le looks down.

They hold each other's gaze. "You," says the boy, lips quivering, "you're my daddy."

IN THAT FRACTION of a second before whip and parasol descend, the image that will become the New World is that of a mysterious and vast garden. In it flowers bloom from a myriad of dreams and far-flung desires, its soil made fertile by love and its endless foibles. The descending sun washes the world in a fiery orange light; the air wavers. Farther out, the crowd stares, their blurred faces aglow with expectations.

Mr. Le didn't see it before, but he sees it now: how far he has traveled. His dream has taken him farther from his homeland in a way that the jumbo jet plane never could. How everything has changed, as if the skin, once broken, will in some way remain forever open to the larger world, just as the borders, once crossed, remain forever porous to the traveler.

In the kitchen his wife is moving about, the dishes clang and clatter, and the air smells of fish sauce and ground pepper. A cool breeze through the living room sways the curtains, and behind them the high-rises of San Francisco appear and disappear. "*Minh oi*," yells Mrs. Le lovingly, "time for supper."

Show & Tell

Mr. K brought in the new kid near the end of the semester during what he called Oral Presentations and everybody else called Seventh-Grade Show and Tell. "This is Cao Long Dinh," he said, "and he's from Vietnam," and immediately mean old Billy said, "Cool!"

"What's so cool about that?" Kevin, who sat behind him, asked, and Billy said, "Idiot, don't you know anything? That's where my dad came back from with this big old scar on his chest and a bunch of grossed out stories and that's where they have helicopters and guns and VCs and all this crazy shit." Billy would have gone on, but Mr. K said, "Be quiet, Billy."

Mr. K stood behind the new kid and drummed his fingers on the kid's skinny shoulders like they were little flapping wings. He tried to be nice to the new kid, I could tell, but the kid looked nervous anyway—the way he hugged his green backpack you'd think it was a lifesaver.

"Cao Long Dinh is a Vietnamese refugee," Mr. K said, and he turned around and wrote "Cao Long Dinh—Refugee" in blue on the blackboard. "Cao doesn't speak any English yet, but he'll learn soon enough, so let's welcome him, shall we?" And we did. We all applauded, but mean old Billy decided to boo him just for the hell of it, and Kevin and a few others started to laugh and the new kid blushed like a little girl. When we were done applauding (and booing), Mr. K gave him a seat in front of me and he sat down without saying hello to anybody, not even to me, his neighbor, and I had gone out of my way to flash him a smile. But right away I started to smell this nice smell from him. It reminded me of eucalyptus or something. I was going to ask him what it was, but the new kid took out his Hello Kitty notebook and began to draw in it like he'd been doing it forever, drawing and scrawling and paying no mind to anyone even when Show and Tell already started and it was— I'm sorry to say—my turn.

Tell you the truth, I didn't want it to be my turn. I can be funny and all, but I hated being in front of the class as much as I hated anything. But what can you do? You go up when it's your turn, that's what. So when Mr. K called my name, I brought my family tree chart and taped it on the blackboard under where Mr. K wrote "Cao Long Dinh—Refugee," but before I even started, Billy said, "Bobby's so poor he only got half a tree," and everybody laughed.

I wanted to say something back real bad right then and there. But as usual I held my tongue 'cuz I was a little afraid of Billy. OK, I lie, more than a little afraid. But if I weren't so fearful of that big dumb ox, I could have said a bunch of things like "Well, at least I have half a tree. Some people, they only have sorry-ass warmongers with big old scars for a daddy." Or I could say "What's wrong with half a tree? It's much better than having shit for brains" or something like that.

Anyway, not everybody laughed at Billy's butt wipe of a comment. Mr. K, for instance, didn't laugh. He looked sad, in fact, shaking his head like he was giving up on Billy, and saying, Shh, Billy, how many times do I have to tell you to be quiet in my class? And the new kid, he didn't laugh neither. He just stared at my tree like he was trying to figure out what it was, but when he saw me looking at him, he blushed and pretended like he was busy drawing. I knew he wasn't. He was curious about my drawing, my sorry excuse of a family tree.

If you want to know the awful truth, it's only half a tree 'cuz my Mama wouldn't tell me about the other half. "Your daddy was a jackass," she said, "and so is his entire family." That's all she said. "But, Mama," I said, "it's for my Oral Presentation Project, and it's important." But she said, "So what?"

So nothing, that's what. So my daddy hangs alone on this little branch on the left side. He left when I was four, so I don't remember him very well. All I remember is that he was real big and handsome. I remember him hugging and kissing and reading me a bedtime story once or twice, and then he was gone. Only my sister, Charlene, remembers him well on account of Charlene being three years older than me. Charlene remembers us having a nice house when my daddy was still around and Mama didn't have to work. Then she remembers a lot of fighting and yelling and flying dishes and broken vases and stuff like that. One night the battle between Mama and Daddy got so bad that Charlene said she found me hiding in the closet under a bunch of Mama's clothes with my eyes closed and my hands over my ears saying, "Stop, please, stop, please, stop," like I was singing or chanting or something. I don't remember any of that stuff. It just feels like my entire life is spent living in this crummy apartment at the edge of the city and that Mama has been working at Max's Diner forever.

So what did I do? I started out with a big lie. I had rehearsed the whole night for it. I said my daddy's dead. Dead from a car accident a long, long time ago. I said he was an orphan, so that's why there's only half a tree (so fuck you, Billy). Then I started on the other half. I know the other half real well 'cuz all of Mama's relatives are crazy or suicidal. There was, for example, my great-great-granddaddy Charles Boyle the Third, who was this rich man in New Orleans and who had ten children and a big old plantation during the Civil War. Too bad he supported the losing side, 'cuz he lost everything and killed himself after the war ended. Then there was my granddaddy Jonathan Quentin, who became a millionaire from owning a gold mine in Mexico and then he lost it all on alcohol and gambling and then he killed himself. And there was my grandma Mary, who was a sweetheart and who had three children and who killed herself before the bone cancer got to her, and there were a bunch of cousins who went north and east and west—and who knows where else?—and they became pilots and doctors and lawyers and maybe some of them killed themselves, too. And I wouldn't be a bit surprised if they did 'cuz my Mama said it's kinda like a family curse or something.

I went on like that for some time, going through a dozen lives before I got to the best part: "See here, that's my great aunt Jenny Ann Quentin, all alone on this little branch 'cuz she's an old maid. She's still alive, too, ninety-seven years old and with only half a mind and she lives in this broken-down mansion outside of New Orleans and she wears old tattered clothes and talks to ghosts and curses them Yankees for winning the war. I saw her once when I was young. Great Aunt Jenny scared the hell out of me 'cuz she had an old shotgun and everything, and she didn't pay her electric bills, so her big old house was always dark and scary and haunted. If you stay overnight there, the Confederate ghosts'll pull your legs or re-arrange your furniture, or worse, steal your underwear. So in summary, had we won the war a hundred years ago, we might have all stayed around in the South. But as it is, my family tree has its leaves fallen all over the states. So that's it, now I'm done, thank you."

Tommy went after me. He told about stamp collecting, and he brought three albums full of pretty stamps, stamps a hundred years old, and stamps as far as the Vatican and Sri Lanka. He told how hard it was for him to have a complete collection of Pope John Paul the Second. Then it was Cindy's turn. She talked about embroidery, and she brought with her two favorite pillowcases with pictures of playing pandas and dolphins that she embroidered herself. She even showed us how she stitches, what each stitch is called and how rewarding it was to get the whole thing together. And Kevin talked about building a tree house with his dad and how fun it was. He even showed us the blueprint that he and his daddy designed to-gether and photos of himself hanging out on the tree house, wav-ing and swinging from a rope like a monkey with his friends, and it looked like a great place to hide, too, if you're pissed off at your Mama or something, and then the bell rang.

"Robert," Mr. K said, "I wonder if you'd be so kind as to take care of our new student and show him the cafeteria." "Why me?" I asked and made a face like when I had to take the garbage out at home when it wasn't even my turn. But Mr. K said, "Why not you? Robert, you're a nice one."

"Oh no, I'm not," I said.

"Oh yes, you are," he said and wiggled his bushy eyebrows up and down like Groucho Marx.

"Oh no, I'm not."

"Oh yes, you are."

"OK," I said, "but just today, OK?" though I kinda wanted to talk to the new kid anyway, and Mr. K said, "Thank you, Robert Quentin Mitchell." He called the new kid over and put one arm around his shoulders and the other around mine. Then he said, "Robert, this is Cao; Cao, this is Robert. Robert will take care of you. You both can bring your lunch back here and eat if you want. We're having a speed tournament today, and there's a new X-Men comic book for the winner."

"All right!" I said. You're privileged if you get to eat lunch in Mr. K's room. Mr. K has all these games he keeps in the cabinet, and at lunchtime it's sort of a club and everything. You can eat there if a) you're a straight-A student, b) if Mr. K likes and invites you—which is not often, or c) if you know for sure you're gonna get jumped that day if you play outside and you beg Mr. K really, really hard to let you stay. I'm somewhere in between the b) and c) category. If you're a bad egg like Billy, who is single-handedly responsible for my c) situation, you ain't never ever gonna get to eat there and play games, that's for sure. "So, Kal Dinh Refugee," I said, "let's go grab lunch, then we'll come back here for the speed tournament, what d'you say?" But the new kid said nothing. He just stared at me and blinked like I'm some kinda strange animal that he ain't never seen before or something. "C'mon," I said and waved him toward me. "C'mon, follow me, the line's getting longer by the sec," and so finally he did.

We stood in line with nothing to do so I asked him, "Hey, Kal, where'd you get them funny shoes?"

"No undostand," he said and smiled. "No sspeak engliss."

"Shoes," I said. "Bata, Bata," and I pointed, and he looked down.

"Oh, ssues," he said, his eyes shiny and black and wide opened like he just found out for the first time that he was wearing shoes. "Ssssues, ssues . . . Saigon."

"Yeah?" I said. "I guess I can't buy me some here in the good old U. S. of A. then? Mine's Adidas. They're as old as Mrs. Hamilton—prehistoric, if you ask me—but they're still Adidas. A. Dee. Das. Go 'head, Kal, say it."

"Adeedoos suues," Kal said. "Adeedoos."

"That's right," I said. "Very good, Kal. Adidas shoes. And yours, they're Bata shoes," and Kal said, "Theirs Bata ssuees," and we both looked at each other and grinned like idiots, and that's when Billy showed up. "Why you want them gook shoes anyway?" he said and cut in between us, but nobody behind in line said nothing 'cuz it's Billy.

"Why not?" I said, trying to sound tough. "Bata sounds kind of nice, Billy. They're from Saigon."

"Bata ssues," the new kid said again, trying to impress Billy.

But Billy wasn't impressed. "My daddy said them VCs don't wear shoes," he said. "They wear sandals made from jeep tires and they live in fuck'n tunnels like moles and they eat bugs and snakes for lunch. Then afterwards they go up and take sniper shots at you with their AK-47s."

"He don't look like he lived in no tunnel," I said.

"Maybe not him," said Billy, "but his daddy, I'm sure. Isn't that right, refugee boy? Your daddy a VC? Your daddy the one who gave my daddy that goddamn scar?"

The new kid didn't say nothing. You could tell he pretty much figured it out that Billy's an asshole 'cuz you don't need no English for that. But all he could say was "no undohsten" and "ssues ad-eedoos" and those ain't no comeback lines and he knew it. So he just bit his lip and blushed and kept looking at me with them eyes.

So I don't know why, maybe 'cuz I didn't want him to know that I belonged to the c) category, or maybe 'cuz he kept looking at me with those eyes, but I said, "Leave him alone, Billy." I was kinda surprised that I said it. And Billy turned and looked at me like he was shocked, too, like he just saw me for the first time or something. Then in this loud singsong voice, he said, "Bobby's protecting his new boyfriend. Everybody look, Bobby's got a boyfriend and he's gonna suck his VC's dick after lunch."

Everybody started to look.

The new kid kept looking at me like he was waiting to see what I was gonna do next. What I'd usually do next is shut my trap and pretend that I was invisible or try not to cry like last time when Billy got me in a headlock in the locker room and called me sissy over and over again 'cuz I missed the softball at PE even when it was an easy catch. But not now. Now I couldn't pretend to be invisible 'cuz too many people were looking. It was like I didn't have a choice. It was like now or never. So I said, "You know what, Billy, don't mind if I do. I'm sure anything is bigger than yours," and everybody in line said, "Ooohh."

"Fuck you, you little faggot," Billy said.

"No thanks, Billy," I said. "I already got me a new boyfriend, remember?"

Everybody said "Oohh" again, and Billy looked real mad. Then I got more scared than mad, my blood pumping. I thought, "Oh my God, what have I done? I'm gonna get my lights punched out for sure." But then, God delivered stupid Becky. She suddenly stuck her beak in. "And he's cute, too," she said, "almost as cute as you, Bobby. A blond and a brunette. You two'll make a nice faggot couple, I'm sure. So, like, promise me you'll name your first born after me, OK?"

So, like, I tore at her. That girl could never jump me, not in a zillion years. "And I'm sure you're a slut," I said. "I'm sure you'd get down with anything that moves. I'm sure there are litters of stray mutts already named after you. You know, Bitch Becky One, Bitch Becky Two, and, let's not forget, Bow Wow Becky Junior," and Becky said, "Asshole!" and looked away, and everyone cracked up, even mean old Billy.

"Man," he said, shaking his head, "you got some mean mouth on you today." It was like suddenly I was too funny or famous for him to beat up.

But after he bought his burger and chocolate milk, he said it real loud so everybody can hear, he said, "I'll see you two bitches later. Outside."

"Sure, Billy," I said and waved to him, "see yah later," and then, after we grabbed our lunch, the new kid and me, we made a beeline for Mr. K's.

BOY, IT WAS GOOD to be in Mr. K's, I tell you. You don't have to watch over your shoulder every other second. You can play whatever game you want. Or you can read or just talk. So we ate and afterward I showed the new kid how to play speed. He was a quick learner, too, if you asked me, but he lost pretty early on in the tournament. Then I lost, too, pretty damn quickly after him. So we sat around and I flipped through the X-Men comic book and tried to explain to the new kid why Wolverine is so cool 'cuz he can heal himself with his mutant factor and he had claws that cut through metal, and Phoenix, she's my favorite, Phoenix's so very cool 'cuz she can talk to you psychically and she knows how everybody feels without even having to ask them, and best of all, she can lift an eighteen-wheeler with her psycho-kinetic energy. "That's way cool, don't you think, Kal?"

The new kid, he listened and nodded to everything I said like he understood. Anyway, after a while, there were more losers than winners and the losers surrounded us and interrogated the new kid like he was a POW or something.

"You ever shoot anybody, Cao Long?"

"Did you see anybody get killed?"

"Say, Long, how *long* you been here, *long*? Haha!"

"I hear they eat dogs over there, is that true, Long? Have you ever eaten a dog?"

"Have you ever seen a helicopter blown up like in the movies?"

"No undohsten," the new kid answered to each question and smiled or shook his head or waved his hands like shooing flies but the loser flies wouldn't shoo. I mean, where else could they go? Mr. K's was it. So the new kid looked at me again with them eyes and I said, "OK, OK, Kal, I'll teach you something else. Why don't you say: 'Hey, fuck heads, leave me alone!' Go head, Kal, say it."

"Hee, foock headss," he said, looking at me.

"Leave. Me. Alone!" I said, looking at him.

"Leevenme olone!" he said. "Hee, foock headss. Leevenme olone!

And everybody laughed. I guess that was the first time they got called fuck heads and actually felt good about it, but Mr. K said, "Robert Quentin Mitchell, you watch your mouth or you'll never come in here again," but you could tell he was trying not to laugh himself. So, I said, "OK, Mr. K," but I leaned over and whispered, "Hey, fuck heads, leave me alone!" again in the new kid's ear, so he'd remember, and he looked at me like I'm the coolest guy in the world.

Then after school when I was waiting for my bus, the new kid found me. He gave me a folded piece of paper and before I could say anything he blushed and ran away. You'd never guess what it was. It was a drawing of me and it was really, really good. I was smiling in it. I looked real happy, and older, like a sophomore or something, not like in the sixth-grade yearbook picture where I looked so goofy with my eyes closed and everything, and I had to sign my name over it so people wouldn't look. When I got home, I taped it on my family tree chart and pinned the chart on my bedroom door, and I swear, the whole room had this vague eucalyptus smell.

Next day at Show and Tell, Billy made the new kid cry. He went after Jimmy. Jimmy was this total nerd with thick glasses who told us how "very challenging" it was doing *The New York Times* crossword puzzles 'cuz you got to know words like *ubiquitous* and *undulate* and *capricious*, totally lame and bogus stuff like that. When he took so long just to do 5 across and 7 horizontal, we shot spitballs at him, and Mr. K said, "Stop that!" But we got rid of that capricious undulating bozo ubiquitously fast, and that was when Billy came up and made the new kid cry.

He brought in his daddy's army uniform and a stack of old magazines. He unfolded the uniform with the name "Baxter" sewed under "U.S. ARMY" and put it on a chair. Then he opened one magazine and showed a picture of this naked and bleeding little girl running and crying on this road while these houses behind her were on fire. "That's napalm," he said, "and it eats into your skin and burns for a long, long time."

"This girl," Billy said, "she got burned real bad, see there, yeah." Then he showed another picture of this monk sitting cross-legged and he was on fire and everything and there were people standing behind him crying but nobody tried to put the poor man out. "That's what you call self-immolation," Billy said. "They do that all the time in Nam. This man, he poured gasoline on himself and lit a match 'cuz he didn't like the government." Then Billy showed another picture of dead people in black pajamas along this road and he said, "These are VCs and my dad got at least a dozen of them before he was wounded himself. My dad told me if it weren't for them beatniks and hippies, we could have won." And that's when the new kid buried his face in his arms and cried and I could see his skinny shoulders go up and down like waves.

"That's enough, Billy Baxter," Mr. K said. "You can sit down now, thank you."

"Oh, man!" Billy said. "I didn't even get to the part about how my dad got his scar, that's the best part."

"Never mind," Mr. K said. "Sit down, please. I'm not sure whether you understood the assignment, but you were supposed to do an oral presentation on what you've done, or something that has to do with you, a hobby or a personal project, not the atrocities in Indochina."

Then Mr. K looked at the new kid like he didn't know what to do next. "That war," he said, "I swear." After that it got real quiet in the room and all you could hear was the new kid sobbing. "Cao,"

Mr. K said finally, real quiet like, like he didn't really want to bother him. "Cao, are you all right? Cao Long Dinh?"

The new kid didn't answer Mr. K, so I put my hand on his shoulder and shook it a little. "Hey, Kal," I said, "you OK?"

Then, it was like I pressed an ON button or something, 'cuz all of a sudden Kal raised his head and stood up. He looked at me and then he looked at the blackboard. He looked at me again, then the blackboard. Then he marched right up there even though it was Roger's turn next and Roger, he already brought his two pet snakes and everything. But Kal didn't care. Maybe he thought it was his turn 'cuz Mr. K called his name and so he just grabbed a bunch of colored chalks on Mr. K's desk and started to draw like a wild man, and Mr. K, he let him.

We all stared.

He was really, really good, but I guess I already knew that.

First he drew a picture of a boy sitting on this water buffalo, and then he drew this rice field in green. Then he drew another boy on another water buffalo, and they seemed to be racing. He drew other kids running along the bank with their kites in the sky, and you could tell they were laughing and yelling, having a good time. Then he started to draw little houses on both sides of this river and the river ran toward the ocean and the ocean had big old waves. Kal drew a couple standing outside this very nice house holding hands, and underneath them Kal wrote "Ba" and "Ma." Then he turned and looked straight at me, his eyes still wet with tears.

"Rowbuurt," he said, tapping the pictures with his chalk, his voice sad but expecting, "Rowbuurt."

"Me?" I said. I felt kinda dizzy. Everybody was looking back and forth between him and me now like we were tossing a softball between us or something.

"Rowbuurt." Kal said my name again and kept looking at me until I said, "What, what'd you want, Kal?"

Kal tapped the blackboard with his chalk again and I saw in my head the picture of myself taped on my family tree and then, I don't know how, but I just kinda knew. So I just took a deep breath and then I said, "OK, OK. Kal, uhmm, said he used to live in this village with his Mama and Papa near where the river runs into the sea," and Kal nodded and smiled and waved his chalk in a circle like he was saying, "Go on, Robert Quentin Mitchell, you're doing fine, go on."

So I went on.

And he went on.

I talked. He drew.

We fell into a rhythm.

"He had a good time racing them water buffaloes with his friends and flying kites," I said. "His village is, hmm, very nice, and . . . and . . . and . . . at night he goes to sleep swinging on this hammock and hearing the sound of ocean behind the dunes and everything."

"Then one day," I said, "the soldiers came with guns and they took his daddy away. They put him behind barbed wires with other men, all very skinny, skinny and hungry, and they got chains on their ankles and they looked really, really sad. Kal and his mother went to visit his daddy, and they stood on the other side of the fence and cried a lot. Then he died. And Kal and his mother buried him in this cemetery with lots of graves and they lit candles and cried and cried. After that, there was this boat, this really crowded boat, I guess, and Kal and his Mama climbed on it, and they went down the river out to sea. Then they got on this island and then they got on an airplane after that and they came here to live in America."

Kal was running out of space. He drew the map of America way too big, but he didn't want to erase it. So he climbed on a chair and drew these high-rises right above the rice fields, and I recognized the Transamerica Building right away, a skinny pyramid underneath a rising moon. Then he drew a big old heart around it. Then he went back to the scene where the man named Ba stood in the doorway with his wife, and he drew a heart around him. Then he went back to the first scene of the two boys racing on the water buffaloes in the rice field and paused a little before he drew tiny tennis shoes on the boys' feet, and I heard Billy say "That's Bobby and his refugee boyfriend," but I ignored him.

"Kal loves America very much, especially San Francisco," I said. "He'd never seen so many tall buildings before in his whole life and they're so pretty. Maybe he'll live with his mother someday up in the penthouse when they have lots of money. But he misses home, too, and he misses his friends, and he especially misses his daddy who died. A lot. And that's all. I think he's done, thank you."

And he was done. Kal turned around and climbed down from the chair. Then he looked at everybody and checked out their faces to see if they understood. Then in this real loud voice he said, "Hee, foock headss, leevenme olone!" and bowed to them, and everybody cracked up and applauded.

Kal started walking back. He was smiling and looking straight at me like he was saying "Robert Quentin Mitchell, ain't we a team, or what?" And I wanted to say "Yes, yes, Kal Long Dinh—Refugee, yeah we are," but I just didn't say anything.

The Palmist

T HE PALMIST CLOSED UP shop early because of the pain. He felt as if he was being roasted, slowly, inside out. By noon he could no longer focus on his customers' palms; their life and love lines had all failed to point to any significant future, but blurred and streaked instead into rivers and streams of his memories.

Outside, the weather had turned. Dark clouds hung low and the wind was heavy with moisture. He reached the bus stop's tiny shelter when it began to pour. He didn't have to wait long, however. The good old 38 Geary pulled up in a few minutes, and he felt mildly consoled, though sharp pains flared and blossomed from deep inside his bowels like tiny geysers, and they made each of his three steps up the bus laborious.

It was warm and humid on the bus, and crowded, and a fine mist covered the windows. He sat on the front bench facing the aisle, the one reserved for the handicapped and the elderly. A fat woman with rosy cheeks who stayed standing gave him a dirty look. It was true: his hair was still mostly black, and he appeared to be a few years short of senior citizenship. The palmist pretended not to notice her. He leaned contemptuously back against the worn and cracked vinyl and smiled to himself. He closed his eyes. A faint odor of turned earth reached his nostrils. The palmist inhaled deeply and saw again a golden rice field, a beatific smile, a face long gone; his first kiss.

The rain fell harder on the roof of the bus as it rumbled toward the sea.

At the next stop, a teenager got on. Caught in the downpour without an umbrella, he was soaking wet, and his extra-large T-shirt that said "Play Hard . . . Stay Hard" clung to him. It occurred to the palmist that this was the face of someone who hadn't yet learned to be fearful of the weather. The teenager stood towering above the palmist, blocking him from seeing the fat woman, who, from time to time, still glanced disapprovingly at him.

So young, the palmist thought, the age of my youngest son, maybe, had he lived. The palmist tried to conjure his son's face in his mind but could not. It had been some years since the little boy drowned in the South China Sea, along with his two older sisters and their mother. The palmist had escaped on a different boat, a smaller one that left a day after his family's boat, and, as a result, reached America alone.

Alone, thought the palmist and sighed. *Alone.*

It was then that his gaze fell upon the teenager's hand. He saw something there. He leaned forward, and did something he never did before on the 38 Geary. He spoke up, rather loudly, excitedly.

"You," he said in his heavy accent. "I see wonderful life!"

The teenager looked down at the old man, and arched his eyebrows.

"I'm a palmist," said the palmist. "Maybe you give me your hand?"

The teenager did nothing. No one had ever asked to see his hand on this bus before. The fat woman snickered. Oh, she'd seen it all on the 38 Geary. She wasn't surprised. "This my last reading, no money, free, gift for you," the palmist pressed on. "Give me your hand."

"I don't know," the teenager said, scratching his chin. He was nervous. He felt as if he was caught inside a moving glass house and that, with the passengers looking on, he had somehow turned into one of its most conspicuous plants.

"What, what you don't know?" asked the palmist. "Maybe I know. Maybe I answer."

"Dude," the teenager said. "I don't know if I believe in all that hocus-pocus stuff." And though he didn't say it, he didn't know whether he wanted to be touched by the old man who had wrinkled, bony hands and a nauseating tobacco breath. To stall, the teenager said, "I have a question, though. Can you read your own future? Can you, like, tell when you're gonna die and stuff?" Then, he thought about it. "Nah, forget it," he said. "Sorry, that was stupid."

The bus stopped abruptly at the next stop, and everyone who was standing struggled to stay on their feet. But those near the front of the bus were also struggling to listen to the conversation. "No, no, not stupid," said the palmist. "Good question. Long ago, I asked same thing, you know. I read same story in many hands of my people: story that said something bad will happen. Disaster. But in my hand here, I read only good thing. This line here, see, say I have happy family, happy future. No problem. So I think: me, my family, no problem. Now I know better: all hands affect each other, all lines run into each other, tell a big story. When the war ended in my country, you know, it was so bad for everybody. And my family? Gone, gone under the sea. You know, reading palm not like reading map. You feel and see here in heart also, in stomach also, not just here in your head. It is, how d'you say, tuition?"

"Intuition," the teenager corrected him and tried to stifle a giggle.

"Yes," nodded the palmist. "Intuition."

The teenager liked the sound of the old man's voice. Its timbre reminded him of that of his long dead grandfather, who also came from another country, one whose name had since changed several times due to wars.

"My stop not far away now," the palmist continued. "This your last chance. Free. No charge."

"Go on, kiddo," the fat woman said, nudging him with her elbow, smiling. She wanted to hear this boy's future. "I've been listening. It's all right. He's for real, I can tell now."

That was what he needed. "OK," the teenager said and opened his right fist. The old man leaned forward, his face burning with seriousness as he leaned down and trailed the various lines and contours and fleshy knolls on the teenager's palm. He bent the boy's wrist this way and that, kneaded and prodded the fingers and knuckles as if to measure the strength of his resolve. He made mysterious calculations in his own language, mumbling a few singsong words to himself.

Finally, the palmist looked up and, in a solemn voice, spoke. "You will become an artist. When twenty-five, twenty-six, you're going to change very much. If you don't choose right, oh, so many regrets. But don't be afraid. Never be afraid. Move forward. Always. You have help. These squares here, right here, see, they're spirits and mentors, they come protect, guide you. When you reach mountaintop, people everywhere will hear you, know you, see you, your art, what you see, others will see. Oh, so much love. You number one someday."

The palmist went on like this for some time. Despite his pains, which flared up intermittently, he went on to talk of the ordinary palms and sad faces that he had read, and the misfortunes he saw coming and the wondrous opportunities he saw squandered by fear and distrust. Divorces, marriages, and death in families he read too many. Broken romance, betrayals and adulteries, too pedestrian to remember. Twice, however, he held hands that had committed unspeakable evil, and he was sick for a week each time, and once, he held the hand of a reincarnated saint. How many palms had he read since he came to America? "Oh, so many," he answered his own question, laughing. "Too many. Thousands. Who care now? Not me."

When the palmist finished talking, the teenager retrieved his hand and looked at it. He found it heavy and foreign somehow. Most of what the palmist said made no sense to him. Sure he loved reading a good book now and then because reading was like being inside a cartoon, but for that same reason he loved cartoons even more. And even if he got good grades he hated his stupid English classes, though it's true, he did write poetry, but only to himself.

But he also played the piano. A singer? Maybe a graphic artist? Maybe a movie star? He didn't know. Everything was still possible. Besides, turning twenty-five was so far away, almost a decade away.

Before she got off the bus, the fat lady touched the teenager lightly on the shoulder. "Lots of luck, kiddo," she said, and wiped a tear from the corner of her eye.

Nearing his stop, the palmist struggled to get up, wincing as he did, and the teenager helped him. The teenager wanted to say something to the old man but he did not. When the bus stopped, he flashed a smile instead and waved to the palmist, who, in turn, gave him a look that he, in later years, would interpret as that of impossible longing. In later years, too, he would perceive the palmist in various lights, cruel or benevolent or mysterious, depending on how he fared in his quest, and once, in a fanciful moment, the palmist would appear to him as the first among many bodhisattvas in his life, and indicate that theirs was an inevitable encounter in the cosmic sense of things. At that moment, however, all he saw was a small and sad-looking old man whose eyes seemed on the verge of tears as he quietly nodded once to the teenager before stepping out into the downpour.

THE TEENAGER LIVED near the end of the line, past the park. As usual, the bus was near empty at this stretch, and he sat down on the bench that the palmist had previously occupied. He could still feel the warmth of the vinyl.

With everyone gone now, he grew bored. He turned to the fogged-up window behind him and drew a sailor holding a bottle standing on a sloop. It sailed an ocean full of dangerous waves. The boat, it seemed, was heading toward a girl with large, round breasts in a hula skirt and she was dancing on a distant shore. Behind her, he drew a few tall mountains and swaying palm trees. He hesitated before mischievously giving her two, three more heads and eight or nine more arms than she actually needed to entice the drunken sailor to her island, and then he pulled back to look.

Among her waving arms, the teenager saw a rushing world of men, women, and children under black, green, red, blue, polka-dotted umbrellas and plastic ponchos. He watched until the people and storefront windows streaked into green: green pine trees, fern groves, placid lakes, and well-tended grass meadows. The park . . . beyond which was the sea.

The rain tapered off, and a few columns of sunlight pierced the gray clouds, setting the road aglow like a golden river. The boy couldn't wait to get off the bus and run or do something—glide above the clouds if he could. High above the clouds, a jet plane soared. People were flying to marvelous countries to take up mysterious destinies.

With repeated circular movements of his hand, he wiped away sailor, boat, waves, and girl. Where the palmist's thumbnail had pressed into the middle of his palm and made a crescent moon, he could still feel a vague tingling sensation. "A poet!" he said to himself and gave a little laugh. He looked at his cool, wet palm before wiping it clean on his faded Levis. "What a day," he said, shaking his head. "Boy, what a day!"

Slingshot

THIS DUDE, RIGHT, a loner and everything, made his sorry ass part of our family, and Mamma insisted that me and Pammy call him Uncle Steve, but I wouldn't. Uh-uh. I called him U.S. for short.

U.S. came to eat at our restaurant a couple of years ago and ordered Mamma's special Hu Tieu soup. Kept saying he hadn't eaten authentic Vietnamese cooking since he was stationed in Nam and such. Next thing you know, dude's a regular. And Mamma and Pammy, sweet, ready-to-please Pammy, started to treat him like a long-lost relative.

"Poor Uncle Steve," Mamma once said in Vietnamese, "he's a nice man and all alone. He fought on your father's side during the war and even knew his infantry. So treat him nice, you two, especially you, Little Monkey."

"Sure," I said, "sure, Mamma. Whatever."

The thing about regulars is that they sometimes get too personal. They, like, totally get on your nerves. They don't leave at closing time. They walk up to the cash register when you're way too busy adding up the bills or something and start kicking it with you, yammering and yacking 'til you get real distracted and lose your place and then you just want to tell them to shut the hell up. I mean they pay for good cooking and give a tip for good service but, 'scuse me, where does it say on the menu that our special dinner combo of spring rolls, salad, and curry chicken for $6.99 comes with psychological treatment?

Some regulars just hang around late, you know, and ask if we need help cleaning up, or if we want an escort to our apartment after we close even if it's only two blocks away, or what dish we're preparing for tomorrow, but like, hello, it's the same menu every day for the last three years. Some of them just didn't wanna go home, period, and I'll tell you why: most regulars are helluva loners.

But U.S. was the worst. Kept telling us how he hated being an American and everything, hated "this damn country," hated how his wife took the kids and skipped out on his sorry ass back to Texas after he came back a little loony-tooney from Nam.

Sometimes U.S.'d get way annoying when he pretended like he's somehow Vietnamese, 'cuz he's been there and knew some stuff. Like he knew all about Tet: "You dress up nice and you go visit relatives and you give money in red envelopes to little children, am I right, Mrs. Nguyen?" About wedding traditions: "The groom's side of the family comes over to the bride's side bearing gifts wrapped in red. They carry a roasted pig on a big lacquered tray and fruits and tea on the smaller ones, isn't that right, Pammy?" And about funeral arrangements: "You wear white headbands, you burn paper offerings to the dead, and you play really sad music. I remember people in the rural areas prefer to live near their ancestors' graves so they can tend to them. Hell, I've even seen graves in people's backyards. Live and die together, that's the way you people are, am I right?"

If that's not enough to yank your chain, there was this helluva annoying phrase U.S. always used when he came in a little tipsy: *Toi cung la nguoi Viet Nam!*—"I'm also Vietnamese!"—and sometimes Mamma, when she's in a good mood, she'd laugh and clasp her hands and answer him with her broken English: "Uncle Steve, you, you Viet-Nam people like us." Whenever he heard that, boy, dude'd be beaming like Mamma'd just announced that he'd won the Oscar for Best Actor or something. But Mamma was only humoring his ass.

I mean, U.S. as a Vietnamese? Who was he kidding? A doofus from Texas with receding blond hair, a thick mustache, and a beer belly who loves to wear obnoxious-smelling cologne and loud Hawaiian shirts on the weekends?

Puh-leeze, put black pajamas on that dude and he'd be looking more like, I don't know, a chocolate truffle or something.

Anyway, soon U.S. got way too friendly. He brought us flowers, irises and tulips and daffodils and roses or what have you. Then he'd send us postcards when he traveled. U.S. travels for free or for very little money 'cuz he's a baggage handler for United Air at SFO. London? Been there. Hong Kong? Been there, too. Morocco? Done that. Even if it's only on a long weekend, U.S.'d be going off to someplace far.

That one time he came back from France, he got gifts for us all. He'd got a little purse for Pammy, a blouse for me, a hat for Grandma Thien—who I called Grandma T. the first day she got hired by Mamma to help out with the cooking a few years ago—and for Mamma, a real kick-ass turquoise necklace. We all said no, no, no thank you, especially Mamma, who kept saying "No gift, Uncle Steve, no gift. Postcard OK, flowers OK, expensive gifts not OK!" and waved her hands in the air like she was hailing a cab, but U.S. wouldn't listen. *Toi cung la nguoi Viet Nam*, he kept saying, *Toi cung la nguoi Viet Nam* until Mamma pretended to be angry and placed U.S.'s gifts in a pile on the table and he had to give up and offer the loot to Grandma T. And Grandma T. took it, too, 'cuz she has more grandchildren than she can feed.

Still it got so that U.S. wouldn't think twice about going back to the kitchen and standing there like he was the chef himself, tasting the soup and chatting with Mamma and Grandma T. about this and that, that and this. It didn't matter even when they were way too busy—U.S. would yap, yap, yap. Sometimes, he'd say something stupid to Mamma like, "Mrs. Nguyen, correct me if I'm wrong, but doesn't the river in Ben Tre rise real fast sometimes in the afternoon, especially when it's monsoon season?" And Mamma would stop what she was doing and nod and squint her eyes and stare at the industrial-size fridge as if she could see the damn river rising from somewhere behind all that steely grayness. Another time, she was preparing *bun tam bi*, a Southern Vietnamese dish that uses coconut, mint, and pork skin and a bunch of other good but unidentifiable stuff, and U.S. came in and said, "Mrs. Nguyen, there's no better coconut than the ones grown in Ben Tre, am I not right?" And Mamma would giggle and answer, "Uncle Steve, you right, you right. Fresh coconuts over there! Only cans over here! Not the same, no good."

Pammy, too, she's real sweet to U.S., but I guess she's sweet to everybody, that's just the way she is. She's a year older than me, but she acts like she's fresh off the boat. Just me, I guess, I'm the one who told the bums to get lost and the doggin' customers to clear out. I'm the one who ambushed Dwayne Kawowski on the bike path that one time at Golden Gate Park on that seventh-grade field trip and shot him in the kneecap with Papa's slingshot using my favorite ammunition, a jawbreaker—a purple one at that—'cuz he kept teasing Pammy, yanking her long braid and stuff. Told that child to cut hers short like mine to avoid assholes like Dwayne, but would she listen? No. So, anyway, dude was lame for a whole week and couldn't even tell people that a girl shot him with a damn piece of candy.

So guess who was the one to tell U.S. waz'up?

Yup, yours truly. Like that one time, right, when U.S. insisted on staying after closing time and helping me and Pammy clean up. It wasn't necessary, we all said, but dude insisted. Then suddenly, when we were all stacking chairs onto the tables to mop the floor, he got all misty-eyed and blurted, "You two are my favorite Mekong Delta girls. So smart. So filial. I mean it, Jesus almighty, I adore you both like my own."

Mekong Delta girls! Ewww, waz'up with that crazy, corny shit? I mean out of nowhere, this gringo's confession, major vomit material. I get totally bugging when he'd be talking like that. Like there we were in a dingy little dive in the Tender-full-of-freaks-loin with the smell of fish sauce and Pine-Sol up our nostrils while the bums milled about outside looking like zombies, and U.S. talked to us like we were those images in the grease-stained brush paintings hanging on our walls: you know, wearing conical hats and planting rice by the river and rowing boats and singing folk songs and leading the oxen home to the village or shit like that. So I said, "U.S., you're crazy if you think we're your girls. That's heinous, all right. We ain't living in your sorry-ass Mekong Delta fantasy shit. Get a grip. We took a trip. We're in San Francisco—like, A-Me-Ri-Ca ? U.S., you ain't no Vietnamese and you know it."

Boy, you should've seen him. Buttsucker had that hurt-puppy look. "You're mouthy, Tammy," he said, shaking his head and sighing, "but I know you got a good heart." Then he said, "I know we're in America. I know I'm not Vietnamese, racially. All I'm saying is that, after what I went through, Vietnam is part of me, too. I don't know, maybe you'll see it someday."

"Yeah," I said. "Sure, U.S. Whatever."

So IT WAS ESCALATING warfare between U.S. and me 'cuz that time of love declaration from U.S. was nothing compared with the other time when U.S. really got me royally bugging and in helluva trouble with Mamma. He saw me and Adam K—you know, bedroom-eyes Adam, tall, brown hair down to his big shoulders, real light skin with the tattoo of a coiling snake with a blood red rose in its mouth on his left arm and with a turquoise earring and the best smile in last year's yearbook. Anyway, we were just walking and holding hands on the street, right, and I didn't see U.S. spying on us or nothing, but when I got to the restaurant he was all nervous and everything. At first I thought he developed a tic or was having a stroke maybe, but then he said, "I saw you with that Tattoo Guy today, Tammy. Hope you don't mind a piece of advice, but I just don't trust the look on that one. I've seen him real chummy with them gangbangers scoring some dope on Hyde the other day. Tell you what I think: he's the type that'll get in trouble sooner or later. So go slow, OK."

Tattoo Guy? I couldn't believe my ears! He was like dissing Adam, my bedroom-eyes Adam. Worse, U.S. be talking to me like I was his own daughta . . . not! No wonder Texan wife and kids took off on his sorry ass. Had to. Either that or hara-kiri. Besides, homey ain't relative no matter how much he fantasized himself to be. A regular's still a customer, and he's not supposed to tell his waitress who to date, period. He's supposed to sit at his table, you know, and order and eat and say "Ah, that was delicious, miss, thank you very much!" and leave a big tip and then leave.

I totally lost it. I said: "U.S., why don't chew do us all a favor and just FUCK OFF!" Unfortunately Mamma heard it all the way in the kitchen 'cuz I said it LOUD and she got real MAD. There were only two Hispanic customers that afternoon and they were too busy looking in each other's eyes like Romeo and Julietta and they didn't give a hoot what we did. But Mamma, she cared 'cuz right away, she came out and made me apologize to U.S. even when she didn't even know a quarter of the story. Now, Mamma, she may not know the true meaning of "fuck off!" but she pretty much guessed that it wasn't no nice, respecting phrase like "Hello, mister, how are you today?" or "Are you ready to order, madam?" But I wouldn't apologize to U.S. Na-uhh, no frick'n way.

"No, Mamma," I said, "no apologies."

"Little Monkey, apologize," Mamma said it again in Vietnamese, her voice steady and cool as cucumber, which only meant one thing: Mount Saint Helen Nguyen was ready to blow serious lava. "Don't be rude to him. Uncle Steve, he's just like a relative."

"Hell no," I yelled. "Why should I apologize? He ain't no real uncle. He certainly ain't my father. He ain't nothing, Mamma, a nobody. So how's he family?"

Mamma didn't answer. She just looked kind of surprised that I blew first. But it was like Mamma didn't even know what happened and she automatically sided with this dude, an outsider. So I went on in this cold, bitchy voice, you know, pretending like I just figured something out that very second. I said, "Oh, oh, wait a minute, Mamma, I get it. He's going to be my new Papa soon, am I right?" and I heard Pammy suck in her breath. I mean, I shouldn't have said that, I know. But I was still bugging, and therefore, went too far and dissed mi own madre in the process. So she slapped me—Slapp!—right in front of U.S. and Pammy and the Romeo-Julietta couple, who abandoned their banana flambé, threw some money on the table and made like *el viento*.

For one thing, no chef should slap no waitress in front of no customers, that's no good for business for sure. For another, no waitress should cry in front of no regulars, but, oh man, I just couldn't help it, I bawled.

"Go ahead, Mamma," I said through my curtain of tears, "you just go ahead and hit me some more to make yourself happy, but I ain't apologizing to this wuz, all right. Who asked him to ha-rass me in the first place? I don't care if he's been to Ben Tre, Mamma. I don't care if he knew Papa's infantry. I mean, what does it matter now? We're living in the Tender-frick'n-loin and Papa is dead, buried somewhere in the re-education camp by the goddamn Viet Cong and nobody asked me for permission to let this wannabe ruin my life."

I geared myself for the next assault, but it didn't come. Mamma's face suddenly changed from being totally bugging to this real sad look. She raised her hand like she was going to re-slap me, but she just turned it slowly toward her own face instead. Then she wept into it like a baby. Oh my goodness, even now, after all that happened, even after I did what I did later on, I can still see her thin shoulders tremble and shake.

Shouldn't have said all that stuff, I know, I know. My tongue, I swear, it's sharper than Ginsu knives. Tell you truly, I'd rather she re-slap me, *no problema*. It's easier to take than her crying. I couldn't bear it. I felt so hurt inside, like somebody was twisting a knife in my guts or pinching my heart with her long, gnarly nails. So I did what came naturally: I grabbed and hugged her, my Mamma, who once held tiny old me and Pammy in her arms when we sailed out to sea in that old stinking, crowded boat from Ben Tre a zillion nights ago, but who felt suddenly so small in my arms now, so frail, so bony, who suffered so much already.

"Oh, Mommy, I'm sorry," I said, "I'm so sorry," and then Pammy came rushing to us for a team hug and we cried, the three of us, like we were in some weird choir practice. So everything—Les Miz, Les *Vietnam*-Miz or whatever—was happening right in front of U.S. And the dude be acting like he was all tied up. He trembled like he was struggling to get out of some invisible rope until finally his hairy arm slowly reached out like an elephant's trunk toward me and Pammy and Mamma, trying to touch us maybe, but before he could accomplish his mission impossible, I shot him my special Medusa laser-ray stare and froze that ex-GI in his tracks.

That was when Grandma T. came out of the kitchen with her ladle. She looked at us for a second or two. Then she sighed and shook her gray head like she'd seen it all before, and she waved the ladle in the air like a magic wand. "*Troi oi, troi!*" she said, her voice low and throaty. "You people are worse than the monsoon. Please, enough with the crying already, my beef soup went sour back there because of your wailing." We all started to giggle 'cuz Grandma T.'s voice was raspy from years of smoking—she sounded like a Vietnamese Darth Vader or somebody cool like that—and her wrinkled-up face was frowning like a sad old clown. U.S. laughed, too, even though he probably didn't get 90 percent of what she was saying, Mr. I'm-Also-Vietnamese. But Grandma T. was stern to him. She pointed the ladle toward the door and said, "Uncle Steve, you should go and handle baggage. Let us women folks take care of things." U.S. stared at us like he wanted to say something, but nothing came out. So he just looked at Grandma T.'s ladle like he was really thinking hard about something and then he nodded and left. Me, I was still bugging and thought the dude got away easy. I don't know—I kind of expected Grandma T. to like turn his sorry ass into a wart hog or something.

U.S. DID NOT come back the next day or the next. A week went by, then another. Soon everyone started to wonder, including all the other regulars, whatever happened to Uncle Steve, the ex-GI who thought he was Vietnamese? Everyone but me, that is. I mean I didn't care. U.S. was finally out of my hair? Good. Why ask why?

It was like having a vacation. It was like it was raining for a week and then you woke up one day and the sun was out and the sky blue. It was, like, too good to be true. The dark clouds came back pretty quickly. After a month or so, just when I got used to the idea that U.S. was really, really gone, we got a postcard from you-know-who. It showed this pretty Thai babe, a dancer in traditional costume with an intricate pointy headset. Her fingers were bent at an impossible angle, her head leaned to the side, and her eyes were wide and flirty. And she had this smile on her like she was real happy, but you could tell that she was just pretending.

Dear Mrs. Nguyen and family,

If you all are wondering whatever happened to your Stephen, well don't you worry. As you can tell from the postcard, I am in Bangkok, on an extended vacation. I finally decided that I need to take a trip back to 'Nam to look at the past. I am heading home in a few weeks after much needed r&r and then I'll have a very, very precious gift for you and this time you cannot possibly refuse, guaranteed.

Affectionately yours,
Steve

P.S. Hello Pammy and Tammy, how are my favorite gals?

"What's Uncle Steve saying, Mamma?" Pammy asked after she was done reading the card out loud for Mamma.

"Yeah," I joined in, "what's so precious that we can't possibly refuse? Don't we always refuse? Didn't you say we don't need any charity? We make our own living, right, Mamma?"

"No charity," Mamma agreed. "Postcards OK. Flowers OK. Expensive gifts not OK." She studied the postcard for a few seconds then pinned it on the board next to the cash register with all the rest like she didn't care, but you just know she was still thinking about it.

So that night, right, when we were getting ready for bed and everything, Pammy dropped the bomb. "I mean, what if Uncle Steve wants to marry Mamma?" she said.

"What?" I said. "Miss P., are you on LSD? Puh-leeze, Mamma and U.S.? Like, they haven't even dated. Wait, what am I saying: Mamma *never* ever dated. I just don't see it, Pammy, she's so . . . virtuous. She lights incense in the altar, praying and talking to Papa and dead ancestors and all that every night, for God's sake. She's like 'I must suffer 'cuz I'm a totally traditional Confucian Asian babe.' "

"Tammy, I swear, someday your tongue will put you in intensive care."

"My tongue nothing. Miss P., if U.S. so much as touches her I'll shoot him right between the eyes with Papa's slingshot, I mean it. He's not right in the head."

"And you are?" Pammy said, rolling her pretty eyes. "You know what, Tammy? You should have put that slingshot away when you were twelve. You're a sophomore now, and you're still playing with that thing. I swear, sometimes I don' t know whether you're going to end up at Stanford or in San Quentin." But that was not the end of that. Pammy paused for a few seconds and then, in this totally different voice in Vietnamese, all demure like, she said, "Little Monkey, Mamma's been alone for so long. Mamma should have somebody. We shouldn't stand in the way."

I didn't answer her. I just turned out the light. In the dark, I did what I usually do when I have a hard time falling asleep: I try to remember Papa.

I have this favorite memory of him, so long ago, when I was four or five, before the asshole VCs took him, but I remember it super clearly. It's a Kodak moment: a late afternoon in Ben Tre, a golden sun shining over the greenest rice fields you'll ever see and the wind is blowing, making the whole field waver like it's an endless green sea. I am sitting on Papa's lap and we're swinging on this hammock in the back of our house looking at that emerald sea. I'm pulling on the slingshot with one hand and try to shoot, but I don't have the strength and the rock flies less than three feet. Papa laughs and rubs my hair: "Little Monkey, you'll have to wait until you're older. By then you'll have to go hunting for wild ducks and rabbits to feed me and your mother."

Papa shows me how he does it. It's so easy for him, so effortless. He puts a rock in the pouch part and holds the handle in his right hand, turns his head slightly so that he's looking at it from the corner of his eye, and then he pulls the sling far, far back. He lets the rock zip into the air as he exhales. *Phhtock!*—it hits the trunk of a star fruit tree growing by the edge of the rice paddies some twenty yards away. All of a sudden there's this commotion and a flock of wild parrots, hidden in the branches, take off from the tree top, flashing their red and blue and yellow and green feathers, a squawking rainbow toward the sky. I remember yelling and clapping my hands. It's magic, Papa. It's awesome. Oh my goodness, it's the best moment of my life.

But the replay button in my head didn't work that night. I mean, I couldn't see Papa's face clearly, not to save my life. Instead I kept seeing U.S. and Mamma holding hands in my head. Worse, when I fell asleep I dreamed that Grandma T. was scooping soup out of a coffin into a bowl and asked me to drink it but I wouldn't. Then I saw Mamma and U.S. rolling around on this big bed made out of a big tree branch in this big old treehouse doing the wild thang and I just sat there by the bed and cried and cried but it was like U.S. and Mamma didn't even see me and that bummed me out, totally.

So maybe it was just sheer luck or maybe it had to happen. Like Grandma T. always said: "Be careful what you hate or God will give it to you on a lacquered tray." So when Mr. I'm-Also-Vietnamese returned one bright Saturday morning to the Tender-freak'n-loin from overseas, he was in my target range. I mean, usually I wouldn't even think of shooting anybody from the rooftop, let alone a paid customer and a regular, no matter how much he gets in my hair. But Adam was with me. And before we saw U.S., we were already on the roof of my building getting stoned on one of his reefers and shooting at the billboard with Papa's slingshot.

The billboard was helluva annoying. It showed this happy couple and their three children holding hands and smiling with im-

possibly white teeth as they walk out of this white castle. So Adam
broke a candy machine the night before and stuffed his army pants
pockets with jawbreakers just for me, so that fake smiling family
didn't stand a chance. We sent one colorful piece of candy after another zipping toward the gringo family. *Phtoock!*—I took out the
oldest girl's front tooth with a red jawbreaker. *Phtoock!*—Adam
shot the mother in the chest and *Phtooock!*—I shot the father in
the forehead. And then I just went for the baby, the one with a
Mickey Mouse hat on—*Phtoock! Phtoock!*—I made Swiss cheese
out of that little boy.

We shot and shot until the roof was littered with broken can-
dies. It looked like a rainbow had shattered and rained down in
pieces. We couldn't stop laughing. It was my second time doing pot,
but the first didn't really count: nothing happened that first time.
So how would I know I was gonna be higher than a kite the second
time around? The stuff, as Adam said, was from Colombia, so it
had extra strength, extra magic. One puff, and I coughed, cursed,
breathed in, breathed out; two puffs, and I had tears in my eyes,
pain in my lungs, and my throat hurt like hell; three, and boom, I
was gone. I was like, oh my God, I'm swimming in this thick, gold,
bright air. My head felt like it had on that gilded traditional hat the
Thai dancer was wearing in U.S.'s postcard. It felt heavy and weird
but kinda cool, too, like the sunshine had found a way inside and
was swirling around.

I was laughing like the mad and messed-up chick that I was
when I saw over the parapet an all-too-familiar shape. He had this
conical hat on his head and a red and yellow Hawaiian shirt full
of flowers and in his arms he had a brown vase wrapped in a red
ribbon. If you asked me, U.S. looked like he was depriving some
village somewhere of an idiot.

"That's him, Adam," I said, giggling still. "That's him. He's back.
That's the dude who's going to try to marry my Mamma. Look, he's
even got a wedding gift wrapped in red for her, see."

"That shithead down there with the funny hat?" Adam said.
"He's the one who called me Tattoo Boy?"

"Tattoo Guy."

"Who gives a fuck," Adam said. Then he had this look on his face, like he just thought of something funny. "Hey," he said, "Tammy, listen, you can prevent a wedding."

"How?" I said and kept staring at the bleeding rose in the snake's mouth on his arm. When he flexed it, it seemed like it was slithering.

Adam turned to look at me like I was real stupid. "What d'you mean how? Look down, babe, that ain't no toy in your hand."

I looked. Papa's slingshot, made of mahogany and smoothed by years of use, was glowing like wildfire. Adam took out an orange jawbreaker from his pants pocket, blew on it for good luck and took my hand. He made me squeeze it, then kissed me. "Do it, baby," he whispered into my face. I closed my eyes. I could taste the sweetness of his breath, feel the intense heat emanating from his body, smell his salty sweat. "Do it. Hurry! Before he's out of range."

What happened next I see it now like watching TV, in slo-mo. I see me putting the jawbreaker in the sling and pulling it far, far back. I see me taking aim at U.S., and then the jawbreaker just flew. It took forever to reach that conical-hatted figure down below . . .

Years . . .

Decades . . .

Centuries . . .

And for a moment I thought it would never reach him. But how could it not? Papa's slingshot was magic. That morning was magic. And so was Adam's candy. It hit U.S.'s upper left shoulder with a small thud, and he automatically jerked forward and yelped, and the vase in his hand fell out of his grasp to shatter on the sidewalk in this nasty, cracking noise.

"No," he wailed and stepped one step forward before sinking to his knees. Then he checked his shoulder to see if he was bleeding, but of course he wasn't. "Who did this? Who did this?" He yelled and took off the conical hat and looked around but didn't see anybody. So he looked down again at the mess. "Oh, Jesus! Jesus almighty."

By then Adam had pulled me back away from the edge, out of U.S.'s sight. "Holy fuck'n shit, Tammy." He kept hugging me and laughing like a madman. "You're my girl! You're in Da House!" but I wasn't even listening to him anymore. U.S.'s voice was the only thing that registered. It sounded so wounded, so hurt down there, like an injured dog.

I pushed Adam away. I went to the parapet and looked again. U.S. was still down there on his knees, busy now gathering the damaged goods into the hat while yelling something like "all that work, all that negotiation . . ." to himself, but his voice trailed off in the morning wind. A strange gray-white powder had spilled from the broken vase and was spiraling upward from his hands and into the sky like smoke.

I must have moved then 'cuz U.S. looked up and our eyes met. Suddenly the giggle went out of me. His eyes were in tears, and his face, tanned and smeared with that gray-white powder, was in such pain and hurt that it took my breath away. I mean, I didn't recognize it at all but, at the same time, it felt like I'd been staring at it all my life.

When he spoke, his voice was all choked up. "These are your father's ashes. I brought them back from Nam. For you . . . for the family."

Something had gone off in my head that moment, a flash, I guess, or a flood of light, and it formed a circle between us. We were somewhere else, another place, another morning. The street below was fast turning into a dark river and the light poles were sprouting silvery fronds. I could almost smell the jasmine fragrance of the rice fields in the air, hear the parrots squabbling somewhere in the sky, feel the burning heat of a tropical sun on my back.

"Your father's ashes," U.S. said again then held the conical hat with its broken urn up higher for me to see, his gift. For the first time since I knew U.S., I didn't have a thing to say to him, not a thing. So I just stared. Then suddenly I couldn't help myself: I raised my arm high in the air and waved over and over again like I was waiting at the dock welcoming him home or something.

Everything Must Go

O N A WINDY MORNING in June, when the fog had finally lifted and the air was cool, they borrowed a truck to drive around Noe Valley in search of garage sales. Along the way they saw many Victorian homes, some of which reminded her of wedding cakes, especially those with white trim, and she said so to him. He agreed with this assessment, though his favorite was the mansion a little farther down the road, one with richly ornate friezes and two distinctive, detailed witches' hats on their spiraling minarets.

When they neared it he slowed down so they both could look. The elaborate gingerbread house caused her to giggle. "Hey," she said, "you're right, very cute. Maybe we should buy it after our first baby."

As soon as she said this, however, she blushed and looked away out the window, and the gesture stirred in him memories of an enamel painting in his family's villa in Hue. The young beauty in it sits leaning out the window with a whimsical expression on her face, her chin resting on the back of her hand. She wears white pajamas, her profile to the viewer, her black hair long, cascading down frail shoulders like a waterfall. On another chair sits her conical hat, half hidden in shadows. It's as if her yearning for the outside world was either restrained or hindered by the blinding sunlight.

Still thinking of this painted beauty, he lifted her hand to kiss it. A warm feeling flowed freely between them as he drove, something like a shared psychic projection of things to come: furniture, a house, a destination, a pouting boy—four years old and talking animatedly—a shared life.

Though neither had discussed it directly, the idea of matrimony had loomed like the city's shimmering high-rises outside their bedroom window, an inevitable progression that presented itself with thrilling alacrity as the days went by. Why else would they buy a loft together after knowing each other for less than six months? A magnificent and spacious 2,300-square-foot upper unit in a three-story Victorian house in Pacific Heights that had everything they could want: a place with a sense of history, lived-in but refurbished with hardwood floors, a generous skylight above the state-of-the-art kitchen with black granite countertops and accent lighting, two fireplaces with blue marble mantels, a back porch large enough for barbecues, and a garden and a small Jacuzzi and tall, double-glazed French windows—windows, framed by flowing white satin curtains, that opened their living room to the Bay.

The wind in their hair, the sun shining, they felt strangely privileged as they drove. It was as if their jubilation and fortune had been providentially bestowed upon them and no one else in the city of fog and sea and intermittent sunshine, of immigrants and cable cars. Contented, he whistled as he drove and, between clutch shifts, rested his hand on her thigh, and she, as if in sync with his music, responded by practicing scales on his knuckles.

A serendipitous meeting: each was driving a red BMW Z8 convertible down Battery Street smack into the Gay Pride Parade. Stuck for the duration, all they could do was watch. But he also watched her, and, as soon as he saw her profile, he inched his car forward until they paralleled.

"Hey," he said. She turned and lifted her dark shades to display mild displeasure. But irritation melted into amusement as he facetiously eyed her car and pursed his lips and, mimicking a pretentious but approving art critic, raised one arch eyebrow and nodded in approval.

It worked; she smiled.

But before any further exchanges passed between them, a float of S&M practitioners slowly passed in front of them, its speakers blasting "Let's Play Master and Servant" by Depeche Mode, distracting them both. At its bow stood an unusually large man with a bearded face and a round belly that protruded from his open leather vest, and in his hand whirled a short whip. Kneeling on both sides of the float were muscular young men in leather shorts and spike-studded leather collars, their torsos bare and oiled, their arms tied loosely behind their backs, their muscular chests heaving glossily under a scorching sun.

The two turned to each other and laughed. "Nice day for a parade," she remarked and rolled her eyes comically.

"Yeah," he said, taking her cue. "Too bad I got here late. I missed my favorite float: Proud Gay Dentists From Bakersfield."

"Well," she retorted, not missing a beat, "at least I got to see mine: Ecstatic Pakistani Lesbian Nannies."

He laughed. As they talked on they found, to their mutual surprise, that they had even more in common than their taste in sports cars or humor: they came from the same country, shared the same history—refugees when they were but children. They quickly exchanged business cards, and, as traffic moved again, he called her cell phone while she was still in his sight and asked if she wanted to go dancing the next day. "Sure, yes," she said and waved backward to him as she eyed him from her rearview mirror. Making a date at Pride with a complete stranger was not something she did on a regular basis, she said, but for him, she would make an exception.

After they hung up he pumped his fist in the air triumphantly the way he had when his high-tech company went public. He turned onto Larkin and elation abruptly gave over to a profound emptiness. He already missed her. Would she show up? He gripped the cell phone, contemplating calling her again to hear her voice, to make sure, but decided not to and winced instead under the harsh sunlight.

A memory came stirring up from somewhere deep inside. Sunshine in a garden, bird songs in the air, the sound of children's laughter. A giggly child, he stood waiting patiently with his two older sisters in the garden with their palms outstretched, waiting for their mother to read their future. His turn and she bent his fingers back so hard he cried and tried to pull away but her grip was a vice. "You'll be a very rich man, quite rich," she announced sweetly. But when she looked into his eyes, her voice was the kind she used to address an adult, a stranger: "What will you do, tell me, sir, with all the earthly paradise you'll inherit?"

It had frightened him. That was in Hue, the Imperial City, in a whitewashed villa overlooking the Perfume River, some time before the war escalated and engulfed the entire country and before his mother's sadness grew to engulf everyone in the household, her nightly weeping turning into his childhood lullabies, while his father faded into a silent, distant figure. He remembered staring at the scratchy lines in the middle of his palm afterward, frightened and confused. He remembered how they had seemed to him like tiny rivers and roads, his palm a map that foretold a mysterious destiny.

She hung up and giggled. A date with a stranger met on gay Market Street. Imagine! She kept laughing as she drove, going slowly from east to west, in a mythic American trajectory, toward the setting sun, trailing for two blocks the dying procession of floats on which sat weary, sunburnt dancers—some massaging their calves and feet while others had fallen asleep among the bed of wilting flowers and broken leis—a rotting Eden on wheels.

SHE SAW IT FIRST and sat up like a cat. "Stop!" she said. He hit the brakes. Stapled to the weathered, cracked wood of a telephone pole riddled with rusted staples was a handwritten sign. They both leaned forward and read.

ESTATE SALE! ESTATE SALE!
861 ALVARADO STREET
EVERYTHING MUST GO BY 4 PM!!!

"Everything!" she shrieked, her voice several notes higher. "I knew it! Oh gosh! Oh gosh!" She yelled and pointed at a small house where people were going in and out carrying lamps and clothes and dishes and a few chairs. It reminded him of a mass looting.

"It looks like . . . ," he said, but she was already out of the truck. "Honey," she yelled, "jackpot! Let's go. Let's go in. Baby, I mean, you park first. Park, OK? I'll get in before everything's gone. I have a good feeling about this."

"Hold on," he said and was about to give her his wallet—she had left her purse at home—but she already had slammed the door and, like a jittery swallow, darted away from him.

The wind on her back, her water-lilies summer dress fluttered like a floating garden against her body—he laughed as she hurried down the block and sidestepped dancer-like to avoid the young couple carrying a coffee table out of the house. At the doorway she turned and blew a kiss to him as if from a cruise ship before a long ocean voyage.

A quaint but not particularly large house: the kind of bungalow built at least half a century ago for ambitious working couples on their way to a larger place. But now, with prices rising in the city, with the working class leaving and high-tech professionals moving in, the place was prime property, given the location. Having hunted for the perfect home for months, she smiled cynically when she thought of how real estate salesmen would describe the place to potential buyers after the estate sale was done: something along the lines of "an enchanting bungalow" or "storybook home."

But its water-stained shingles and listing white wooden fence evoked nothing enchanting. Or rather a quiet sobriety rose in her that renewed her resolve. Got to get what's there before it's all gone.

She had been poor. She had even been homeless. Unlike him, who, thanks to his family connections, came to America by plane even before the war ended, she was, like most of the others who fled afterward, a boat person. She had lived most of her childhood in various refugee camps, subsisting on handouts and charity.

Chicken wings in red plastic buckets; wet, gooey rice in rusted tin pails; bunk beds that sheltered whole families; tick bites and rashes; unbearable heat and odious stench. Everyone lived under oppressive corrugated hangars, where fights broke out daily, where practically every week someone would hang himself or herself in the latrines, and where hurried and banal and careless sex went on behind flimsy, ragged curtains, and on the other side children played hopscotch and sang.

For months in one refugee camp she had kept a piece of treasure from America, a page from a Sears catalog that had wrapped her boiled peanuts. It was smeared on one side, but on the other, oh the beauty! Bed frames and mattresses, colorful pillows fluffy as clouds, and flower-print sheets that blossomed into sprawling gardens and red-tiled haciendas in her recurring dreams.

She kept it all the way to America and threw it out the first week after she saw what was available at a nearby shopping mall, where she spent the bulk of her teen years yearning for a better life. Sometimes she would walk to a nicer neighborhood and peer into the lighted windows, stealing glimpses of the décor and the elegant life within.

At seventeen she fled. She did not miss the cockroach-infested rented home in Irvine she'd shared with her family of six. Granted a full scholarship, she went to Berkeley, read *Elle* and *Vogue* and *Cosmopolitan* and *Better Homes and Gardens*. She discovered she could shave her annoying Vietnamese accent off her tongue by adopting a slightly British one. Unlike her siblings, she never looked back, never wanted to take up residence near her parents after college to show her filial piety. Then to work—to a sophisticated life *sans* the stink of fish sauce wafting from a grease-stained kitchen and the coughing fits of her chain-smoking father and the sorrowful-sounding Buddhist chant of her mother each morning.

But now, she'd come full circle, hadn't she? Now she'd found a man that her parents couldn't help but approve of, an upper-class man from the old country, a sales executive at a high-tech company.

With him, she'd created a golden nest in a worldly setting, something the rest of her family, who clung to the often churlish and nostalgic culture of Little Saigon and resisted the offerings of the larger world, could only gawk at in awe.

A fat woman in her mid-forties sat at the end of the dark hallway behind a small Louis Quinze side table. She greeted everyone who entered with rehearsed joviality and a slogan: "Everything's gotta go, we've got to close by four. So come on in. Cash, checks, credit cards—we take them before four, we take them all."

"Is that side table sold already?" she asked breathlessly. She could tell that it was an antique.

"Good eye," the fat lady said. "But I already sold it. You can tell when it's written 'Sold' on the tag here, see? Plenty of good stuff inside though," winked the fat lady, "if you're quick." At her plump feet sat the kind of crocheted bag old ladies keep for yarn and needles and half-made sweaters, but instead it bulged with a cloisonné enamel bowl, two silver candlesticks, a wine bottle from Bordeaux.

She walked farther in. The house was chaotic. And dark. And vaguely odorous—the smell of decay. She sighed. And took a deep breath. Better get used to it now.

As she moved, she kept her focus, paying attention only to things and their price tags: furniture and kitchenware, silverware and ceramics, and price tags that didn't yet say "Sold." There was a nice wedding cabinet, but the door was broken—too big anyway for the truck. Next to the cabinet stood a lovely rosewood armoire. For $100, it was a bargain. She could tell that it was well-kept and something of an antique. The carved bookcase, on the other hand, was too scratched to fix, and its blond wood, alas, wouldn't match the furniture she already had bought.

She turned away. There must be other pieces still available. She made a mental calculation: two big things could possibly fit on that truck, no more. What indeed might fit where and what might go with which pieces in their loft, and how, and what color scheme and pattern for which room were overwhelming her vision. She had been fancying something in the Mission style, though not strictly so, of course, for this was the post-modern age, after all. Varnished rosewood and mahogany would shine under the intricate lighting and creamy beige walls of the drawing room and chrysanthemum William Morris wallpaper to provide understated elegance in the dining room. She pictured a hand-knotted wool rug of fern motif, envisioned on the walls a few abstract paintings by an artist friend, all in dark green and white, which he called *Monsoon Rains.*

"Excuse me," she said as she jostled past a woman to get to the dining table. The table was sold but on it were silverware, vases, and wine bottles. She saw a beautifully carved teapot made of some black stone, and reached for it before a young woman with pink hair holding a carton box full of plates across the table could. "Finder's keepers," she said and tried to soften the blow with a wink. If the woman had muttered "bitch!" under her breath, she didn't care to hear it. She was too busy studying the exquisite pot, which was heavy in her hand. The stone's smooth texture had lit her on fire. She whistled. It was an antique, she could tell, with images of Chinese gods and fairies attending a banquet in the clouds, and a summer pavilion by a lake. It was a definite buy. She hugged it to her bosom. The price tag said $20. She could see it on their coffee table; it would fit. Perfectly. If only she could find the stone cups that went with it. She searched and searched. But she could find none.

An oily, sticky film coated everything, including the sofa and doorknobs and windowpanes, which, with the stained, yellowed curtains, obscured the sunlight despite the bright afternoon outside. She grew frantic. The place was crawling with good stuff, hidden among the junk. It was as if several people with incongruous tastes and economic means had lived in the same house. It was a challenge to pick the good from the bad.

If only she'd arrived in the early morning! Out in the hallway, the fat lady sang out in a melodic voice, as if to admonish her for being late: "Buy one, buy all, everything's gotta go by four!"

When he entered the house, it was as if a flea market had decided to move inside a very small place. People talked, argued, pushed, and jostled about in the tight, cramped space. They touched and turned things over and around, pots clanged against pans in the kitchen, and desk and cabinet drawers shuffled in and out repeatedly as if the entire house were host to a poltergeist.

A fat woman stood at the end of the dark hallway giving change to a couple, each holding a varnished mahogany nightstand. She greeted him without looking. "Great sale! Great sale!" she said. "Buy them up, buy them now, we'll bargain, we'll take checks, cash, credit cards."

A faint but unmistakable odor of disinfectant and stale urine reached his nostrils and caused him to shudder. A familiar smell, it immediately brought back memories of the hospital in Boston where his mother lost her fight with bone cancer some years ago. Or was it her sadness that seeped into the marrow, the bone, and poisoned her?

In the crowded living room someone was removing the chandelier while standing on a very expensive-looking chair. It was dark in the house. A man grabbed his arm and he turned. "Sorry," said the man, "for a minute there I thought you were my brother."

Before he could say anything someone dropped some chinaware in the kitchen; the sound of the thing shattering set his teeth on edge. Two middle-aged men argued over a stained-glass cabinet, their voices angry. They had drawn a small crowd. "I saw it first, asshole." "Who cares," said the other. "Lots of people saw it. I already asked the lady for it."

He shook his head and made a face. He called out her name, tentatively at first, almost in a whisper, then found his voice and repeated it several times. No answers came, though a few heads turned. He kept moving. He tried to hold his breath, and failed, and fought the retching.

Where is she? He took out his cell phone only to remember that hers was in her purse, which was left on their bed. He walked slowly, pushing people out of his way, not in a panic exactly, avoiding carton boxes, but wondering where she was. He tried to focus on human shapes and voices, saw no signs of her. A strange thought rose in him, that she was, as if in a horror film, abducted and gone, and he fought quickly to dismiss it. Somewhere in the next room a child shrieked repeatedly before bawling.

He stumbled into the main bedroom and saw what caused the smell. Behind a handful of people busily inspecting a bookcase and a large oval mirror stood a metal hospital bed. Draped under a white sheet, it was ignored by all. He imagined a body under it, and, though he knew it was only his imagination, he instinctively backed out and stepped on a woman's foot. An aged blonde with a closed face yelped as she clutched at a large pink vase in her arms dramatically. "Watch out," she said, "you jerk!"

"Sorry," he mumbled. The woman glared at him.

Out in the hallway, the fat lady sang with humor. "Everything's gotta go, we've got to close by four. So come on in, folks."

He massaged his temples as he leaned against the wall. Somehow he'd fallen through a trap door to some other place not of his city. With eyes closed, he saw morphine dripping and heard the low, persistent groans of the infirm. Then, among the various noises, he heard someone calling for him: *Duyen!* But his girlfriend never called him by that name. He turned around. He looked at the hospital bed again and felt goosebumps rising.

IT WAS BRIGHTEST in the dining room. In it, he saw a Chinese in-laid cabinet. It had circular perforated doors with two carved brass doorknobs that formed the shape of the Chinese word *happiness*. They were veiled now in a green patina. One of its doors had slipped off its hinges, threatening to fall off, and the wood, once deep red, had faded to beige, marred by years of use. It was going for $80. It could be restored, he supposed, but it would take time and effort, and, anyway, it wasn't up to him to decide. He trusted her taste and aesthetic instincts and, moreover, he relied on her enthusiasm.

The contents inside, on the other hand, drew his attention. Forty or so dolls of different sizes and shapes and representing different countries, lined three shelves as if they were in a pageant. A few had already been bought, leaving white spots on the shelves. The dolls, those made of porcelain or wood, looked expensive to him, but the most expensive went for $20, and his eyes fell on one in a red *ao dai* dress and conical hat that went for $5. He grabbed it. It vaguely hurt him that he was participating in the breaking up of someone's collection, but he hadn't seen a doll like that since he was a child, the kind that tourists bought in Saigon or Hue in souvenir shops, and nostalgia stirred in him. Besides, she would get a kick out of it, he thought, wherever she was.

IN THE BASEMENT, on top of a treasure.

She first saw a door in the kitchen that she thought would lead to the pantry, but it led her down to the basement. She went tentatively down the steps, and at the bottom, behind two middle-aged men sifting through stacks of old magazines and records in carton boxes, was the writing desk—a true blue Stickley. She could tell right away what it was, having seen one just like it that went for $8,900 in an antique shop on Battery Street a month or so ago, out of her price range. She thought she knew its origin—crafted sometime around 1910, a roll-top desk with original finish, great ebony color.

She held her breath as she walked toward it. When she saw the price tag she sighed with relief and put down her teapot and the stained-glass art deco lamp she'd found in one of the three bedrooms. No one had bought it yet. It had suffered minor wear but was still in fine condition. And at $300 it was practically a giveaway. She tore the tag off, sat on the desk, then picked up her teapot and held it tightly, as if preparing to use it as a weapon on anyone who would stray too close. A dream of a find, it made the two Morris chairs they bought last week mere junk.

She cursed herself. If she had her purse, it would have been "Sold." Then she could go and look at other possible treasures. But she quickly calculated: she must have this desk first, no matter what. The couple rummaging by the carton boxes finally looked at her. Was she acting suspicious? There were other treasure hunters around, she could tell. She smiled amiably to make sure they knew it was hers, the price tag she had hidden in the teapot. "I'm waiting for my husband," she said, "to help me carry this monster."

She could be amazing, she had boasted to him more than once, when it came to getting what she wanted. She had proven herself an expert last month at a flea market in Marin County. Although she had forgotten almost everything else about her homeland, she still remembered, strangely enough, how to bargain. She'd ingested the art of haggling from her simple but hard-working mother. Cajole, appeal to the seller's better nature, lose one's temper, point out the defects in question, sigh and pout, and when the object is bought at the determined price, look unhappy, as if you're doing the seller a favor.

The last time they went looking for garage sales, they found two perfect chairs. "If my job at Schwab didn't pay so well," she had told him as they put their newly bought chairs in the truck, "I'd quit in a minute and go into the antique business. Like the Kenny Rogers' song says: 'You've got to know when to hold, know when to walk away.' If you're too attached to the object you desire, baby, you'll lose, you'll lose."

Furniture thrilled her. Immensely. Especially antiques, with their elegant sheen that held fabulous histories, their dark wood surfaces touched by many hands over the centuries; these things stirred something deep in her soul.

A few more minutes passed. Damn it, where was he? She grew frantic for the want of things—treasures among junk—to be found in the bungalow. If he found her now she could start grabbing the small stuff—china and antique lamps and carved picture frames and lacquered cigar boxes and urns—while he bought the desk for her. She chastised herself for leaving her purse at home—stupid, stupid!—and now she was dependent on him for the purchases. There was possibly one other great piece she'd spotted in the bedroom closet, a highboy made of polished oak. And who knows, there might be a chair that went with this desk somewhere, of the same period. But how could she leave her Chippendale? She had found a few good pieces before at estate sales but this—this was the mother lode.

Did he know there was a basement accessible from the kitchen? She wanted to yell. "I'm down here! Come down to get me! Come down now!" She felt at once trapped, overwhelmed, abandoned, and giddy. She had fallen into a well and found herself on top of a mound of gold coins and was waiting for her prince charming to throw her a rope.

"Where is he?" She said it out loud this time and one of the men laughed. "I've been saying that all my life, honey," he said. His companion elbowed him in the ribs and in a catty voice said, "Yeah, me, too. Listen, settle with what you've got. Don't hold your breath."

She laughed and, when they left to go back upstairs, sighed and wiped the cold sweat off her neck. She walked around the desk. Her hands caressed its surface, feeling where it was scratched on its otherwise elegant smoothness, and she imagined herself writing a letter on it. She opened the drawer and the smell of old wood and camphor rose to fill the air. Inside was a small, framed photo. It was a faded sepia of a woman, pretty but not beautiful, with curly blond hair. The woman was smoking a cigarette through a long, white cigarette holder, probably made of bone or ivory. She held it in the upturned cupped palm on which she rested her chin. She wore a simple blouse and her fingers were long, elegant, but her half smile was enigmatic. She was seeing something very far away, seemingly unaware of the camera.

"Hey," she heard him and turned. He was holding a doll out to her, smiling. There was a look in his eyes that she hadn't seen before, something between sad and hopeful.

"God, where have you been?" she asked, visibly relaxed. "I've been waiting and waiting down here."

"I didn't know there was a down here here," he said, trying to humor her, but she didn't wait for him to finish. "Did you buy that?" she said. "Honey, it's ragged. The porcelain ones are more valuable. Still, they're all, I don't know, too kitschy, don't you think? Won't fit in our place."

He looked at the doll in his hand and looked again at her. "Did you find anything?" he asked, his voice flat and lacking energy. "This place gives me the creeps. Some old guy died here and it smells awful."

"My guess: it was this woman," she said and held out the photograph. "I doubt a man would collect dolls. Started out rich, ended up poor. Got a little loco near the end, became a pack rat. You know the deal."

She looked at his watch. "Damn! Most of the good stuff is probably already sold by now. You should have given me your wallet."

He was still studying the photograph. Then he looked at her as if to assess her anew. "Whatever," he said impatiently. "Let's go."

"Are you kidding? We can't go. It's an estate sale, honey," she said, rolling her eyes. "That's what happens at estate sales. Someone dies so others can buy."

"Well, that's crass," he said. He couldn't tell if she was being funny or serious from her tone. In the dim light she seemed to be smirking at him, which made him feel like an obtuse child in the schoolyard who was the butt of some joke.

"We can't go," she said again. "Not now. Not yet." In a conspiratorial tone, she whispered to him so that the old man who had come down after him and was now rummaging at the other end among carton boxes couldn't hear her. "Baby, jackpot! I'm sitting on a true blue Stickley writing desk. For 300 smackaroos." Then she kissed him, a quick peck on the nose.

"Oh," he said, but he didn't look at it. He was too busy looking at the doll in his hand. He wanted to say "Good job, honey," but another urge came rising up instead, as if he needed to validate something. He pushed himself against her and kissed her hard. While doing so, he reached out with his other hand and touched her breast. She did not resist at first, but when his hand wandered down toward her crotch, she hit him instinctively with the teapot.

"Ouch," he said.

"Sorry," she hissed. "Shit. Did that hurt?"

"It hurts," he said, annoyed. "More than you know."

"Well, what were you thinking?" she said defensively, gesturing with her chin at the old man who was now watching them. "We just had sex this morning. Don't you ever have enough?"

"Don't you?" he replied.

"Well, who's crass now? You or me?" she asked, matching his venom.

He took a quick breath. "Come on, let's get out of here."

"No!" she said, rather sourly. "Look, I'm sorry. I really am. But we've got, at the very least, to get this desk and this pot. Oh, and this lamp, too."

An accusing look flowed from his eyes then, but he said nothing. In the dim light, she seemed different to him somehow, a little haggard-looking, and older, too. And her hand was gripping the teapot with a kind of jealous ownership as if she had no intention of sharing any of the things she'd found.

But what had he been thinking? He didn't know. If he had to venture a guess, he'd kissed her to make sure that she was there and not an apparition, that it was still OK between them.

"I don't know," he finally said, though he meant to say I don't know what I'm thinking, and somehow the sentence was left unfinished.

"One those moods again, huh?" she said. "If you're afraid of ghosts, why don't you wait in the truck?"

He drew himself in from the comment. He'd never heard her use that tone of voice before. He was not afraid. Not of ghosts, nor of the dead. He was afraid for her, for them. Why, exactly, he didn't know. Still, the accusation hurt. "It's just an old desk," he said. His voice shifted a little; it had more confidence and a sense of brashness in it, the kind of voice he used at work. Then it built a rhythm and he found his stride. "Frankly, I don't think it's any good. It's scratched over here, see. That's too much for $300. And it'll be difficult to take it out of the basement. We could get hurt. We should go." He stepped back away from her, as if ready to leave.

He had the wallet, after all.

She watched him move farther away from her. She opened her mouth to say something but changed her mind. Win an argument and lose the Stickley. A light came over her face then; she smiled seductively. "Wait, honey," she whispered. "Tell you what: I'll make you a deal."

He looked quizzically at her. He could hear the flirtation in her voice, chased with humor. So he matched hers. "Yeah," he said, "what kind of deal, sweetheart?"

"Come 'ere," she said. He complied. When he was close enough, she leaned forward and whispered the deal in his ear. There was no one else around. The older man had gone back upstairs. She could see him blushing despite the dim light at the proposal. He cleared his throat. "You'll do that, if I give you my sky's-the-limit gold MasterCard?"

"Uh-huh. Once we get home."

"Oh, I don't know," he said. He, too, could bargain. She was not the only one who had that gift. "How about we raise the stakes? What about if I, uhm, I mean, we do it here?" She scowled but quickly recovered. "Here?"

"Yeah, here," he went on. "And I'll help you carry this beautiful desk afterward, plus whatever else you want to buy. My shop-'til-you-drop gold card is all yours."

She looked at him. She could feel herself blushing. It was no longer funny. But she wanted the desk. She envisioned it in the study, a perfect match with the Oxford display cabinet. "Fine," she said. "And I'll buy whatever I want without you saying another word."

She left the pot and lamp on the desk and took his hand and they went behind the furnace and she promptly got down on her knees and unzipped him. She took out his penis. But he couldn't get hard. In fact, he was still having trouble breathing.

"Listen," he said after a minute or two, grabbing her hands. "I'm sorry. I didn't know you were going to go through with it. I was just kidding. I shouldn't have . . ."

"Whatever," she said and stood up and fixed her hair and brushed the dirt off her knees. She held out her hand. "Credit card, please." Then she added, a little breathless. "We've got to get the desk before four."

He zipped up, took out his wallet, and gave the credit card to her. "Here you go." She snatched it and started to go upstairs with it.

"Oh, honey, and get the hospital bed, too, if you want." He meant it as a joke, but there was hostility in his voice, and with the mood they were in, it didn't register as funny to either of them.

She looked back at him. "At least I have a passion. I don't wallow in self-loathing."

They stood staring at each other and the moment filled with their helplessness. He felt as if some mysterious malevolent force had come and pushed them away from one another.

"Listen," he said. "I'm sorry."

"You said that already. Just go get the truck, OK?"

He nodded miserably. Their first fight, and it somehow ended up all wrong. You were supposed to have sex after your fight, not in between, and you weren't supposed to remain angry after.

He wanted to say more, but she'd already rushed past him up the stairs to search for the fat lady.

WHEN HE EMERGED from the house the weather had turned. Thick white clouds drifted above him and it was windy and cold. For a moment he stood staring at the churning clouds; his eyes, having been in the dark for so long, had trouble adjusting. The world seemed luminescent and constantly changing, and even those distant hills, kissed now by low-flying clouds, were moving as well. He blinked and blinked, trying to readjust his sight, but the world still possessed that odd, transparent quality, as if everything were made of the clearest water. The wind billowed and howled in his ears. People all around him were carrying things out of the house—china, books, gilded mirrors, chairs, pillows, paintings, a vanity—assigning a biography to oblivion.

He looked down at his hand. He'd been holding the little doll with the conical hat in a tight grip, the price tag still tied to its arm. He had picked it up on the way out of the basement without thinking, without paying for it, and now, in the sunlight, he could see that she was right. The doll's red dress, moth-eaten, had tangled up in her raised arms, revealing her pale, plastic flesh underneath. He stared contemplatively at the doll for some time before fixing her dress, smoothing her hair, and rearranging her conical hat. In a cracked blue casserole on top of a pile of broken junk someone left on the sidewalk, he laid her down gently, almost ceremoniously, as if she were a dead baby.

His Rolex said 3:44 p.m. Another few minutes and everything would be gone.

They broke up in late October, though the sky remained blue and the weather hardly changed at all. It was amicable: she bought him out of his half of the loft, and he generously offered to give all the lovely furniture they'd bought together to her, his departing gesture, as it were, but she wouldn't hear of it. "I'm not petty," she said and paid him his half of what they'd paid, though not the furniture's real worth at antique stores, and the writing desk did turn out to be an authentic Stickley that was worth quite a bit of money.

It didn't really matter. He became a multimillionaire soon thereafter. His company was sold to a multinational corporation, which eventually merged with another, and all these frantic transactions made him immensely rich. He wisely pulled out before the economy overheated and then went sour. He invested in real estate as more garage sales went up around the city. He retired at a very young age, then took off and traveled to India and China and Tibet, and, upon returning to the States, decided to once more go back to Boston to be near his older sisters and their families.

She did not do badly herself. She went into the antique business with a well-to-do French boyfriend. They opened a shop on Union Street and, with her instincts and connections, it became quite successful. The centerpiece of her shop was the writing desk—her desk now—and it was the only thing in the store that was not for sale.

When she was idle, or when she was on the phone, she would mindlessly let her fingers trail over the desk's surface, its carved edges, the scratches on its otherwise elegant smoothness, and this calmed her. Sometimes, though, late at night and alone, doing accounting on the sales of the day, under an incandescent light, she would, with the carefulness of a jewel thief, open the desk's left drawer. She'd rescued the photograph of the woman with the ivory cigarette holder in her mouth. She would study it carefully, trying to imagine the life of this stranger who smiled her mysterious smile. Inevitably, the vague mildew and mothball smell rising from the drawer would remind her too much of the events of that strange day and, filling with despair, she would quickly close the drawer, sentencing the photograph once more to the dark.

He, too, often thought of her, recalling his last image of that afternoon. After the goods were bought and bargained for and bundled and secured with ropes, especially the desk, she told him that she would sit in the back of the truck to make sure things wouldn't fall off. "But you'll be cold," he protested meekly. "Anyway, neither of us have a jacket. It's so ridiculous."

"What's so ridiculous?" she snapped. "A little wind? I'm not wimpy."

Like veterans of some long-fought war, they looked warily at each other, bruised and scarred by the things they'd been carrying. "Suit yourself," he shrugged and climbed in the truck and slammed the door. He drove with the heater blowing oppressively, parchingly, and felt like he was roasting in an oven. Occasionally he would steal glances at her in the rearview mirror. She was there, all right, against the cold, gray sky, beautiful once more but expressionless, showing no fear of the weather, and hovering over his right shoulder as if flying, her hair a silky black flag flapping in the wind.

Grandma's Tales

THE DAY AFTER Mama and Papa took off to Las Vegas, Grandma died. Lea and me, we didn't know what to do. Vietnamese traditional funerals with incense sticks and chanting Buddhist monks were not our thing.

"We have a big freezer," Lea said. "Why don't we freeze Grandma? Really, why bother Mama and Papa—what's another day or two for Grandma now anyway?"

Since Lea's older than me and since I didn't have any better idea, we iced Grandma.

Grandma was ninety-four years, eight months, and six days old when she died. She had seen lots of things and lived through three wars and two famines. She lived a full hard life, if you ask me. America, besides, was not all that good for her. She had been confined to the second floor of our big Victorian home as her health was failing, and she did not speak English and only a little French. French like "*Oui, monsieur, c'est evidemment un petit monstre.*" And "*Non, Madame, vous n' êtes pas du tout enceinte, je vous assure.*" She was a head nurse in the maternity ward of the Hanoi hospital during the French colonial time. I used to love her stories about delivering all these strange two-headed babies and the Siamese triplets connected at the hip whom she named Happy, Liberation, and Day.

Grandma died a quiet death really. She was eating spring rolls with me and Lea. Lea was wearing this real nice black miniskirt and her lips were painted red and Grandma said, "You look like a high-class whore." And Lea made a face and said she was preparing to go to one of her famous San Francisco artsy-fartsy cocktail parties where waiters are better dressed than most Vietnamese men of high-class status back home and the foods are served on silver trays and there is baby corn, duck paté, salmon mousse, and ice sculptures with wings, and live musicians playing Vivaldi music. "So eat, Grandma, and get off my case, because I'm no whore."

"It was a compliment," Grandma said, winking at me, "but I guess it's wasted on you, child." Then Grandma laughed, her breath hoarse and thinning, her deep wrinkled face a blur. Still she managed to say this much as Lea prepared to leave: "Child, do the cha-cha-cha for me. I didn't get to do much when I was young, with my clubbed foot and the wars and everything else."

"Sure, Grandma," Lea said and rolled her pretty eyes toward the chandelier. Then Grandma just dropped her chopsticks on the hardwood floor—clack, clack, clatter, clack, clack—leaned back, closed her eyes, and stopped breathing. Just like that.

So we iced her. She was small enough that she fit right above the TV dinner trays and the frozen yogurt bars we were going to have for dessert. We wrapped all of grandma's five-foot-three, ninety-eight-pound lithe body in Saran wrap and kept her there and hoped Mama and Papa would get the Mama-Papa-come-home-quick-Grandma's-dead letter that we sent to Circus Circus, where they were staying, celebrating their thirty-third wedding anniversary. In the meanwhile, Lea's got a party to go to and I've got to meet Kayden for a movie.

It was a bad movie, too, if you want to know the truth. But Kayden is cool. Kayden has always been cool. Kayden's got eyes so green they make you want to become an environmentalist. Kayden's got this laugh that makes you warm all over. And Kayden is really beautiful and a year older than me, a senior. The movie is called *Dragon*, starring this Hawaiian guy who played Bruce Lee. He moaned and groaned and fought a lot in the movie, but it just wasn't the same. Bruce Lee is dead. Bruce Lee could not be revived even if the guy who played him had all these muscles to crack walnuts and lay bricks with. Now Grandma was dead, too.

So Kayden and I got home and necked on the couch. Kayden liked Grandma. Grandma liked Kayden. Though they hardly ever spoke to one another because neither one knew the other's language, there was this thing between them, you know, mutual respect, like one cool old chick to one cool young dude thing. (Sometimes I would translate, but not always 'cuz my English is not all that good and my Vietnamese sucks.)

What's so cool about Grandma is that she's the only one who knows I'm bisexual. I mean, I hate the term, but I'm bisexual, I suppose, by default 'cuz I don't have a preference and I respond to all stimuli and Kayden stimulated me at the moment and Grandma, who for some reason, though Confucian born and trained, and a Buddhist and all, was really cool about it. One night, I remember, we were sitting in the living room watching a John Wayne movie together and Kayden was there with me and Grandma while Mama and Papa had just gone to bed. (Lea was again at some weird black-and-white ball or something like that.) And Kayden leaned over and kissed me on the lips and Grandma said, "That's real nice," and I translated and we all laughed and John Wayne shot dead five mean old guys. Just like that. But Grandma didn't mind, really. She'd seen Americans like John Wayne shooting her people before and always thought John Wayne was a bad guy in the movies and she'd seen us more passionate than a kiss on the lips and didn't mind. She used to tell us to be careful and not make babies—obviously a joke—'cuz she's done delivering them. She also thought John Wayne was uglier than a water buffalo's ass, but never-you-mind. So, you see, we liked Grandma a lot.

Now Grandma's packed in 20-degree Fahrenheit. And the movie sucked. On the couch in the living room after a while I said, "Kayden, I have to tell you something."

"What?" asked Kayden.

"Grandma's dead," I said.

"You're kidding me!" Kayden whispered, showing his beautiful white teeth.

"I kid you not," I said. "She's dead, and Lea and me, we iced her."

"Shit!" said Kayden. "Why?"

" 'Cuz she would start to smell otherwise, duh, and we have to wait for my parents to perform a traditional Vietnamese funeral." We fell silent for a while then, holding each other. Then Kayden said, "Can I take a peek at Grandma?"

"Sure," I said, "sure you can; she was just as much yours as she was mine," and we went to the freezer and looked in.

The weird thing was the freezer was on defrost and Grandma was nowhere in sight. There was a trail of water and Saran wrap leading from the freezer to her bedroom, though, so we followed it. On the bed, all wet and everything, there sat Grandma counting her Buddhist rosary and chanting her diamond sutra. What's weirder still is that she looked real young. I mean around fifty-four now, not ninety-four. The high cheekbones had come back, the rosy lips. When she saw us, she smiled and said: "What do you say we all go to one of those famous cocktail parties that Lea's gone to, the three of us?"

Now, I wasn't scared, she being my Grandma and all, but what really got me feeling all these goosebumps on my neck and arms was that she said it in English, I mean accentless California English. I mean the way Mrs. Collier, our neighbor, the English teacher, speaks English. Me, I have a slight accent still, but Grandma's was like that of an announcer on NPR.

"Wow, Grandma," said Kayden, "your English is excellent."

"I know," Grandma said, "that's just a side benefit of being reborn. But enough with compliments; we've got to party."

"Cool," said Kayden.

"Cool," I said, though I was a little jealous 'cuz I had to go through junior high and high school and all those damn ESL classes and everything to learn the same language while Grandma just got it down cold—no pun intended—'cuz she was reborn. And

Grandma put on this nice brocade red blouse and black silk pants and sequined velvet shoes and fixed her hair real nice and we drove off downtown.

Boy, you should've seen Lea's face when we came in. I mean she nearly tripped over herself and had to put her face on the wing of this ice sculpture that looked like a big melting duck to calm herself. Then she walked straight up to us, all haughty like, and said, "It's invitation only, how'd y'all get in?"

"Calm yourself, child," said Grandma. "I told them that I was a board member of the Cancer Society and flashed my jade bracelet and diamond ring and gave the man a forty-dollar tip." And Lea had the same reaction Kayden and I had: "Grandma, your English is flawless!" But Grandma was oblivious to compliments. She went straight to the punch bowl to scoop up some spirits, and that's when I noticed that her clubbed foot was cured and she had this elegant grace about her. She drifted, you might say, across the room, her hair floating like gray-black clouds behind her and everyone stared, mesmerized.

Needless to say, Grandma was the big hit at that artsy-fartsy party. She had so many interesting stories to tell. The feminists, it seemed, loved her the most. They crowded around her like hens around a barnyard rooster and made it hard for the rest of us to hear. But Grandma told her stories all right. She told them how she'd been married early and had eight children while being the matriarch of a middle-class family during the Viet Minh Uprising. She told them about my grandfather, a brilliant man who was well-versed in Moliere and Shakespeare and who was an accomplished violinist but who drank himself to death because he was helpless against the colonial powers of the French. She told everyone how single-handedly she had raised her children after his death and they all became doctors and lawyers and pilots and famous composers.

Then she started telling them how the twenty-four-year-old civil war divided her family up and brothers fought brothers over some stupid ideological notions that proved terribly bloody but pointless afterward. Then she told them about our journey across the Pacific Ocean in this crowded fishing boat where thirst and starvation nearly did us all in, but we survived to catch glimpses of this beautiful America and become Americans.

She started telling them, too, about the fate of Vietnamese women who must marry and see their husbands and sons go to war and never come back. Then she recited poems and told fairy tales with sad endings, fairy tales she herself had learned as a child, the kind she used to tell my cousins and me when we were real young. There was this princess, you see, who fell in love with a fisherman, and he didn't know about her 'cuz she only heard his beautiful voice singing from a distance, and so when he drifted down river one day, she died, her heart turning into this ruby with the image of his boat imprinted on it. There was also this faithful wife who held her baby waiting for her war-faring husband every night on a cliff, and one stormy night, out of pity, the gods turned her and her child into stone. In Grandma's stories, the husbands and fishermen always come home, but they come home always too late and there was nothing the women could do but mourn and grieve.

Grandma's voice was sad and seductive and words came pouring out of her like rain and the whole place turned quiet and Lea sobbed because she understood. Kayden, he stood close to me, put a hand on my shoulder and squeezed slightly, and I leaned against him and cried a little, too.

"I lost four of my children," Grandma said, "twelve of my grandchildren and countless relatives and friends to wars and famines, and I lost everything I owned when I left my beautiful country behind. Mine is a story of suffering and sorrow, sorrow and suffering being the way of Vietnamese life. But now I have a second chance and I am not who I was, and yet I have all the memories, so wherever I go, I figure, I will keep telling my stories and songs."

There was this big applause then, and afterward a rich-looking man with gray hair and a pinstripe suit came up to Grandma and they talked quietly for a while. When they were done, Grandma came to me and Lea and Kayden and said goodbye. She said she was not going to wait for my parents to come home for a traditional funeral. She had a lot of living still to do since Buddha had given her the gift to live twice in one life, and this man, some famous novelist from Colombia, was going to take her places. He might even help her write a book. So she was going to the Mediterranean to get a tan and to Venice to see the festivals and ride the gondolas and maybe afterward she'd go by Hanoi and see what they'd done to her childhood home and visit some long-forgotten ancestral graves and relatives and then who knows where she'll go after that. She'll send postcards, though, and "Don't you wait up."

Then before we knew it, Grandma was already out the door with the famous novelist and the elevator music started playing and I swear, if those ice sculptures of swans started to fly away or something, nobody would have been surprised. Kayden and I ran out after Grandma when we got through the hugging frenzy, but she was already gone and outside there was only this beautiful city under a velvety night sky, its high-rises shining like glass cages with little diamonds and gold coins kept locked inside of them.

Mama and Papa came home two days later. They brought incense sticks and ox-hide drums and wooden fish and copper gongs and jasmine wreaths and oolong tea and paper offerings—all the things that we were supposed to have for a traditional funeral. A monk had even sent a fax of his chanting rate and schedule so we could choose the appropriate time because he was real busy, and the relatives started pouring in.

It was hard to explain then what had happened, what we had always expected as the tragic ending of things, human frailty the point of mourning and grief. And wasn't epic loss what made us tell our stories? It was difficult for me to mourn now, though. Difficult 'cuz while the incense smoke drifted all over the house and the crying and wailing droned like cicadas humming on the tamarind tree in the summer back in Vietnam, Grandma wasn't around. Grandma had done away with the normal plot for tragedy, and life after her was not going to be so simple anymore.

Hunger

"EAT," MR. NGUYEN tells his little girl, "eat, you must eat, please, for your Ba," and she cries. "No! I won't," she says through runny nose and tears, "no meat, no meat." As she is saying this, Mr. Nguyen quickly spoons the stir-fried pork into her mouth, but she spits it right back out. They both stare at the piece of pork on the table as if waiting for it to crawl away and escape. After a few seconds, however, Mr. Nguyen covers it up with a blue paper napkin and sighs.

His little girl eats only rice and steamed tofu and sometimes, if he is successful in his begging, a fried egg. Because of this she looks like an aged dwarf—high cheekbones and sunken eyes, thin, dry hair, and the size of a four-year-old, though actually she's already six. Scrawny little thing and miserable-looking, Mr. Nguyen calls her his Easy-to-Love.

"Please," he begs again, "please, Easy-to-Love, just chew like your Ba, like this, look," and he picks another small piece of sautéed pork from its pond of caramelized fish sauce and puts it in his mouth and chews it with lots of rice. He pretends that it tastes very good. "Hmm, hmmm," he says, making obligatory noises that convey deep appreciation for tasty food, rubbing his stomach and, still chewing, trying to smile like a happy fool. But he can't fool her. He sees from her teary but watchful eyes that she knows he hates the taste of meat as much as she does, its unmistakable feral stench, its chewy texture abhorrent to his tongue and teeth.

But Mr. Nguyen continues to chew as the little girl stares at him coldly. "Hmmm, so delicious, there, see, precious, wasn't that easy?" He swallows pork and rice in one big gulp and tries hard not to grimace. "Now, it's your turn, yes, yes?"

"No, Ba, no meat," she says.

"And why not?" he asks. "Do you know how much happier you would make your Ba feel if you would just eat? Don't you remember in the camp how we had to live on porridge and salted eggs? Eat and be resilient. Eat and be strong and beautiful. Eat and soon— soon you'll forget all your bad dreams and nightmares. So, here, eat, my Easy-to-Love, please?"

"No, no," his little daughter shrieks as the spoon carrying another piece of pork approaches her. She shakes her head violently, her tiny hands raised to cover her mouth. "No, I don't want it," she says through her fingers. "Go away. I want Ma."

As soon as he hears this, Mr. Nguyen drops bowl and spoon and sautéed pork and gathers his little girl into his arms and weeps.

"LET HER EAT whatever she wants," says Mr. Nguyen's cousin, Eddie. His cousin's Vietnamese name is Thanh, but in America it's Eddie. He lives fifty miles south of the city, in San Jose, among a large community of Vietnamese who have benefited from working in the high-tech industry. The cousin started as an assembler of computer chips and is now a manager of forty people. He is the only relative Mr. Nguyen has in America. "Brother, my children eat whatever they want. Children are kings and queens here in America; the adults have no say."

"But your children eat meat and ice cream, and they drink milk," Mr. Nguyen protests meekly. "My daughter doesn't. She needs to eat if she is to grow up healthy and beautiful like your children, not frail like me. She eats like a Buddhist nun, practically a vegetarian. Brother, what can I do?"

The cousin sighs but he has no reasonable answers. "Look, if my wife weren't such a bitch, you'd be staying here, you know that, right? She thinks you're cursed. After she heard what happened on that boat and to your wife, well, the bitch will divorce me if I even mention your name again. Still, we have to find a way for you to get out of there."

The cousin thinks Mr. Nguyen should move to San Jose to be among their people at the first opportunity. "I'll keep an eye out. Something will come along. But you've got to be willing to work."

"Sure, but how? Easier said than done," Mr. Nguyen sighs warily. He feels it is his duty to explain it all again to his cousin: "I am half-crazed, my daughter is half-starved—we are not what you would call the most resourceful of Vietnamese in America. I am on disability, Section 8. The Catholic Charity Services woman, Mrs. Cindy, said we are lucky to even qualify for this low-income housing in San Francisco after having arrived only a few months ago."

But his cousin won't listen. His cousin says, "How many Vietnamese started out rich and established in America?" He's heard it all before, so please, he told Mr. Nguyen, don't tell him the same thing each time he calls.

"Brother, in America time speeds up," the cousin says in a serious tone. "The main objective here is to climb up the social ladder. You should know this term, it's a funny term—but people believe in it. It's called the American Dream. Everybody can be middle class here, at the very least, if they're willing to work hard."

"American Dream?" asks Mr. Nguyen skeptically, looking out to the concrete courtyard where the broken swings lie inert, and the walls of the buildings across from his are sprayed with all sorts of graffiti. Last week his daughter collected used hypodermic needles from the playground. Some had dried blood in them, and he made her throw them all away and wash her hands thoroughly. "Brother, we barely have enough money to live on. It's hard to dream. I used to dream back home, the Vietnamese Dream, and look where it's gotten me. Death and horror. Now my daughter and I live off your kindness. We wear clothes you gave away. Our TV, toaster, pots and pans came from you, too."

"You can have many things, better things, if you really make an effort," the cousin says in a hopeless voice. "I think Vietnam and that horrible trip have addled your mind."

Perhaps. But what can Mr. Nguyen say? An American Dream for his cousin, maybe, but only a nightmare for him. He feels as if they had been reincarnated, and his cousin drew a red number while he drew a black. His cousin turned into a phoenix, rising from that miserable dust of war. Whereas Mr. Nguyen . . . he is cursed for coming over too late, an old man already at middle age with heart trouble and traumatized from the carnage on that boat, and worse, no skills to speak of except for farming. It is all he knows. But where can he farm in a world of concrete and asphalt?

"Brother, do your children like turkey and cheese?" Mr. Nguyen asks suddenly, not knowing what else to say. "The Catholic Charity woman, Mrs. Cindy, came by and gave us so much. You can come and pick them up. I have these fancy things and we don't eat."

His cousin laughs again, but his voice is stern and reprimanding. "Do you think I would take food from a man on disability and living in a housing project? For God's sake, my fat wife keeps our two refrigerators filled with food. I'm on a diet myself, too much cholesterol and high blood pressure. Please, don't talk to me about food. This is America. Look around you. Even the poor here are very fat, fatter than the rich, for sure. Think of progress, improvement, education. Think of living well and prospering. Think of getting out of that crazy and violent black village full of losers, for God's sake."

THEY HAD BEEN very close, once, a long time ago, back in their own country. But his cousin escaped right after the war ended, and soon, in America, he sent back photos and letters that told of his success. See the two-story house in the suburb with an apple tree in front? See the children laughing in the sparkling pool in back? See the pretty, red-lipped, jewel-bedecked wife waving from their Volvo parked with the Golden Gate Bridge in the background, which Ly, Mr. Nguyen's wife, noted was not gold at all but rusty red? See the cousin in a blue suit laughing at a wedding banquet, clinking a champagne flute with well-dressed friends, their faces shiny from the flashbulb? On the table, the Peking duck sparkles in the light next to a large plate of steamed fish and a mound of fried rice. If you squint really hard, you can even see the shrimp mixed in the rice. Back home, that photo made everyone's mouth water; they shook their heads and imagined themselves at the banquet and clicked their tongues in admiration.

When their baby was born, Mr. Nguyen's wife had a hard time nursing her. She was thin, didn't have enough milk. They had no money. They were living in Bac Lieu, a small town in the Mekong Delta, with his wife's family. They worked the farm with her clan but barely fed themselves. They borrowed money to buy pig knuckles for soup each Sunday so that Mr. Nguyen's wife would lactate. This way they nursed their daughter past the age of one, but they owed money they couldn't repay. Then, catastrophe hit. The new government co-opted their rice field. The whole clan, twenty people in all, became tenant farmers on their own land. When his daughter turned two, she was very thin and her eyes grew sad—they had the look of someone in mourning. So husband and wife, studying the photographs sent by the cousin for the hundredth time, decided to *vuot bien*—to cross the border and escape. They borrowed more money from his in-laws, sold furniture and the portion of the house that his wife owned. Then they took the cousin's photos with them as if they were talismans that could protect them from all possible dangers, and, one moonless night, sailed down the river out to sea.

His daughter misses her mother, and her body suffers. Some nights she wakes crying, and he turns on the nightstand lamp and holds his precious in his lap on their creaky bed as they watch their combined shadows dance on the wall. He tells her stories like he did back in the refugee camp, "Look, that's where your mother is now. She lives where our shadows are combined, in the shadowy

world, see. She moves with us, watches over us, follows us everywhere, see, see, she blesses us with her love," and he waves his arms
and the shadow's arms wave back and his daughter stops crying
a little to watch. These gestures amuse her more than toys. And
this way they giggle together, feeling as if they are one whole family
again. On the wall the shadows—two heads, one large, one small,
four arms, two long, two short—waver and dance in restricted,
drunken, seasick motions. After a while, when his Easy-to-Love
tires, he sings an old lullaby his wife used to sing for her back home:

> *Saigon's lights, some green some red*
> *Bac Lieu's lights, some sad, some bright*
> *You go learn right from wrong*
> *Nine moons I'll wait*
> *Nine moons I'll wait*
> *Ten Autumns, darling*
> *Ten Autumns I'll stay true*

And her tiny body relaxes in his arms as she falls back to sleep.
Sometimes his little girl listens as she watches the shadows on the
wall. Late one night a few weeks ago, however, she lost interest
in the shadow game very quickly and started to cry so loud that
the noise aroused the big black woman and her teenage son next
door from their slumber. They banged on the other side of the wall
where the shadow danced, and his daughter, frightened, immediately stopped.

EXCEPT FOR THE MILK, which his daughter drinks sporadically
if Mr. Nguyen puts chocolate powder in it, he doesn't know what
to do with Mrs. Cindy's groceries, the cheese and butter and that
big turkey.

He tried to fry one drumstick early this morning after his
daughter went to school, but he couldn't eat it. As he sits and watches television, he hears his neighbor's door slam. He thinks of the
large black woman, the one who pounded on his wall. Maybe she

will take it. Maybe she will forgive Mr. Nguyen and his daughter for making so much noise some nights, though to be fair, her son plays music loud enough to wake the dead when she's gone to work.

The trouble is they have never talked before. He and his daughter have been here at Sunny Dale Housing Project for almost two months, and they have exchanged no more than a nod or two. But to waste otherwise perfectly good food is the ultimate sin where he comes from. So he opens the fridge and takes the turkey out, minus the one leg and carries it next door and knocks.

It is the son who opens it. "What d'you want?" he says in a low, angry voice.

Mr. Nguyen's English is very poor, and he doesn't know how to say the word "gift." "I have turkey," he says. The tall, black teenager is wearing a sleeveless shirt and his biceps bulge glossily in the sunlight. "So?" the boy asks. But before Mr. Nguyen can muster an answer, the boy looks down and yells, "Damn, nigger, it's dripping on my shoes!"

Mr. Nguyen looks down and sees that this is true. He looks up and opens his mouth to say something, but the boy punches him on the left side of his face, hard, and the turkey falls to the ground. Mr. Nguyen staggers and falls to his knees. He is stunned, too stunned, in fact, to be scared or angry or hurt or to run away. Instead of defending himself, his mind starts to wander. He stares at the turkey sitting idly on the concrete in front of him and thinks, "What if?"

What if they had a turkey on the boat? What if he and his wife, Ly, didn't leave the land of their ancestors? What if they never saw the photographs that Eddie sent? What if he never was born? What if he dies now, who would feed his Easy-to-Love?

The black teenager is saying something above him. The boy pulls his eyelids back toward his ears, making them slanted. Mr. Nguyen's English is poor. All he understands is "chink" and "motherfucker" and something about shoes, but for some reason he starts to giggle. He can't help it. He has tears in his left eye where the kid hit him, and it throbs now with pain, but he keeps on giggling. He is appreciative of the boy's clownish face—so exotic and strange to him that it stops him from dwelling on the what-ifs that eat at him every morning and every night.

The boy has a beautiful face. Mr. Nguyen imagines him in a leather loincloth, his face and body painted with squiggly white lines. Perhaps, he muses, he should hold a spear like in the movie he saw the other day on TV. Perhaps he should stab me with it, he thinks, get my life over with. He imagines this while waiting for more punches to rain down on him. But the teenager begins to lose his nerve. He seems confused, as if he doesn't know what he should do next.

"Rash'ad, you stop it!" says his mother, who appears from behind Mr. Nguyen, holding a grocery bag. "Stop it right now! Leave that poor man alone. Go on, go back in this second."

The boy turns away then, scowling and mumbling to himself without giving Mr. Nguyen a second glance.

Mr. Nguyen doesn't know which action, the black lady's yelling at her black son or his laughing, spared him from a possible beating. He's already been punched by another group of black kids who robbed him of his wallet a week after he moved in, and he lost twenty-two dollars, plus his Social Security card. The black lady tries to help him up, but he pushes her away. So she stands at the threshold of her home, large and intimidating herself, and stares at him with her grocery bag in her arms. She shakes her head, trying to apologize for what her son did and not knowing how. Mr. Nguyen, humiliated and in pain, just stares like a hurt child at the one-legged turkey on the ground, refusing to lift his face to meet her gaze.

MR. NGUYEN'S COUSIN calls a few days later. He's very excited on the phone. He says, "Have you heard of *60 Minutes*? It's a show on TV. Channel Five. Brother, your golden opportunity may be arriving soon." The cousin tells Mr. Nguyen that he has a way for Mr. Nguyen to make money. "But you must be willing to tell your story," he says. "That's how you can change your life."

"My story? On American TV?" Mr. Nguyen asks, appalled. The idea sounds to him as ridiculous as making dinner out of mud.

"You must tell what happened on that boat. You must tell it like you told me, everything, so that Hollywood would want to make a movie."

Mr. Nguyen thinks of the horror he and his daughter endured on the trip, and what happened to his wife and the other passengers. His mind goes blank. He trembles a little. He wonders who's crazier, he or his cousin? He wants to hang up the phone and never talk to the man again. What's there to tell? The boat captain and his crew killed his wife and two others, the weakest, the dying, when their boat was stranded on a coral reef for fourteen days, and ate their flesh and drank their blood in order to survive.

"Have you heard of Amy Tan?" his cousin asks. "She's a Chinese woman who writes about Chinese tragedies, and Americans eat them up. It made her very rich, a multimillionaire in Oakland."

Mr. Nguyen has never heard of Amy Tan. He regrets having told his story to his cousin and to his wife, who has since then refused to speak to him, even on the phone. He can barely hear his cousin's voice because a sharp, burning pain suddenly shoots outward from somewhere deep inside his stomach, like fireworks. He feels as if he is bleeding. His head is heavy and dense, and the pallid living room of his apartment fades from him. He feels seasick once more, weak in the knees, his throat is parched, his eyes are hurting from an unforgiving sun.

He sees Ly again, frail and bony, her black hair matted against her burned face, dying in his arms. Her lips are dry, cracked. They move, but no words come out. He thinks she is trying to say their daughter's name. He leans over and wipes her face with a wet handkerchief soaked with seawater. Two weeks have passed since their boat was stranded on the coral reef. Their food ran out days ago, water, too. A few ships passed after the U.S. warship gave them food and water and told them to wait, but no one has come to rescue them. They are very weak, and the boat is taking in seawater, about a meter so far.

Then a shadow stands over him. "We need food to survive," the captain of the boat says. He says this almost politely. We need food to survive! So simple a sentence, and Mr. Nguyen, being a rice farmer, is more than inclined to agree. Except that the captain, still a robust man despite hunger and thirst, had said it two days before when, with the help of three crew members, he killed a boy dying from drinking saltwater.

"We need food to survive." How true! But isn't this the start of all Mr. Nguyen's troubles? He raises his fist as if to strike at the man or perhaps at the cruel, inescapable truth of that statement, but either way it's a feeble attempt. He can barely sit up, let alone protect himself and his family.

Next to him, his daughter is sleeping, a tiny bundle hidden under a conical hat, and perhaps dying, too. He instinctively puts one arm over her. Three men descend upon them, and next thing he knows his wife is gone.

"Brother, are you there?" asks his cousin on the phone, but Mr. Nguyen does not answer. "Are you there?" He leaves the phone off the hook and goes to sit on the sofa and cry.

Yet he can't help himself. While his daughter is playing outside with another child among the swings, Mr. Nguyen turns on the television just in time to see the boat captain crying to the blond reporter of *60 Minutes*. They are standing on the beach near the jail where the boat captain is being held for what he did.

The boat captain seems very thin to Mr. Nguyen, as if he had never regained the weight he lost on that trip, but, for that matter, neither did Mr. Nguyen. The reporter, on the other hand, looks healthy, with rosy cheeks. She looks like Mrs. Cindy, except prettier and younger, like her daughter maybe. She listens with concentration as the captain confesses with the sea in the background.

"There were ninety-two of us on a boat that was thirteen meters long, two meters wide. On the sixth day our food ran out, our water a couple of days after that. We were hungry and thirsty. Then the boat got stuck on a coral reef. On the thirteenth day, three died from weakness. We threw them overboard. That same morning, a U.S. warship appeared. It came within two hundred meters of our boat. They told us: 'Wait for rescue by the other ships. They will come in two days.' They gave us some food and water, and then they left and never came back. We waited another week. Food and water ran out again. So I had to make a decision . . ."

"The sad thing is," the captain says to the reporter later on when he finishes telling his story of what happened on the boat, "no one wants to sponsor me to America now. Not even my own mother. They all think I'm a monster. But I am not a monster. I did what was necessary. I saved lives."

THE NEXT AFTERNOON, a drizzling Monday, Mr. Nguyen opens his door and sees his cousin smiling brightly. Standing behind Mr. Nguyen's cousin are a pretty Chinese woman and a fat cameraman with a goatee wearing his baseball cap backward. The cousin steps up and says, "Channel Five is here." He keeps repeating "Channel Five, Channel Five," as if he can't believe it himself. "Channel Five, Channel Five, that's a CBS station." The pretty Chinese reporter smiles sweetly at Mr. Nguyen and the cameraman behind her turns on a very bright light from above the large camera on his shoulder. He beams it at Mr. Nguyen's face. Mr. Nguyen winces, hurting from the light. "What's this?" he asks. "What's this?"

"Brother," says his cousin, holding his hand, looking sad and sympathetic, "would you talk about it? I know it is sad, but this, I guarantee, this will get you out of your hellhole. I'm telling them that I'm your agent and interpreter, if it's all right with you."

"What's this? " Mr. Nguyen asks again, confused and a bit angry. He pulls his hand away from his cousin's. "Why didn't you tell me you were coming? Why did you bring these people?"

"Why? Because you wouldn't agree to anything if I told you ahead of time," says the cousin in a soft, coaxing voice, trying to sound reasonable. He affects a sad look on his face. "But think, think really hard, brother; do you want your daughter to starve or do you want to be beaten up every other week by these savages?

I guarantee you, if this story is told, we can sell it as a book, and maybe, who knows, even a movie. At the very least, people will send you money. So it's up to you. You want to stay here until your heart gives out? Do you really want your daughter to grow up here? Or do you want your daughter to have something of a life and even prosper? If you don't, just give the word. I'll leave."

Then his cousin's voice changes to a threatening tone. "But, you know me, this is my last effort. I won't come back."

Mr. Nguyen thinks about it really hard. His old dream, the one he shared with his wife back in Bac Lieu while looking at the cousin's photographs—a house, lots of food, and a daughter growing tall and beautiful and happy—comes surging up from some forgotten place inside. He thinks about his life in America without his cousin. He thinks about life in the housing project and the probability of a good life for his daughter. "I will tell a little but not too much," he says in a whisper, "but please, not much."

The pretty Chinese TV reporter asks all sorts of questions, and the cousin interprets and elaborates. Mr. Nguyen answers, but he keeps thinking of his daughter as the floodlight shines in his eyes. His daughter, he notes to himself, is at school and won't be back for a few more hours, and these people will be gone by then.

The most difficult question to answer is the one everyone wants to know. Did you eat human flesh yourself? And did your daughter? Did you and your daughter eat your wife?

The answer takes a while to explain, and much coaxing from the cousin. He and his daughter only ate part of his wife and it was because it was his wife that they gave him and his daughter some of the blood and flesh. That's how he and his daughter survived. She was mostly unconscious and too weak to know what she was eating. But as he is telling them this, he wonders if it's true. But she was so young, barely three years old and weak from thirst and hunger, how can she remember anything?

Mr. Nguyen thinks of his dead wife, what remains of her, bones and hair, lying at the bottom of the sea, and he bursts into tears. He walks away several times from the camera to wash his face in the bathroom. Each time his cousin manages to get him to come back, then they talk some more, and Mr. Nguyen tells his story while he keeps repeating to himself like a mantra, "She will grow up a beautiful young lady. She will eat well and grow up beautiful."

NIGHT, AGAIN. On television the pretty Chinese reporter woman, whose name is Caroline Wang-Reed, says his name, "Mr. Binh Nguyen," and footage of ragged-looking boat people standing on rickety boats appears behind her, followed by some footage from *60 Minutes* from the night before.

Then Mr. Nguyen appears on television. It's the first time he's seen himself, and he finds it very strange. He sees himself sitting where he is sitting now, on a worn, checkered sofa. On screen his face is tearful and sad but also very large. Mr. Nguyen is thinking, I don't look as skinny as I think I am. He touches his jaw. He looks more healthy on TV, he notes, has more flesh.

He hears himself confessing on TV, with his cousin's voice-over in English, and then the story ends. Much of what he told had been cut. The bald news anchorman shakes his head a little and asks a few more questions, but Mr. Nguyen doesn't understand enough to follow.

Caroline Wang-Reed answers the bald anchorman thoroughly. She answers as if she knew the story by heart, telling it with many details and with so much animation that Mr. Nguyen feels that it is no longer his story. And, for a brief second, he becomes confused. He imagines the Chinese reporter as his own Easy-to-Love, all grown up and articulate and well-adjusted and successful, and that makes him smile approvingly.

The bald anchorman falls silent for a second after the story is told, then says it's a very sad story. Mr. Nguyen knows this sentence very well. In the Palawan Refugee Camp, his beautiful Filipina English teacher used to encourage her students to tell their stories in English and then corrected their sentences. After each story was told, she would sigh and comment, "It's a very sad story." This English sentence, his first, Mr. Nguyen had memorized.

Presently the bald anchorman looks straight into the camera and, in a more urgent voice, tells of other bad news, a flood in another part of America, a typhoon in Hong Kong, and something about a riot in India. Mr. Nguyen knows the word *India*, and on screen he sees Indians running away from the mounted police, their faces full of blood.

IT IS LATE. Mr. Nguyen can't sleep. The television is off once again, as it should be, he thinks, from now on. How can he sleep? His poor Easy-to-Love refused dinner tonight and only drank a little chocolate milk. She could tell that he was very worried, however, and had kissed him on the cheek and did not cry at all before she went to sleep. But, they are still here, he and his daughter, in the low-income housing called Sunny Dale, with nowhere to go. Worse, far worse, it slowly dawns on him that now everyone knows—and how will they live this down?— that he and his daughter are cannibals.

He hears knocking at the door.

Mr. Nguyen immediately thinks it's his wife. Maybe she's come back from the dead. "Ly?" he says out loud, though he knows ghosts don't need to knock. Maybe the television people are back. What else do they want? They already got his story. Maybe gangster kids.

He remains frozen in place. He hopes whoever is at the door—ghosts, thieves, evil spirits, or American reporters—will go away. But he hears knocking again, louder this time. Then he hears a woman's voice. He gets up and looks through the little hole in the door. He barely sees a silhouette wavering there against the pale street lamps. Nevertheless, he recognizes his neighbor. He takes in a deep breath, unhooks the latch, and opens the door. He has no turkey and wonders what he can give her this time. Maybe the butter and cheese?

"Hi," the big black lady says. She rattles off a series of sentences that Mr. Nguyen fails to understand except for the "I saw you on TV" part. Then she says, "It's all so crazy."

Mr. Nguyen thinks that the woman asks if he were crazy doing what he did on that boat, and he nods sadly and says, "Yes, I have Section 8."

His big neighbor laughs. She takes a step forward. He takes a step back. She lets herself in without asking. She passes him on the way to the sofa. She has a strong body odor and, mixing with it, a fruity perfume. It suggests all at once grapes, watermelon, and peaches, and the rivers of his past. He closes his eyes, inhales, and imagines a fertile field in her wake.

Now in the pale light of the living room he sees that she has on a necklace full of silver bells that peal softly as she moves. She also has a new hairstyle. It is braided and filled with colorful beads, and they clatter like rain when she moves. In her plump hand she holds a bag of chocolate chip cookies.

"Sit, please," he says. "I make tea."

"You go ahead," she says, but she does not sit down. The black woman follows him to the kitchen instead. She goes on talking to him in a deep timbre as he boils water and he keeps nodding, saying "yes, yes," without understanding much but trying nevertheless to be polite. There is a kind of excitement in her voice when she talks, at times girlish. It sounds as if it's ready to roar up in anger or burst out in unrestrained laughter at any moment.

The black woman tells him her name. She places her well-manicured hand on her left bosom and says, "My name is Kathy, Katherine Lee Washington." She repeats it again, and he takes her cue. He tells her his name, sounding like an ESL student back in the refugee camp.

"My name is Mister Nguyen. Binh Nguyen. I am forty-three years old. I am glad to meet you."

She laughs then slaps him on his bony back. "I know who you are. I heard it all on TV."

On the worn sofa they sit and drink tea. Mr. Nguyen pours tea. Mrs. Kathy Lee picks up the teacup with her plump fingers whose nails, he notices, are long and lacquered red. Then something on his face catches her eyes. She puts down her teacup and touches his left cheek. He flinches. Her nails scrape softly against his tender skin. The bruise. It has subsided, but a slight, purplish ring remains. It hurts a little but not so bad, he wants to say but does not have the words for it, so he smiles. "I'm sorry," she says and shakes her head. "My son, Rash'ad." Mr. Nguyen doesn't understand anything else the black woman says after that, but after a while she stops talking and opens the paper bag and gives Mr. Nguyen a cookie.

They eat and drink and say nothing for a time. When Mrs. Kathy Lee finishes her third cookie she starts talking again, but her voice has a new seriousness to it. She points at the dark television screen and says, "I was on it, too, when my husband died."

"Husband died?" Mr. Nguyen asks attentively and nods to assure her that he, at least, has an idea of what she's telling him. Husbands died, wives died, children died, we almost died on the boat. Die, dies, have died, had died, dying, will die, will be dying—*to die* was among the first few verbs that he and other boat people learned to conjugate thoroughly for their pretty Filipina English teacher.

"Yes," she says through a sigh, "I done buried him three years ago." Then she shows Mr. Nguyen how her husband died. She forms her hand into the shape of a gun and points it to her heart. "BAM!" she says, and Mr. Nguyen's own heart jumps. He can feel the floor vibrate from the gunshot. He thinks of the war when he was younger. He can hear faintly the echoes of the exploding bombs. When he was a boy he used to put his hands over his ears to block out the war to go to sleep. He resists doing it now. He thinks of his daughter sleeping in the bedroom. Then he thinks of his dead wife and dead father and dead mother and all the dead, long ago or recent, buried in rice fields, blown to pieces, or drowned at sea, and is suddenly fearful that the black woman's voice can somehow rouse them all.

"BAM!" Mrs. Kathy Lee says it again, pointing this time at her own temple.

Mr. Nguyen nods and reaches out to pour more tea into her cup. "It is a very sad story, Mrs. Kathy Lee," he says.

Mrs. Kathy Lee seems a little surprised at Mr. Nguyen's complete sentence. "Yeah," she says, shaking her head, "sure is. Sad and crazy."

She gets up and goes to the refrigerator and takes out a milk carton. She seems very much at home in Mr. Nguyen's apartment now, and it suddenly occurs to him that his place is exactly the same size and shape as hers, and for some reason this comforts him. She comes back and pours milk into her teacup and tells him another story.

Mr. Nguyen can tell from the tone of her voice that it is a different story. Mr. Nguyen wishes that he could understand every word, but he can't, and he resorts instead to listening to the deep timbre of her voice, which is warm and rhythmic, its sadness.

"Damn drugs," Mrs. Kathy Lee says. Then she says something about her son, Rash'ad, then she says, "Lord! Lord!" and breaks into tears. But before Mr. Nguyen can reach over to pat her hands, her hands suddenly go up in the air to describe something. It has something to do with her past, Mr. Nguyen reasons, something to do with gathering fruits or harvesting. "I came from Georgia," Mrs. Kathy Lee says. "Worked in the field, night and day. My granddaddy, my daddy, my Ma, my brothers, we all worked the field."

Mr. Nguyen nods. "Yes . . . ," he says encouragingly, "yes."

Mrs. Kathy Lee keeps on talking. She even hums a song. Listening to Mrs. Kathy Lee, Mr. Nguyen thinks of folk songs his wife, her relatives, and he used to sing together while they, too, worked in the fields at harvest time. He is barely aware that he has stood up and is now making gestures of working in the fields. His back bent, his hand holding that rusted scythe once more, he slashes back and forth at the golden rice blades that spring off the stained carpet of the dimly lit living room.

"This I do in Bac Lieu," he says to Mrs. Kathy Lee and smiles. "In Vietnam."

"Yeah, I hear you," says Mrs. Kathy Lee. He goes on harvesting for some time, then he straightens up and wipes the imagined sweat from his forehead and she laughs. Now that he has her complete attention, he goes on to show Mrs. Kathy Lee how he used to catch catfish with a bamboo trap with his pant legs all rolled up and the muddy water to his knees. Throughout all this, Mrs. Kathy Lee keeps nodding her head, saying, "I hear you" and "Uh-huh, uh-huh," as if she could see life in his village very well. She keeps humming while Mr. Nguyen continues to gesture.

In the middle of all of this, his daughter cries, her sobs ringing out from the bedroom. "Excuse me," he says. In the bedroom the little girl sits, rubbing her teary eyes. Mr. Nguyen sits down next to her and smoothes her hair. "Go back to sleep, Easy-to-Love. . . ." But his daughter looks past his shoulders. He hears the tiny sounds of bells and turns. There, in the dim light, leaning against the wall, stands Mrs. Kathy Lee, looking down at them.

"Ma?" his daughter says in a sleepy voice as she rubs her eyes.

"No, she's not Ma, precious," he tells his daughter and cradles her in his arms. "She's our neighbor, Mrs. Kathy Lee, she's come over for a visit. Don't be afraid. She's a very nice woman."

His daughter stares at Mrs. Kathy Lee with concentration. Mr. Nguyen looks back and forth between the two. He sees what his daughter sees: Mrs. Kathy stands where their combined shadows have often danced on the wall. Mr. Nguyen points at his daughter and then to Mrs. Kathy and smiles timidly. "My daughter see you, Mrs. Kathy, like Mama."

Mrs. Kathy hangs her head back and laughs and laughs at the statement. Mr. Nguyen watches in awe as her body shakes. She opens her arms to the girl.

Mr. Nguyen hesitates. He doesn't know how his daughter will react. But it's his daughter who decides: the girl raises her arms toward Mrs. Kathy Lee, and the woman cradles the child in her bosom.

"I'm Mrs. Kathy Lee Washington," she says in a low, warm tone. "And what's your name?"

"Amy," his daughter says. "I'm in first grade."

Amy. Amy Nguyen. It's a name that his daughter had chosen for herself. She touches Mrs. Kathy's silver necklace, and the tiny bells jingle. "Kat," his little girl says, smiling shyly, "Miss Kat Lee."

"Yeah," Mrs. Kathy Lee says, chuckling, "that's me, all right," and sits down on the old bed, which creaks painfully. Her weight creates a crater on the mattress that causes Mr. Nguyen to tilt forward, and he has to hold on to the mattress's edge lest he fall toward her.

Mrs. Kathy Lee begins to hum that same song again, but it is Mr. Nguyen, and not his daughter, who suddenly grows very sleepy. He resists the impulse to let go and let gravity pull him forward and rest his head on her bosom. Instead he holds on to the mattress's edge tighter and closes his eyes and listens. Her voice rekindles in Mr. Nguyen's mind's eye the fertile landscape once more, but it is populated with people previously invisible to him. No freeways, no two-tiered suburban houses, no smiling successes, no clinking champagne glasses there, just blood and soil and sweat and people singing sad, knowing ballads, people celebrating their hard lives, people telling stories.

Mr. Nguyen grows lightheaded thinking about this new country. His eyes still closed, he sees his daughter sitting under a tall tree with generous branches and heavy with strange fruits. Next to her Mrs. Kathy Lee is carving a large Butterball turkey and humming her song, and, for the first time in a long, long time, his stomach growls with hunger.

Birds of Paradise Lost

Mister Qua's oolong tea from Guangdong was wasted that Thanksgiving morning. As usual we sat at our corner table at the Golden Phoenix, Mister Qua's restaurant, chatting when Mister Huy ran in as if chased by a ghost. "Undone, absolutely undone," he yelled and waved the *San Jose Mercury News* expressively above his bald head. "Mister Bac has committed self-immolation."

"Self-immolation?" I mumbled, and the words vibrated in my throat, swirled between my ears, reigniting that terrifying flame of long ago. The flame blossomed quickly, a flower on fire, a restless, transparent bird of paradise in whose pistil serenely sat a Buddhist monk. "Self-immolation!" I repeated the words again, the meanings sank in finally while the flame soared and flickered, and the monk fell backward, his charred body went into a brief spasm or two and then was perfectly still. "No!" I said. "No!"

Mister Qua in the meanwhile had stood up and taken the newspaper from Mister Huy's hand as if the two of them were engaged in some desultory septuagenarian game of relay. "Are you joking?" he yelled loudly. Heads turned. His three waiters in their red jackets and black bow ties paused with their trays balancing precariously on industrious fingers. "How can this be?" he asked loudly. "I just had lunch with him here last Monday!"

Mister Huy shook his head and sighed. "Read, read," he said. He was almost out of breath, tiny beads of perspiration glistened on his liver-spotted forehead. "Mister Bac went all the way to Washington, D.C., to do it."

What immediately struck me were not the words themselves but the two photographs that accompanied the article. One, the larger, was a blurry image of a figure on fire, a human torch swirling in a fiery circle on a landing of the Capitol building, his face lifted skyward, arms raised above his head as if waiting for a benediction from the heavens. The smaller was the photo of Truong Hoai Bac's driver's license, the one I readily recognized: Old Silver Eagle, publisher of the *Vietnam Forever*, smiling with mischievous eyes to the camera. As I studied the two disparate photos—life versus death—I heard Mister Qua say rather impatiently, "Out loud, Thang, read it out loud, please; you're the professor."

Thus, on that morning, with the oolong's bittersweet aftertaste lingering on my palate, I heard myself recite in English to a gathering crowd what turned out to be my oldest and dearest friend's unexpected obituary:

Late Wednesday afternoon a man doused himself in gasoline, marched up the steps of the Capitol building and, upon reaching the first landing, lit a match. John Learner, a tourist from North Dakota, managed to capture a photo (see far right) of the self-immolator who was later identified by the police as Bac Hoai Truong, 65, a Vietnamese American, and an editor and publisher of a Vietnamese language magazine in San Jose, California.

According to his youngest daughter, Theresa Truong, 21, a senior at Georgetown University, Mister Truong did not give any indication as to what he was about to do. "He said he came to visit me since I couldn't go home for Thanksgiving," she reported through tears. "Then this morning he borrowed my Georgetown U sweatshirt and my car keys. He said he wanted to go for a walk around the monuments but he never came home."

The article went on to say that Mister Bac had left a suicide note, one that the paper translated and printed as a sidebar. So at the urging of my friends, I skipped the rest of the reporting and read our friend's last words and testimony:

Letter to the people of the free world,

Communism has ruined my country. My homeland is in shambles. I am tormented by thoughts of my people living in despair under the cruel communist regime. I cannot sleep at night thinking about their suffering. I close my eyes and all I see are boat people drowning in the South China Sea and dissidents languishing in horrid prison conditions.

Human rights violations in Vietnam are among the worst in the world. I denounce its re-education camps, its malaria-infested New Economic Zones and its continuing arrests of clergymen and intellectuals without due process.

I have lived a full life. I have been blessed with comforts and a supportive family. But considering the plight of my people, I cannot be so selfish as to live the remains of my days in peace. My conscience demands that I must act and offer myself completely to the cause of my country.

May my insignificant body serve as a little flame that shines in the darkness that has befallen my country. May my death reveal to the civilized world the evil of the communist ideology and Godless demons who continue to drink the blood of my people.

I wish you all a healthy, peaceful and prosperous life.

Good-bye,
Truong Hoai Bac

I finished reading and felt strangely parched. I took a deep breath. Exhaled. Took another. Exhaled even slower. But this calming exercise, learned from my long-dead father to combat my childhood bouts with asthma, had the opposite effect that day. For instead of calm, after more than a dozen years since I quit smoking, I imagined a cigarette smoldering between my lips. I could almost feel its smoky residue warming my scarred lungs.

A beam of sunlight had come slanting through the window, highlighting our ruined faces. Mister Qua was struggling to keep from sobbing, his long and deeply wrinkled face contorted, while

Mister Huy, like a hurt child, was intermittently wiping his teary eyes with the back of his hands.

A profound sadness welled up from deep inside me, too, and I had to close my eyes. I heard a child's cry, a woman's shrill laughter, men's low bantering, and speculating voices. I smelled that complex aroma of *pho* soup, its beef broth spiced in star anise combined with the terrific smell of freshly roasted coffee to scent the air. Everything was the same that morning, yet everything had changed. When I opened my eyes again and looked at Mister Bac's empty chair, it forced me to look away, out the window, to the busy sun-drenched thoroughfare of Santa Clara. Old Silver Eagle, poor soul, was really gone!

WHEN I THINK of him, "the first" is always what comes to mind: the first to start a newspaper in exile, right in the Guam refugee camp as a matter of fact, with Vietnamese typesets he had brought along while escaping Saigon. The first to organize anti-communist rallies in San Jose, the first to put together cultural shows and Tet festivals at the Santa Clara fairgrounds, and, as it turned out, the first (and only) to commit self-immolation in America to protest Vietnamese communism.

A restless spirit, Mister Bac always pleaded and urged many to "do something for our homeland." Have we, he often asked, forgotten the past? Who among us hadn't suffered under communist hands? Are we so afraid, so near to the grave, to speak up?

Imagine then, four old men in black pajamas sitting inside a flimsy bamboo cage on Lion Plaza at the end of Tully Road in San Jose, demonstrating against Hanoi's unjustifiable arrests of clergymen and dissidents back home. The cage was so flimsy that my adorable seven-year-old granddaughter, Kimmy, could break out with ease, and her equally adorable five-year-old brother, Aaron, could squeeze through without touching the bars. Still, for four straight days and three consecutive nights, with the South Vietnamese flags, gold with three blood-red horizontal stripes, flapping heroically in the summer wind about us, we starved. Shoppers walked by, waved hello, and children giggled as they stared at the sight. We would talk to anyone regarding the sorry state of Vietnam, the life lived under communist oppression. Young supporters stood by and passed out literature on the subject, and a few shoppers even posed with us for photographs. I remember one blond child asking Mister Bac whether we were living in a zoo. This made him laugh very hard and answer: "Yes, this is what it's like to live under communism."

Still, as far as hunger strikes go, it ranked no doubt among the Rolls-Royces. After all, how many political prisoners back home had Old Qua's cellular phone so that he could instruct his restaurant staff? And it is very doubtful that those prisoners were provided with sleeping bags and pillows by caring relatives. Trang, my wife, scented mine with her trademark Toujours Moi to remind me that this old goat had something to come home to. Last but not least, how many have a cardiologist, my youngest son to be exact, with whose family my wife and I now live, to come out and monitor their heart rates and blood pressures daily? True, each time, without fail, Tinh chastised our act of protest as "pure folly" and "most unhealthy," and we each had to promise him that it would end soon. When we finally made the front page of the *San Jose Mercury News* on the fourth morning, indeed, the hunger protest mercifully ended.

THAT AFTERNOON AT the Golden Phoenix we saw a procession of mourners. Old friends and acquaintances, strangers who heard the news, all dropped in by the dozens to express their shock and dismay and sadness. We all wondered: what could have happened and why?

We didn't learn until pock-faced Hung, now an insurance salesman, came in and brought more news about our beloved comrade. "The publisher of *Saigon Today* suggested that Mister Bac Truong was facing bankruptcy due to the lack of readership and advertisements," he told us. "He said Mister Bac committed suicide out of desperation and deep depression. I was curious. So I checked it out this morning with John Le, the CPA, and it turned out Mister Bac did file for bankruptcy last week. John said he's dubious about Mister Bac's motive."

The news stunned us. What Hung heard next was our protests. I, for one, never liked that owner of *Saigon Today*, a young computer engineer with lots of money to throw around; his rag of a magazine is full of gossip and lewd Vietnamese starlets. But his attack of Mister Bac's good name less than a day after his demise was insulting to the bone.

It was as if Hung's news galvanized our thoughts and feelings. "Motives? But there's only one," intoned Mister Huy with all seriousness. Once a judge in the municipal court in Saigon, he could be imposing when necessary, and he certainly rose to the occasion. "He lived for Vietnam and he died for Vietnam. What else is there to know? Why go digging for things that do not exist?"

"Agreed. Agreed," added Mister Qua. "A hero and a role model."

I, drawing inspiration from the old days when still lecturing in Saigon on Vietnamese history, one full of heroes and strife, told him that I knew nothing about the bankruptcy, that Mister Bac never mentioned it, not to me, not to Mister Qua nor Mister Huy. When we saw him last, which was only a week earlier, I said, we shook hands and promised to meet as usual here at the Phoenix, and he was as calm as a Zen rock garden.

I told everyone who listened that I knew no one more dedicated to the cause of human rights in Vietnam than our recently departed comrade. He lived in exile dreaming of the day that Vietnam would be liberated from the communists, so why shouldn't he die calling for attention to the same causes? After all, who among us didn't suffer under communism? Mister Huy lost his wife when they fled on a boat in '79 to Thailand. Mister Qua lost his brother to a Viet Cong's bullet in '67. And Mister Bac's parents were executed as landowners in Hanoi. And, last but not least, me. I lost my first son, Tuyen, who never made it past his twenty-first birthday, in '74, a year before the war ended. "Mister Bac spoke his heart and mind through his letter that the *Mercury* published," I said. "The

Vietnamese exile community owes him an enormous debt for his selflessness and should commemorate his passing."

"Well spoken," Mister Huy said.

"Bravo," Mister Qua agreed and applauded.

Pock-faced Hung looked a bit ashen. "I'm sorry," he announced rather defensively. "I am just reporting what I heard. Don't slay the messenger here. I do know about his accomplishments. But I wonder, do you think the way he committed suicide was characteristic of who he was?"

"Not suicide, not suicide," Mister Huy corrected him. He tapped his teacup on the tabletop repeatedly, imagining it, perhaps, as a gavel. "You mean sacrifice. Sa-cri-fice. Mister Bac was a martyr. He sacrificed his life for Vietnam."

Hung nodded dumbly and smiled as if trying to show that he was on our side. But when he was about to ask another question, an irked Mister Qua stood up, raised his snifter. We had switched from tea to cognac. "Brother Bac," he said, "let me drink to your bravery regardless what others say or think. You are a shining example to our community and our country."

Mister Huy joined him. The two began to address Mister Bac's ghost directly and ignored Hung altogether.

"Brother Bac, may your ghost return to Vietnam and haunt all those bastards in Hanoi in their sleep."

"Come back, brother, and witness this tragedy. You're not even buried and people are already slandering your name. So much for gratitude. Damn it all."

Their voices grew sadder and more plaintive with each toast. Then it was my turn. Perhaps I wanted to outdo them, carried away as I was by the success of my previous speech. Perhaps that was why I said it. I stood and raised my snifter to Mister Bac, and in a low, solemn voice, I said: "Brother Bac, don't be surprised if I follow your footsteps. We'll show the Americans, not to mention the younger generation, what old men are capable of." But before I drank the cognac, both Mister Qua and Mister Huy looked nervously toward the entrance where I saw my son Tinh staring quietly at me.

THE NEXT MORNING, as the American expression goes, the shit hit the fan. When I showed up at the Golden Phoenix, Mister Qua looked at me and shook his head. He shoved the paper across the table toward me. "Another article?" I said.

"Your son," Mister Qua said and looked down at his teacup.

My son apparently had written a letter to the editors.

> . . . To live fighting for something is different than to die in its name, especially when it was absolutely uncalled for. Others have said that he's a hero, but I wonder: A newspaperman like him, why would he commit self-immolation on a late afternoon before Thanksgiving? It's one of the loneliest days in D.C. Were he of sound mind, he would have remembered that the media and Congress and their staff are already gone, that Capitol Hill is but an empty structure. I hate to be so cynical, but you can't protest like this twice. Not that he should have, but why not on a Monday morning and waylay the Speaker of the House on his way to lunch? *That* would call the attention of the front page of all the major newspapers across the country, not to mention television coverage, say, CNN and commentaries in the op-ed pages of *The Washington Post* and *New York Times*. If he intended to call the world's attention to the cause of Vietnam, really, why shy away from the world at the very end?

The letter went on to say that Mr. Bac was not of sound mind. That he did not represent the community by killing himself.

I could barely read on.

So when he came and picked me up at the usual time, I said nothing. We were very quiet, too, on the way home. Instead, I sat and marveled at my growing resentment of America—how she snatches immigrant and refugee children from their parents' bosoms and turns them into sophisticated, razor-tongued strangers.

Tinh drove calmly, his right index finger dancing back and forth in vivacious arcs above the leather-bound steering wheel while Vivaldi's *Four Seasons* followed one another in their inevitable succession. I noted his hands then, strong but ordinary, and wondered how many sternums had they cracked, and how many failing hearts had they massaged and mended, and how many had they failed altogether.

The more beautiful the music, the more I found being in his car unbearable. "Well," I said finally, "I hope you're happy. Tomorrow our community will think of our family as a miserable lot." Tinh turned to me and feigned surprise: "Sorry? I don't get it."

"You *get* it perfectly," I said. "If you don't watch your mouth, you won't have any Vietnamese clients left. Our people will boycott your office for what you said today. They'll wave flags in front of your clinic and call you a communist sympathizer. That's what I'm saying."

My son sighed. "Do you mean to suggest that my Vietnamese patients would rather stay home and suffer coronary blockages, arrhythmias, and strokes simply because I disagreed with you? Or should I prescribe self-immolation as some healthy form of stress-release?"

"Oh, don't pretend to be so naive," I said, matching venom with venom. "You're not the only cardiologist in town, even with your good reputation, a reputation which is about to be smeared. You know the community. Gossips abound. Who knows? Tomorrow we might be a laughingstock! I can see those Vietnamese rags writing up that wretched article right now as we speak: 'Son vs. Father Over Fiery Protest: Generational Rift in Vietnamese Community.'"

Tinh shook his head and sighed—he has that particular way of disapproving of someone without ever saying a word, a trait inherited, surely, from his mother. "Father, I simply questioned whether it was worth dying for something you believe in instead of living and fighting for it. It's a question of logic. I may have sounded disrespectful but . . ."

Before he could finish his sentence, I slapped the polished wooden dashboard and startled him. "Please! No more. No more of this logic. I don't want to hear any damn logic. My best friend just died, and my son called him a lunatic in public. How am I to take it? How am I going to show my face at the Golden Phoenix now?"

Tinh expressed nothing except for heaving another sigh. As soon as we came to a quiet neighborhood, however, he parked the Jaguar on the side of the street rather abruptly then reached for yesterday's *Mercury News* in the back seat. "Listen, Father," he said as he unfolded the paper, his voice rising, "let's get it off our chests, shall we, before we go home for a lovely Thanksgiving dinner."

I said nothing, a little surprised that he had stopped the car in the middle of nowhere. "Good," he said, monitoring my expression. "For one thing, don't condemn logic, I beg you. Passion without logic can lead you astray. I did not call Uncle Bac a lunatic and you know it, but I'm afraid the rest of the world might think so. Listen to this—this is the guy who took that photo, Mister Todd somebody. This is what he said: 'At first I thought it was a flag-burning protest. Only when I zoomed my camera did I realize that it was some guy on fire. It's madness!' "

Tinh looked at me triumphantly. I felt myself at that moment an unfortunate, helpless old man, someone caught in a Confucian tragedy where son lectures father. "It *is* absolute madness, Father," he said, his voice rising admonishingly. "If that tourist hadn't been there, Uncle Bac's story would have been on page five with two paragraphs at the most, if that. You know what I think? I think ultimately he's selfish, suffering from an incurable martyr complex, and it robbed him of his common sense. Did he do his daughter any favor? Or his suffering wife? His friends? I heard what you said yesterday. Is that what you want, father, to be 'some guy on fire'? Do you seriously want to be remembered by Kimmy and Aaron that way? Do you want to die so that you don't have to go on hurting from what was robbed from you, from us?"

My son wasn't aware that the newspaper in his hand had crumbled in his grip. I closed my eyes. I saw again Tuyen's coffin being lowered into the ground, saw his handsome smiling face peering out of a black and white photo on the wooden altar behind white snapdragons and daffodils as if trying to speak to the living. I saw, too, burnt paper offerings at Tuyen's newly covered grave and incense smoke billowing against a gray sky, and my wife's crouching form in her white mourning *ao dai* dress as she wept, and little Tinh hugging himself from grief. I began to itch all over. I couldn't stand to be inside that luxury car any longer. I felt parched and heated. Before I knew it I had opened the door and climbed out.

"What are you doing?" Tinh asked. "It's freezing out . . . Father?"

I said nothing. I started walking.

After a few steps I felt a gentle grip at my elbow and turned to see my son looking at me, bewildered, his breath a wafting cloud between us. "Please, Ba," he said in a very different tone of voice now, the kind that he used to speak to me when he was young—that is to say, intimate, and without rancor. "Ba, please, come back inside. I'm sorry. Really, I went too far just now, I know, it's just that . . . Oh, never mind. Ba, please! Huyen and Mother have been cooking all day and the children are waiting."

"Look," I said. "You go home first. I just need a good walk."

My son studied my face for a second or two and relented. He took off his overcoat and draped it over my shoulders. I did not refuse his kindness. I put my arms through its sleeves, then began walking. For several blocks he trailed me in his car, driving so slowly that drivers passed him, honking. To put an end to his pursuit, I turned into a one-way street, away from the direction of our house.

I kept moving. The streets opened themselves to me as if they were an entirely new landscape. What was vaguely familiar from the view of a moving car or bus turned foreign on foot. Tree branches hung over the sidewalks, their leaves rustling in the wind. And an odor of burning wood from someone's fireplace reached my nostrils, and I was momentarily seized by memories of a time before the war when I was a child and my mother a young woman singing in a smoke-stained kitchen.

At a neighborhood grocery store, I purchased my first pack of cigarettes in many, many years and a fluid lighter. I leaned against a tree and smoked. The taste? Disgusting. Or should I say, wonderfully disgusting? Like an old lover's kiss. The smoke burned the membrane in the back of my throat, seared my lungs; my body convulsed. I coughed, spat, felt guilty for breaking my vow to my wife, but it was, after all, an emergency. When I was done with my first, I lit yet another. By the third, it felt as if I had never given up. How I missed the way the plumes escaped from my mouth and nostrils and rose elegantly to the sky!

I resumed walking. Twilight, and the world—leaves, walls, roofs, grass, windows, barren trees, and parked cars—bathed in the violent radiance of dusk.

I DIDN'T KNOW where I was going. But I kept moving. In my unsettled mind, I saw Mister Bac as if in a newsreel, swirling in slow motion, cocooned in a flickering fire, and I kept thinking: did he scream? How painful was it? Did he cry for help? Or did he die like Thich Quang Duc, that holy monk of 1963, muted and silent and ethereal as a statue of an orator?

My son's question plagued me. Where should love for country end and where should common sense begin?

Could I pour gasoline on myself and light a match? Should I? Why should I? I could see myself running into a burning building to save my grandchildren without thinking twice, but I am not so unsophisticated as to dismiss my son's logic nor to be unaware that what I did in San Jose or Washington, D.C., carried very little weight, if any, in Hanoi. Still, if I knew for sure my death could bring freedom for my people, I should do so gladly. But how could I ever be sure? I couldn't, despite what I declared at the Golden Phoenix.

A car approached. Its bright headlights woke me from my torments. I squinted and thought for a second that it was my son coming back for me, but it passed by without slowing. When it was gone, I felt so disappointed that I nearly wept. I stared longingly down the dimly lit street, but all I saw was the darkening gloom.

What surprised me most then, what I didn't dare think about until that moment, was that, along with the sadness that weighed down my heart, there was something else. This was what I was thinking: no more hunger strikes, no more talking to the press and no more shaking fists in the air and waving flags and banners and posing for the photographers in black pajamas. From now on, without Old Silver Eagle, I would be able to sit at home and tell my grandchildren fairy tales with sad endings and the adventures of my youth.

I felt so ashamed and exasperated at this selfish thought that it actually caused me to stop walking. I stood in the middle of nowhere for some time until I heard what sounded like flapping wings. I turned. A piece of newspaper caught in a tiny whirlwind danced hauntingly before me. For almost half a minute, it glided up and down, down and up, graceful and elegant as a winged ballerina. A flock of dead maple leaves accompanied it in an eddy of air, and the sounds of their rustling were melodic.

The twirling ended. The paper came to rest against a metal wire fence where it flapped like some snared, wounded bird. I stared at it and found myself overcome with an inexplicable desire to set it free. But instead of picking it up, I childishly squatted down next to it and took out my lighter and lit its corner. By the second try, the fire caught and spread, a brilliant, mysterious flower blossoming in the night.

I could barely make out the headline of a story in the paper. "New Home Sales Rise . . ." it said, but the fire already had devoured the rest. I reached out then to the flame, not knowing what I was doing exactly, seeking, perhaps, to still my mind or find solace from the cold or find communion with the dead. To my surprise, my hand retracted instinctively at the first searing. The pain exploded inside my head and I saw in the fire that monk once more falling backward. I saw, too, burning buildings and heard the screams of children.

I stared into the fire, mesmerized. This thing, this gift and curse, is a terrifying beauty. It had devoured my best friend, but it would not, in the end, devour me. Contained, it hints of elegance, drives our world; out of control, it engulfs homes, cities, souls, flesh. It creates. Seduces. Overpowers. It attracts. It destroys.

The flame flickered and died, the paper was now but an ultra-thin skin, the color of night. At my clumsy touch, it crumbled into bits and fragments and scattered in the wind.

I took a deep breath. I struggled to my feet, my joints aching. I looked about, into the lighted houses. It seemed that I had entered an elegant neighborhood where I had never been. Satellite dishes sat on tiled rooftops, unknown trees and shrubs wavered under a starry sky. I felt like a stranger in a strange land, a thief in the night.

I inhaled deeply. I exhaled. I felt hunger pangs. My burned fingers throbbed painfully. But I kept on walking.

Sister

SHE'S IN THE MIDDLE of doing her taxes when her brother calls. "Sister, guess what I've just done?"

"Little Demon," she says, "how can I guess? If you have something to say, say it so it's told."

"No, no, not that easy," he says in the little boy's voice he uses when he's very excited. "Sister, *you* have to guess."

She tries not to give in to laughter the way she used to when they were kids. She writes down the six-digit number on line 13, where it says, "Business income (or loss)," and he says, "C'mon, guess!"

So she guesses—wrong. She hears her brother groan on the other end and has to suppress a laugh. It's as far-fetched a guess as can be. Her brother, cute but shy, and strangely immature, has yet to find a girlfriend, let alone do what she just guessed.

"Such a dirty mind for an older sister," he says. "No one's pregnant. No birth, no marriage, no sex-crazed guesses, puh-leaze."

She writes down the capital gain not reported on line 14 and recalculates the estimated interest of her income on her calculator, her practiced fingers darting over the numbers in a blur. "Listen," she says finally in English, "no more playing games. I got to do my taxes."

"OK, OK," he says, sounding a little deflated. "I'll give you a clue." He starts to sing, his voice warm and without even a trace of a Vietnamese accent. She feels as if she were listening to a native-born American, not her brother, crooning on the other end.

"Reach out, reach out and touch someone. Reach out, reach out and just say . . ."

"Stop, please," she says. "What is this game you play?" She grows a little frightened and does not know why. She closes her tax folder. "Little Demon," she says, "if you have something to say, *say* it quickly. I need to get back to business."

"All right," he sighs. "You win." But he pauses instead and a little silence ensues. She notes the swaying white curtains on the sliding door to her deck and, beyond them, sunshine among the lilies and tulips in her garden, and, even farther out, in a dreamlike distance, San Francisco's high-rises shimmering reassuringly across the gold-freckled surface of the bay.

"It's really incredible," her brother whispers breathlessly. "Promise you won't get mad?"

"No, no more promises. Spit it out, you."

"Fine. You won't believe this but *I just called home.*"

"Home? Aren't you calling home now? I'm your only home in the world."

"No, no," he says. Then he sighs again, "I mean, yes, of course, you're right. I meant home-home. Home as in over there—cross the Pacific, yonder and long ago, home once-upon-a-time home."

Her mouth goes dry. She clears her throat.

"You know," her brother continues, "tamarind trees, guavas, kite festivals, moon cakes, lanterns, sweet rice with coconut, monsoon rain. Home-home."

"Stop it, Jaden," she hisses as she absent-mindedly grips the calculator; meaningless numbers appear on the panel in red, flashing, ruining her calculation. But her brother doesn't stop. "You might not have heard it, but AT&T performs miracles. It connected the

U.S. to Vietnam a few months ago—I saw it on CNN—so I did what I always wanted to do: I called home. Same number."

"Home?" she says, still incredulous. Then, despite herself, she hears her own voice reciting a number. "*Nam muoi bon sau tam?*" "50-468?"

Her brother gives a little laugh. "That's right," he says, encouraging her, "that's right, you remember it, too. *Nam muoi bon sau tam.* . . . Sounds like a Buddhist sutra, doesn't it. Except, now you have to call the international code, 32, then add an 8 for the city code in front of it. Can you believe it, still the *same* number after all these years?"

But she does not listen anymore. With her eyes closed, she tries to remember the calculation for line 14. She tries to remember the number of houses she sold last year.

"Sister, there was an old lady. She had a Hanoi accent, and *she* answered. '*Ano, Ano,*' she said. Isn't that funny?"

"Listen," she says abruptly, surprised by her own loud and angry voice. "I don't care. To hell with AT&T. Fuck your Pac Bell and MCI. How stupid can you be? There's no home to go back to, no one there to call. Besides, why, of all your ludicrous pranks and tricks, why talk to killers and robbers?"

Then before her brother can muster an answer, she slams the receiver down, hard, where it belongs.

"HELLO? EEVIE, YOU there? Oh Christ! Listen. I just wanted to know who lives there now. That's all. When we left, it was emptied out. The old lady who answered, she's no killer or robber. Sis? Listen, don't be mad. It's true—you're my only family in this Wild Wild West. Ivory, pick up the phone. . . . Eevie?"

SHE NEEDS HER warm sun. From her deck she sees white sails flutter on the water like a flock of butterflies. She takes in a deep breath, vague odors of wild herbs, burnt grass, sweet sage. Beau, her orange cat, emerges from the garden below and rubs himself against her leg. She scoops him up and hugs him, hiding her face in his fur.

"Ooh, lucky little cat, aren't you?" she coos into the back of his head and neck. She feels overwhelmed in the sunshine. "Beau, oh Beau, you don't know what month this is, do you? It's April. April's the cruelest month. And taxes must be done."

The phone in her study rings again and her heart jumps. The cat, too, jerks his head, ears perked, whiskers lifted. She hugs him again, harder, and he meows and claws at her arms until she lets him go. She stands near the phone, reaches out for it, then pauses. It might be her brother again. She's in no mood to talk. It stops after the fourth ring. She studies the phone as if she'd never seen one before and turns away.

"Think," she says aloud, "think line 14 of the tax form, think house on Brunswick on Saturday, sale signs and potential buyers and sign-in list and business cards. Think dinner, what to make." She feels restless and heated inside. She starts to hum an old Beatles song: "She loves you, yeah, yeah, yeah!" as she looks out to the bay. But blue sky, distant mountains, mellow sun, Golden Gate Bridge, glassy high-rises, wild herbs perfuming the air, and even the old Beatles refrain—all fail to banish a very old phone number that has begun to echo like a steady chant from somewhere deep within her skull.

50-468. *Nam muoi bon sau tam.*

From: MIT SYSTEM ADMINSTRATOR Page 1 of 1
To: Ivory Tran Calder
Date: Tuesday 7, Apr 1996
Fascimile: 510-456-5532

Eevie. Since you won't answer my phone calls, a fax then.

Why'd I phone home? It might be a mistake to tell you, but who else *would* I tell? Sis, I called because I wake in the night and see our villa fresh from my dreams, see Mama and Papa sitting on the balcony, drinking chrysanthemum tea, talking politics, music, poetry. I hear humming and cannot tell if it is my computer or the cicadas from the old tamarind tree. I know it's spring in Boston, but I *smell* summer in Saigon. The roses are blooming.

Last week I had a strange dream. In it I was zooming down a highway made of fiber optics. Broken into bytes and bits, I was somehow reassembled on a million screens across the globe. A part of me emerged in a mirror of a house and I recognized it as our old home (you know the mirror, with the dragon carved on top?), and a little boy was looking at me. And he said: "Oh, look, an American!" and clapped his hands.

I woke up in tears, Eevie!

I felt so alone, I don't know why. It was so wild yet wildly familiar.

That dream haunted me. I wanted to tell you that before you hung up. Sis, I did what I felt I had to. I called but didn't expect to reach the right house. I tried without really trying. Didn't expect an old woman to answer. Didn't expect her to confirm that I had reached the right address, the right house. I just had to share it. You are the closest human being to me on this earth. It was wrong of me, in retrospect, considering all that happened.

But now, hear me out for once, please. I learned something. Now I know. I mean *really* know. Vietnam exists, Sis, that house exists. I needed to confirm that, to feel it in my guts. Vietnam didn't roll up like a scroll to be stored in some dark attic. It's just gone on without us.

Let's talk soon.

I love you very much.

Your Bro

P.S. I'm flying out as soon as finals are over, like it or not.

HER SLEEP IS MADE fitful by unwanted dreams. Awake, she begins to feel color in the air—a vague lavender hue seeps into everything, even her coffee. The azaleas are bluer, too, somehow, and the silverware a little pink.

Last night she tossed and turned, and her husband asked in a sleepy voice: "You OK, Ivory? Honey? One of those nightmares?"

She mumbled something to deny it, to calm his worries, then cradled his head in her arms and kissed his forehead as if it was *he* who suffered from flashbacks and insomnia.

"It's all right, Michael," she said to him. "Shhh, everything's all right."

But everything is not all right. Everything is slightly off center. The recurring pain acts up. A familiar sharp pinch in the back of her neck shoots pain down her left shoulder and causes her arm to tingle. Lifting a glass of water to her mouth is painful. Cutting a slice of bacon is an effort. Now that her husband has gone to work, Ivory stares at her coffee cup and sees familiar images from the dream coming again to the surface. Frail hands reach out above the dark waves. She hears faint cries, wailing voices. A crescent moon hangs above her, half hidden behind black clouds. A corpse drifts slowly by. The sea roars. Faintly, she hears her own brother call for her, "Sister! Sister!"

But it is not the memories of the storm and shipwreck that displace her now. She is, in many ways, inured to those old images and can banish them like familiar ghosts back into the watery darkness almost at will. She's numb to that old horror. No, it's the voice of a weepy child whose life depended solely on her willpower, her strength to survive, that she suddenly finds disturbing and somehow very different, as if the past can be reimagined and changed.

Her brother had wanted her to hold him tighter. She, in spite of her failing strength, did just that. Still, a vague and irrational feeling, completely unfamiliar to her, keeps creeping up from the dark. And it tells her that she had somehow let go, that he'd somehow slipped away from her grip and, despite all of her valiant efforts, had gone, like their mother, under the sea.

It's irrational, but there it is. Years after she saved her brother's life, Ivory can't forgive herself for having somehow lost him.

Business income (or loss): She stares dumbly at her tax folder and calculator. She turns on the calculator, but that is as far as it goes. A red zero stares back at her. She read somewhere that during the Cold War, American spies were arrested in the Soviet Union because, though they spoke Russian with ease, they could not do math in the same language with the same facility. They hesitated and stuttered and betrayed themselves. She feels like a spy herself, a fraud, and math is the first thing that fails her. The phone rang several times earlier this morning, but she ignored it. She can't even look at it now, let alone pick it up and answer or dial. Shiny and vaguely ominous, it is a direct assault on all of her senses.

Nam muoi bon sau tam. 50-468.

The house on Brunswick is built in Tudor style with distinctive chimneys decorated with different-colored bricks, and its walkway lined with black stones. A lovely four-bedroom and three-bath home with a view of the San Francisco Bay, all for $1.6 million. For music, Ivory chooses Ella; for snacks, brie and crackers with soft drinks and Chardonnay. Out the window of the living room she studies the pristine sky and sparkling water below. How many homes has she sold over the years? Almost a hundred. A sense of wonder comes over her. She has done well, very well, for someone so young.

"Ivory!" An older woman's voice, low and smoky. "How are you, dear?"

Startled, she turns to see Mrs. Littman standing in the doorway dressed in a gray cardigan sweater that matches her hair. "Yes, it's me," smiles Ivory as she moves to shake the woman's hand. "And you're my first victim."

Mrs. Littman cackles, and her laughter echoes throughout the empty house. "Goodness," says the older woman, who forgoes the handshake and leans over to kiss Ivory's cheek. "No need for violence, dear. I surrender."

The woman has the look of someone who was once pretty but has, despite the clothing and makeup, been mistreated by time. Now, cosmetic surgery leaves her skin smooth but her face expressionless, with the exception of her gray eyes, which sparkle inquisitively.

Mrs. Littman has been a difficult client, a perfectionist looking for a perfect home for herself and her busy, highly mobile husband. Ivory, having driven her to see six houses, gave up on the possibility of a sale. She's a little surprised to see the older woman here.

"Let me show you the house," Ivory says. "And here's the info sheet."

Mrs. Littman takes the paper and leans closer and places her hand on Ivory's arm. "Are you all right? You look a little pale."

"Oh, no, not at all, Mrs. Littman. I just slept badly a few nights ago, and now I have this pain in my neck and my arm."

"Oh? Have you tried acupuncture? I have arthritis in my left knee, and let me tell you, Mr. Chew, my acupuncturist, really performs wonders. If I may say so, your ancient cultures are just as sophisticated as our western technology—more wise and far less toxic."

On the stereo, Ella is singing "They Can't Take That Away From Me."

"Would you like a drink, Mrs. Littman?" Ivory asks quickly.

A month ago, while driving with Ivory for the first time to look at a house, Mrs. Littman wanted to know where she came from, and the moment Ivory divulged the information, she regretted it. The older woman immediately boasted of her anti-war accomplishments and how horrified she was of all wars. Ivory can still hear it, tidbits of that excited, condescending, I'm-so-sorry-for-what-we-did-to-your-people monologue.

"I adore that country of yours, Ivory. We didn't sail, mind you, but my husband and I flew in from Hong Kong, where we'd docked our yacht. . . . Those atrocious bombs and mines and Agent Orange, ugh. . . . Mind you, I protested against that war like everybody else, I really did."

Ivory had said nothing. She'd gripped the steering wheel and tried her best instead to divert Mrs. Littman's attention to talk of square footage and escrow, to houses and gardens. She chastised herself: why hadn't she said she was Chinese? It would have worked nicely. She wouldn't have minded in the least how terrible Mrs. Littman might have felt for the Chinese after the rape of Nanking.

This time, however, she is saved from Mrs. Littman by a young, smiling couple who come in holding hands. Newlyweds, she can tell. They're curious about the house and not the saleswoman's biography. Soon, surrounded by a handful of potential buyers, Ivory finds her stride.

"Termites? It's been inspected. If you find any, we'll pay to take care of the problem."

"Earthquake? Listen, frankly, if you're afraid of earthquakes, you'll have to move away from the Bay Area, really, to Fresno maybe, and who wants to live in Fresno? But if you risk it like the rest of us, this is the best view there is."

"No, Cindy, I understand, but there isn't enough space for a pool, really, considering the slope of this hill. You can look all you want on this hill and the next and the next, but you'll be hard pressed to find a pool anywhere. It's Jacuzzi country, I'm afraid—you can soak but you can't stroke."

A young woman with a baby sleeping in her stroller comes up to her. She has a favor to ask. She wonders if Ivory would look after her baby while she runs upstairs for a quick peek.

"Sure thing," Ivory volunteers. She has a good feeling. Someone will make an offer today.

"Sure you don't mind?" asks the young mother.

"Absolutely not."

Ivory goes right on talking, joking, giving out numbers, turning on her charm. But then the baby wakes, and, not seeing her mother, starts to cry. "Oh there, there," says Ivory and picks up the baby. She walks around with the baby, and she stops crying. The baby gives no sign of being fearful. In fact, she now smiles brightly up at her. Her small hand wraps around Ivory's index finger with a strong and persistent baby grip. "You are so pretty, aren't you, little baby?" Ivory asks, forgetting all about the house, the milling potential buyers, Mrs. Littman's inquisitive eyes from the foyer. "You're so friendly. You're not afraid, are you?"

She goes and sits down by the bay window so she can play with the baby.

But Mrs. Littman's shadow falls over them. She has some more questions. Something about the age of the pipes in the kitchen. "Oh, they're new," Ivory answers absent-mindedly. "Everything is new in the house. It was remodeled just two years ago. If you care to, have an inspection again, Mrs. Littman. It won't flood, and it won't leak."

But Mrs. Littman sits down. She, too, wants to play with the baby. She leans forward to touch the baby's rosy cheeks, and this irks Ivory. The air around the older woman smells of rose petals and expensive perfume. Ivory wants to stand up and walk away from Mrs. Littman. Instead she concentrates on the smiling infant in her arms. She hears Mrs. Littman say something else, but she doesn't pay any notice. When Mrs. Littman repeats it, she looks up and sees the woman's painted lips pantomime words that she suddenly fails to understand. It's as if English has been stripped from her brain. Everything slows down. She feels like she's watching her English as a Second Language teacher of long ago. Ivory squints her eyes. Concentrates.

"I've been meaning to ask. Home . . . back home . . . Ivory, have you been back?"

A dog barks excitedly somewhere in the next house. The murmurs of conversation between strangers hum in her ears, and the baby is waving up at her as if saying goodbye.

Her lips quiver, but she says nothing. Instead, she grips the baby. Some familiar memory of her old life, like a splinter, edges up from somewhere deep inside. She remembers a little villa with tamarind trees in the garden, a girl with long black hair, a little boy swinging on the swing, laughing, a doting mother with a passion for knitting. The sunlight is bright and the girl's shadow elongates as she descends the spiral staircase. The smell of fried fish is redolent in the air.

"How can I?" she says finally. "Go back to what?"

She hadn't noticed it at first, then she realizes that her voice, out of character and loud, has carried in the empty home and has startled the older woman. Heads turn. In her arms, the baby is bawling.

"MAKE LOVE TO ME, Michael."

"Honey, have you been drinking? I smell vodka."

"Shhh!! Michael."

She closes her eyes. She can hear them, the cicadas are humming. It's summer again and a beautiful glow radiates throughout the villa. Sunlight on a mosaic tile floor, the marble staircase shines like gold, and the tamarind tree's shadow sways on the white-washed walls, the silhouette of a girl washing her hair. She tastes Michael's lips, his hot breath, his neck. She feels his heart drumming fast against her. But everything also reminds her of the ocean: his blue eyes, the salty taste of his skin.

"What did you take, Ivory?"

"Huh?"

"What did you take?"

"Let's see. Xanax for stress, codeine for aches and pains, two martinis for not being super-duper happy."

"Oh shit. You took my Xanax? How many?"

"Two. Michael, I'm a little seasick."

"We'll have to get you into the shower. I'm sorry, honey. It's for your own good."

"Hmm."

"Here, lean on me. I'll unbutton your blouse."

"He was so heavy after a while. Mama said hold on. But she let go."

"I know, baby, I know."

"So heavy."

"Here, let's take this off."

She closes her eyes. A sunset on an island and a velvety black curtain enshrouds the world. A plane takes off from Jakarta to the Philippines to the cold night of San Francisco. Clouds everywhere. Sunset. Sunrise. A stewardess with golden hair says, "Please fill out this form," then Ivory opens her eyes to see a handsome American looking at her with worried blue eyes, and it is raining. She's naked. He is wearing his white shirt and it is soaked.

"Are you OK? Tell me what day it is."

"Michael," she says, her voice a raspy whisper, her throat on fire.

"Yes, baby."

"Tell me something."

"I'm here."

"If you were me, would you let go?"

HER PSYCHOLOGIST GRINS upon seeing her. "Long time," he says. She thinks he's secretly in love with her. He is about to say something else, but his pager beeps. "Excuse me," he says and looks at it, then fumbles to turn it off. "Welcome to the information age, eh?"

He is trying to be funny, she can tell. Yet this irks her somehow. The beeper. The apology. Everything here, come to think of it. The office, elegant with its redwood wall panels, and skeleton hanging from a hook next to his desk, provokes in her the feeling of being inside a coffin. And she resents his slight parental tone despite their being almost the same age. He shifts uncomfortably in his chair. He has aged well, this one, or hardly aged at all. He still reminds her of a diligent, bespectacled boy she once knew in college in Econ 101 at San Francisco State, always taking notes, always asking questions, overanalyzing everything, thinking too hard, and blushing too quickly. Nerd.

"So, how are things at home?"

She does not answer. Instead she tells him of her nightmare. Then of the radiating pain down her neck.

"Are you stressed?" he asks. She scowls at him. "Do you think, that, uh, these flashbacks are signals of your . . . ?"

"Listen," she interrupts him, wincing from a sudden sharp pain down her neck. "I'll get to the point. I can't sleep at night. My shoulder hurts. It's worse than before. Maybe it's psychosomatic. Maybe it's all physical. Both, maybe. But my business is affected. I can deal with hands coming out of the water, out of the fricking wallpaper sometimes. I always have, haven't I? I'm not afraid of ghosts. But he's leaving me. He's going to some place I don't know. I can't deal with that."

Then she cries. She hasn't admitted that much before—not to Michael, not to herself—though she isn't sure what she's just said exactly. She hugs her stomach as if she's having cramps and wails loudly. A couple of minutes later, with the psychologist's hand on her shoulder, she whispers, "You don't understand. He was very heavy after a while. It took all my strength. All of it."

TWO TIMES TWO is four. Four times four is sixteen. Once there was a boat full of people. Then it sank. And only sixteen survived. Once there was a garden full of lavender-colored roses, then it was abandoned. Once there was a family of four. Then the father died in battle, and the mother drowned at sea. The children, well, the children inherited only bitter memories.

This is life. If you belong to the losing side in a civil war, you become a boat person, a refugee, an exile—an enemy of history. You must remake your life elsewhere. She accepted that long ago. She's closed that thick novel with its bloody pages, and after so many weepy nights, said goodbye to it all, hasn't she?

Ivory blames herself for having relied too much on the sappy ideas of America. America had offered itself to her first as a vision of stability and progression. She saw it long before she came. She saw it sleeping on the cold, hard ground of the refugee camp in the Philippines. A house, a car, a job, a husband—a future. She saw America's promises as dependable formulas against bad memories and horrid fates. In America, her vision came true. She got especially good at selling the American dream to others. She knows architectural styles and interest rates and mortgage deals inside out. She encouraged transactions, movement, refinancing, 20 percent downs.

But somewhere in the back of her mind she always knew: optimism is no fortress against the hunger of memories. Like now, when the taxes are done and the house on Brunswick is finally sold and the pains in her shoulder have faded. As she stands idle in her kitchen looking out to the neighbor's yard where three children are running back and forth over a sprinkler and shrieking hysterically, a scene in the refugee camp suddenly comes back to her.

She stood at the entrance of her little hut and looked out to sea and saw her brother among a group of children playing on the beach. They gathered sticks and palm fronds and strands of seaweed around an oval shaped rock and a tall boy found a piece of plank. He placed it on the sand a few meters away from that rock while the others watched.

There was something urgent, something potently ceremonial in the way they gathered. It came to her then what they were doing. They were playing Drowning and Rescue, a game her brother had mentioned the day before. Five little children gathered on that piece of wood—their boat—while three others fought to be on the rock. She could see her brother among the fighters, their voices were loud enough to reach her. On the wooden plank, two smaller children were pushed out onto the sand where they were forced to play drowning victims. Similarly the three boys fought to stay on top of the rock, which represented a big merchant ship. The winner got to throw the rope made of seaweed down to either the boat people or the drowning victims. Those who caught the rope were rescued.

Her brother, who'd won the privilege, stood with an air of determination about him at the imaginary ship's bow. Below him the children pleaded. He didn't hesitate. He threw the rope to the drowning victims.

Ivory is suddenly swept by the poignancy of that gesture. But she remembers what happened next. The two boys on the rock conspired to throw her brother down onto the sand, and though he struggled to keep his footing, he wouldn't let go of the rope. She remembers reaching out toward her brother, as if she could somehow, despite the distance, steady him on the rock before he fell. And this memory is so overwhelming that Ivory has to resist the impulse to repeat the same gesture years later.

"Little Demon! Little Demon! Come up if you dare," one of the two boys called out to her brother. Was it then that the sobriquet stuck, she now wonders?

Still her Little Demon was no victim. He ran after another boy who had lurked about with a little coconut frond sticking out the back of his tattered shirt, and they wrestled briefly until her little brother took the frond from him. As the other boy ran away crying, Little Demon got to play the role of the hungry shark.

IVORY HEARS FOOTSTEPS. She turns from the window. And sees the shadow of that strong-willed child replaced by the vision of a tall, lanky young man in Bermuda shorts and a tie-dye psychedelic T-shirt who blocks the doorway to her living room.

"Sister," he says.

It is late in the afternoon and his skin is golden. But his eyes glimmer with tears. "Eevie," he says, and before she can react, he rushes to hug her. He hugs her so hard that for a moment she is lifted above the wooden floor. "I'm so stupid," he says as she feels the air go out of her. She's overwhelmed by the weight and heat of his body. He looks down at her now, breathes peppermint breath onto her face. Her throat constricts with the sudden onset of love. She wants to say "I forgive you," but she catches herself: he hasn't asked for any forgiveness. And then she thinks, "And really, for what?" Instead she puts her hand on his tear-stained cheeks and strokes gently.

"Why didn't you call ahead? Michael could have picked you up at the airport."

"You should ask," he says accusingly, giggling. "And who would have answered my phone calls? Besides, I wanted it to be a surprise." He sits on the couch and stretches and yawns.

She ignores the comment. "Little Demon," she says, "did you finish all of your finals?"

He smiles guiltily. "I missed one. But it's OK. I don't have to retake the damn class. I'll just have to take the finals again next quarter since I did so well."

"It's just so like you to do something like that," she says, but there's no accusation in her tone.

"Sorry," he says in a clownish, nasal voice. But then his face changes. He takes a deep breath. "Eevie," he says, "do you believe in God?"

"What! What the hell are you talking about?"

"I'm thinking of getting a PhD in religious studies."

"And quitting MIT? Are you mad? Don't you dare."

"Oh no, no," he says quickly. He puts his hands on his temples and massages them slowly. "I'll finish my master's. For sure. No problem there. But don't you believe in God? I think I do."

She sighs and closes her eyes. Already her brother tires her out.

"We'll talk about gods and demons later, *especially* demons."

"Ha-ha."

Beau emerges from under the sofa. He rubs against her brother's leg, purring. Jaden bends down and strokes the cat's head absent-mindedly.

"You hungry?" she asks.

"No, it's cool," he says, lifting the cat to his chest and burying his face in it. Then he changes his mind, his eyes mischievous. "Actually, I am hungry. Very. Do make me something, Eevie."

It's familiar ground. She cooks. He eats. Peace will be restored.

"Go up and shower first," she says. "You stink."

He laughs, and just like that, he is gone. She shakes her head. How did he get to be so tall? Were they in that water now, he'd have to carry her, and *she* would have to hang on to him for dear life.

In the kitchen she can hear the shower upstairs and her brother whistle the tune from *Gilligan's Island*. She looks out the window to the bay and imagines herself as a young girl holding onto him with one arm, a much smaller version of him, of course, and the three empty plastic water jugs with the other. Her prudent mother had tied them together using her headscarf and fabric from a blouse when dark clouds began to gather. "Just in case," her mother had said.

She is remembering this as she absent-mindedly pulls at the refrigerator door handle. But it resists her halfhearted effort. Ivory is genuinely surprised by the resistance. She looks at her arm again. Though it no longer bothers her, there's still a dull ache, as if from phantom pain.

"Did you ever think of letting go?" Michael asked when she told him the story for the first time, before they married.

"No. Not once."

She knew then that if she'd let go and waved to that Belgian ship, which she thought had failed to see them, what would be the point? If she'd let go, how could she have possibly gone on? So she held on. She held him that way, a weeping child whose head was barely above water, and even after they were rescued and even after she lost the power of her arm for nearly a month—even then, she sometimes draped it over him like a blanket while he slept.

Even now . . .

Nam muoi bon sau tam.

50-468.

Just dial the international. Add an eight.

She hears the shower being turned off. She hears more whistles—a new tune that she doesn't recognize, an upbeat melody, perhaps the kind of song that American children sing. A strange sensation sweeps over her. Her skin tingles, she trembles. Through tears, she starts to see two of everything—two suns out the window above the sea, two orange skies, two Golden Gate Bridges, two overlapping horizons.

Ivory raises her hand close to her face and studies it with a kind of detached awe, her vision traveling the length of it. This hand, these fingers—this arm—it has carried the weight of the living. She looks at the phone on the kitchen wall. She watches her hand reaching toward it.

Just dial the international number, Eevie. And add an eight in front.

How difficult is it to let the past go?

Yacht People

How are you doing tonight? Hot? Yeah, sure *is* hot. We're having a tropical heat wave, folks. So hot, it reminds me of coconut trees and thatched-roof huts. It makes me think of myself as this impossibly handsome little boy playing with his dog, or, as so many of you are fond of putting it, playing with his food.

Yeah, as I was saying, I was playing with Next Week's Menu getting him to roll over in fish sauce and lemongrass, jump in the wok, and play dead, when suddenly Mamma, right, she showed up with this bag and said, "Kids, we got to blow this joint!"

Well, actually Mamma didn't say that, exactly. She said—now, listen, 'cuz this is from Vietnamese to English. OK? Like with a bamboo flute going off in the background, so hear me out:

"O filial first son. From the sacred land in which our umbilical cords are buried we must take leave due to communist cruelty. They put your honorable father in the re-education camp. If we stay they'll send us to the New Economic Zone. We have no choice but to commit this forbidden sin. Please go bow to your ancestors, light incense and beg for forgiveness before we leave. And filial first son, don't forget your toothbrush."

I was seven years old. I was like, "What? What'd I do now?"

I'm telling you, it's just like Vietnamese mothers to make everything YOUR OWN GODDAMN FAULT! Think about it: the commies gonna fuck you up and send you to the New Economic Zone so you have to escape out to this big, bad ocean, and somehow it's you who has to beg for forgiveness? And from DEAD PEOPLE?

Grandpa, great-grandma, oh ancestors of eight generations back to the Chink dynasty, please forgive us. We can't clean your graves no more. Clean them your lazy-ass selves. We got to go to America before the VC fuck us up the ass or put us in graves next to you all. So, OK. Goodbye.

We loaded up this fishing boat, right, and move the Mekong-Deltoids to Beverly Hills. Entire clan that is. Vietnamese. Boat People. All climbing in this rickety fishing boat, and when the next village saw us, half of them came along, too. Hell, it's twenty-one by six feet, so why not? When Americans say maximum capacity is forty-five, Vietnamese automatically add a zero to it. You know how it is: tell us it's a boat and we'll find a way to fit.

What? Who said that? What did we do with the dog? I see you. You so fat, you're feeding me lines now? Well . . . thank you.

The dog? Hell, we tied a recipe with some lemongrass around his neck and sent him to our neighbor as a parting gift, you know, kinda like a Vietnamese version of meals on wheels. That's right, don't boo. You heard me. Seriously though, I really miss my Next Week's Menu.

Anyway . . . we live on top of each other, we sit on each other's lap, we shower together to save water, we sleep five to a bed—so no, there's no personal space 'cuz hell, if there's space, there's a PERSON taking it, all right?

Crowded to a Vietnamese is not a family living in one room, that's just normal middle class. Hell, we didn't have *Better Homes and Gardens* magazine back in Nam. Na-ah, we had *Shanty, Thatch & Hut Newsletter*.

Crowded on that boat is, like it takes you from Saturday to Monday to get to the toilet, and until Wednesday to get back. Crowded is, if you bend down looking for your plastic slippers, you'd lose your cherry. Crowded is, when you have the hiccups and that fat lady a few people down from you gets multiple orgasms.

When my siblings and me, all three of us, came to America and we saw the two white kids next door playing that game Twister, we thought, "Phssaw, you call that a game?"

"It's Twister," said Suzie and her gayish brother, Leon.

We didn't know Twister, but we knew about living in tight spaces. "Nah-ah, it's Life-On-The-Boat," my little brother and sister immediately corrected her. All three of us showed Leon and Suzie right then and there how to play it properly. OK, so do you know how you can tell when Vietnamese boat children play Twister? We'd be like connecting red and green and yellow dots, WHILE helping each other do math homework, that's how.

Hell, it was so crowded that when them Thai pirates came and took some of us over to their boat for our poontangs, the rest were thinking, "Well, at least now we can stretch our legs."

No, don't boo. Seriously though, them pirates, man, I got me an AK-47 then, I'd have blown them out of the freaking water. Swear to God. Mean-ass mofos. Funny thing was, there were twenty of us to one of them, and they were just opportunistic fishermen with knives and one spear gun, that was it, but we were a bunch of morons and burnouts. So crammed in, so weak, dehydrated, what have you, we just let them have our poontangs and jewelries without even so much as a protest, man. Well, I hope they rot in hell.

We were just unprepared. Period. We had no idea where we were going, no idea how long it'd take. And people bring the craziest shit when they flee, let me tell you.

Like, listen to this. One woman brought land with her. Yeah, you heard me. I'm serious. Food and water make sense, right? Cup O Noodles? Sure. But dirt? We ran out of water and food after a week, and this crazy bitch was crying constantly. Man, I know I shoulda felt bad for her. But honestly? I hated her ass.

She complained and complained, and then, when she ran out of food, we found out that last bag she'd been sitting on was no family heirloom. It was a kilo of dirt that belonged to her garden. What the hell was she thinking? I'm escaping out to sea to who knows where, but I got a bag of Vietnamese dirt? Why not rice? Or maybe a bag of Cheerios? Even them pirates were laughing at her. They tore open her bag and just shook their heads. Dirt!

Then another guy, old dude, right, he had a bonsai. It was like this old, fugly dwarf of a tree that's like a thousand years old. Then another brought keys to his house and cabinet with him. And get this—this old lady, she brought mango seeds. Mango seeds! She said she wanted to grow them wherever she was going to end up. We didn't know she got them seeds til it rained, right, and they sprouted from her pockets.

We were robbed of everything and starving and dying of thirst, and can you imagine it: there's mango saplings coiling from right under the old lady's sagging tits? She should've gotten together with the dirt lady so they could grow mango trees so by the time we got to the Philippines maybe we coulda got something to eat.

What? Huh? You again. Shoulda brought the dog? Ah—ladies and gentlemen, let me introduce you to my man here. Yeah, fat man on the fourth row on the right—the one who found his Thrill by *being* The Blueberry Hill. Hey, man, what's your name? Huh?

Kevin. Kev, yeah, my personal heckler, man. Give it up for Kevin, everybody. . . .

Yeah! Kevin. God, you so fat! You so fat if you were on that boat, you'd be sittin' next to everybody. You so fat, if you fell into that ocean, the Japanese be harpooning your humpback ass.

Sure, Kev, we should have brought Next Week's Menu. Should have brought a whole lot of everything. Sure. But we didn't, all right? There's a lot of shit we ought to do that we don't do. Like you, Kev, going on a diet, for instance. Or donate your liposuction fat to Our Merciless Lady of Irony to make candles and soap so they can make some money and feed the poor.

Seriously though, reality is weirder than fiction. You're escaping out to sea, to who knows where, and the stats were that one out of two wouldn't make it, due to drowning and starvation and pirates and the overwhelming generosity of the merchant and navy ships that honk their horns and let you wave and wave til your arms drop. So what do you take along? Rocks and a dwarf tree and mango seeds. Keys to an old cabinet—what the hell you gonna do with a bunch of damn useless keys? That's a riddle for the rest of your life, man. Rusting keys to a lacquer cabinet in a country you don't intend to ever, ever see again.

You hear Vietnamese are so damn practical, right, studying to be doctors and engineers and computer programmers and shit like that, but did any fool on that boat bring a life jacket? Hell no. A gun? A flare? Hello—maybe a map and compass?

Nahh-ah—that would be like THINKING AHEAD.

So—we ran out of food and water. My youngest bro, he was like three years old and he was dying. So guess what my Mamma did? You won't believe this shit, but it's the godawful truth, I swear. She cut her finger and bled into my baby brother's mouth. It was gross. It was so awesome, man. Mamma fed him like he was little Vampire Lestat. She nearly died from that experience 'cuz she was already dehydrated herself, but like she was not like ever gonna let him die.

That kid, right, he's all grown up now, six feet tall and as handsome as Bruce Lee, but guess what, folks? Scarrrred for life! Yearrrrs of therapy ain't gonna change da fact that Mamma gave life to him not once but TWICE, and she nearly died that second time, and he remembered it. Hell, as if she'd ever let him forget. She bled into him so he better go to med school, be a surgeon, and that's that. He majored in psychiatry and brain surgery, and I think he was like his own first patient. I gave a couch to Honorable Son Number Two so he can lie on it and take notes and talk to himself.

I mean, I'm not sure what Freud would say about it, but we can safely assume that big U-Haul permanently parked outside his new house is for all for my bro's emotional baggage. She owns him, man. Mamma got him wrapped around her finger now, no pun intended.

He wanted to be in a rock 'n' roll band at seventeen, right, 'cuz he's really good with them drums, but she wanted him to be a doctor and he started to kick it back to her about American individualism and American dream and shit like that, and Mamma she just held up her finger with that little scar, and that shut him the hell up.

But she stopped saying shit like "O unfilial Son Number Two. The blood that throbs through your ungrateful veins is my blood, my sacrifice," like she used to.

Now she speaks her own version of Vietninglish. So listen.

"I bleet for chew. I keep chew alai. What four? So chew can be heevy-meetal rock-carr? No Back Si Reet boi for chew. Chew be Mma Dee in-steed. No drum, no rockeen-roe. Chew lull cho Mamma, chew study EMMER-CAT."

My bro, he wanted to date Suzie, right, and Mamma'd be wagging like this with her finger in the air. "OK, chew date. Mamma just go keel her sell to assk ang-cesster for four-giffness. Firest one no good. Mamma no have no-ting if chew no good numba two. But befour Mamma go, Mamma wan only one ting: give back two gallon of Mamma's blood. OK?"

My bro, man, he'd be breaking down, weeping like a baby. "I'm sorry, Mamma. I'll be a doctor, Mamma. I'll be a brain surgeon. Don't cry, Mamma. I'll forget Suzie." She gets her way, my Mamma. 'Cuz you know why? Unlike driving in L.A., I'm telling you, in my family, giving somebody The Finger takes on a whole different meaning.

Me, on the other hand, no-good dishonorable first son, I am the only one who got to slap my Mamma and get away with it. Once, right, she took her favorite cocktail, Rum and Robitussin, and she fainted right there on the kitchen floor. Everybody was acting like they were chickens without heads. My sister, Le-Ann, was doing her prissy, ditsy maid *Gone-With-the-Wind* routine: "Mamma gonna die! Mamma gonna die!" So I slapped her first to shut her up.

Did the pre-med boy do anything? Na-ahh. He froze. It was up to me—the yellow sheep, the strayed lamb, the screwed-up among scholarship kids—to become a Mamma Slapper. So I dropped and rolled. And straddled my Mamma right there on the kitchen floor and slapped her.

Wake up, Mamma, wake up. Slap! Slap!

My siblings, they both stared: they were shocked. I looked over my shoulders and there was also this awe in their eyes. They were like, "You slapped The Saint!"

The truth was, I was doing something that they all fantasized about in their deep, dark, wet dreams but never admitted it: I was bitch slapping The Queen Bitch-Slapper. Mamma not only believes in corporal punishment, she holds seminars on it in Little Saigon, sort of like Confucianism and the Joy of S&M 101. "Mama sho chew love wit kain. No-oh . . . not shuega kain. Bamp-bu kain."

Mamma used the rod on our tender asses. Mamma slapped us every other week for sassing and what not. Especially Le-Ann, who needed to be slapped like every five minutes to stop peering over the fence to make goo-goo eyes at Leon. Well, I was slapping Mamma, and Le-Ann, she was just downright envious. I could see her wanting to get in on it. Her hand was rising in the air mimicking my slapping like she was trying to give me pointers on how to do it.

See, we barely survived and then we were shipwrecked and were like stranded on a deserted island for like a month before we got rescued. I'm telling you, that was rough. Our diet consisted of coconut, oysters, and seaweed. What's for breakfast, Mamma? Coconut.

"What's for lunch, Mamma?"

"Boiled seaweed."

"What's for dinner, Uncle?"

"Seaweed and oysters and coconut, now shut up!"

Oysters. Oysters and seaweed. We were lucky if we caught a fish and small crab, that was like Thanksgiving dinner.

Oysters. I swear, when you're a kid, a warm, quivering oyster was the nastiest thing you can ever imagine putting in your mouth, right? If you look real close, you can even see its membranes quivering. Why? 'Cuz it's scared! It knows what's next. Nastiest shit ever.

Took me years in America to get used to eating oysters again, folks. And only when it's on ice and comes with vodka and a horny, smiling chick who thinks that shit is an aphrodisiac. But it's crazy. For one thing it was like, "Why the hell do I have to pay so much money for them when we had to be slapped silly before to eat it?" For years whenever I see an oyster, I get nauseated. I'd feel like I'm on fucking Gilligan's Island again. Fuck that. Give me a Quarter Pounder, man, you know what I'm saying?

My sister, Le-Ann, she nearly starved on that island, she was downright anorexic. She cried every time she had to eat an oyster. She threw up so many times 'cuz it was so absolutely nasty. This is her description: "It's like eating a big thick wad of somebody else's three-day-old phlegm soaked in piss." My mother had to slap that girl to make her eat. "No, Mamma. I can't." Slap. Slap. Slap. "OK, OK, OK, Mamma, I'll eat."

Funny how Miss Finicky grew past puberty and, suddenly, how many nasty things she'd be willing to put in her mouth, no slapping necessary. She wanted Leon's oysters, all right. "Oh Leon! I want your three-day-old phlegm. Yeah, give it to me!" I know what you're thinking, you people are nasty!

So back to Mamma on the kitchen floor: when I was slapping my Mamma, I was slappin' for all the horrors we experienced.

"Wake up Mamma!" Slap. Slap.

I was slapping her on the behalf of all oppressed Asian kids who had to do our homework and eat the shittiest food—like catfish in stinky-high-to-heaven shrimp paste when everyone else in the neighborhood had macaroni and cheese with Spam. I was slapping her on behalf of emasculated Asian boys who grew up under the fiery breath of dragon ladies and all the teasing we got for being poor FOBs. I was slapping her for making me leave Next Week's Menu behind.

"Wake up, Mamma!"

Oh, she woke up, all right. We knew she was OK 'cuz she opened her eyes, right, looked at me, and with her Terminator's GRIP, she grabbed my hand in mid-slap, and she started slapping me with it.

Mamma survived. Hell, we ALL survived. The truth is Honorable Number Two did really well. And so did Le-Ann. They're doctors now.

Last year, Honorable Number Two bought a big yacht when he moved to Sausalito. He took us all around Alcatraz and Angel Island. We drank champagne and waved to all these skinny blond people on their yachts who looked over at us kinda funny. Why?

Maybe 'cuz Mamma, she brought her rice cooker, and she wore her conical hat, black pajamas, and Prada purse and squatted right there on the deck to make us lunch.

But so what? We ain't Fresh Off the Boat, ain't FOBs no more.

We've got Fab-ulous Oriental Booties!

We're Flamboyant Oriental Balladeers!

We've got Fantastic Oto-Biographies!

It's like, look at us now, man. I mean, really *look!*

We're yacht people now!

Bright Clouds
Over the Mekong

IT WAS UNFATHOMABLE, but there he was. One bright afternoon the door of her restaurant opened to admit a tall man
who limped a little, like someone trying to stay steady at sea.
When he neared her, he said, "*Chao co, manh gioi*?"—in an awkward tone delivered by an inflexible tongue. She looked up and saw
a pair of ice green eyes, and it took her a full second to realize that
he was smiling.

She'd never seen that smile, but she remembered those eyes.
And that voice! She tingled all over. It couldn't be! Could it? No!
Not possible.

"Miss, are you all right?" he asked and touched her lightly on the
elbow, his forehead creased with concern. She looked again into
those eyes and felt hollowed by the force of recognition. Where he
touched her she felt a tiny vibration. She hugged her elbows. When
she spoke, her voice was under control, almost detached. "Fine. A
bit windy when you opened the door."

"Ah," he said and made a gesture toward the door, but already it
had shut on its own, "I'm sorry."

"No, never mind," she said, smiling. "Hey, you speak good Vietnamese, by the way!"

"*Cam on,*" he said. Thank you.

She gave him table six, poured ice water with a lemon slice into his glass, then handed him the menu. Through it all, she resisted an appalling yet powerful impulse to grab the conical hat hanging on the wall and lie down on the polished wooden floor and cover her face with it. If she did, she would squint her eyes just so, then she would hold her breath, lying as still as the dead and imagine the sun bearing down on them like long ago, so she could, from that vantage point, make sure that it was him.

It had been so many years, but it *was* him, she was sure of it, 95 percent. How could she possibly forget that face, the glare of his eyes? Older now, sure, and looking distinguished in a gray business suit, and very sad or depressed somehow. The sadness she did not expect. Nor the gentle and shy demeanor. Otherwise, it was the man. Factor in the passage of time, the wrinkles and deep laugh lines, the spider webs under those eyes, a little gray to the black hair, and a little more flesh that blurred the firm jaw lines of a younger man's face and, yes, yes, it would be him, exactly.

She had to make sure, of course. She had made a couple of mistakes before. A few times over the years she thought she had seen him. But the other men, on closer scrutiny, had blue or hazel eyes, and none had ever served in Vietnam.

This man was different. Apprehension burned in her blood; she swept in a stream of mysterious water. She told him her name.

When he offered his, she boldly asked for his business card. Her hand trembled slightly as she read it. Jay Harrison, VP of Human Resources, Phelan Accounting & Audit. In a casual voice, Kathy Nguyen asked Jay Harrison how he'd learned her language.

And he told her. She listened with clenched teeth. Right place. Right time. Bingo.

"Did you see a lot of fighting?" she asked. Murderer! You—your platoon. You murdered! Back in Vietnam, you killed!

He looked up at her and gave it some thought. "No, not much," he said. "Thank God. But it was crazy enough. I got this shrapnel in the leg, hence the little limp. I'm sorry I volunteered for the army, I'll tell you that much."

She contemplated calling her daughter, who was now a medical intern in New York. But she did not call. They hadn't talked since their last argument a year ago. Her headstrong daughter disapproved of her latest romance. But then, what would she say to her? "Come back and watch Jay Harrison, VP of Human Resources, the man who shot your father, eat my food? Watch me stab him in the eye?"

Besides, she was too busy watching him, lest he'd somehow disappear. There at table six he sat, solemn and self-contained, unarmed and stooping a little, poring over the menu made of cotton paper as if it were a love letter from some secret admirer.

She had seen him a long time ago, from the vantage point of the dead. Smeared with her cousin's blood and wounded herself, partially hidden under her cousin's body, she lay very still among the wavering rice blades, her conical hat shading her face. Above her GIs milled about, their walkie-talkies buzzed and crackled, their boots sloshed mud.

Through nearly shut eyes, she watched.

A tall officer stood above her husband, a cigarette dangling from his mouth. "*Viet Cong*—Charlie—where? *VC dau? Dau?*" he asked. "*Hong biet! Hong biet o dau*," her husband answered loudly, shaking his head like an epileptic. She studied his face. It was badly bruised, lips split and bleeding.

Her husband stole glances at his rusted scythe nearby, though his wrists were bound. One of the soldiers, a freckled, red-faced teenager, prudently kicked the scythe away. Her husband made fists with his bound hands, every muscle on his torso tensed and rippled as he muttered to himself: "*Song tao tra thu. Chet thanh ma tao tru*"—"Live, I'll take revenge. Dead, as a ghost I'll haunt you."

Her body twitched hearing his words. She sensed a strange, heated stillness in the air. She wanted to yell, to crawl to his side and tell him, "Don't. I'm still alive. The baby is still alive. So tell them lies. Tell anything to survive."

But she thought of the baby inside, four and a half months along, and she willed herself to lie still and watch. A gust of wind, the rice blades rustled—the sound of late summer rain. A whiff of the foreigners' sweaty odors assaulted her nostrils. The wound on her breast burned slowly, her flesh seeped fire from deep inside. She was parched.

"*VC dau*?" asked the officer again with a quiet, almost friendly voice, but her husband shook his head angrily. The GI slapped him. Hard.

"*Viet Cong* where?"

Abruptly, her husband rose to his feet and spat blood on the officer's face. That was his answer.

The men stood, awestruck. One of them mumbled something to the others, and they snickered. The men waited. It was suddenly very quiet. She could hear the cicadas singing in the distance. The officer stepped back and, without wiping away the spit, took out his carbine from his hip holster and—Pop! Pop! Pop! Pop!—shot her husband point-blank in the chest.

The shots, sounding like firecrackers during Tet, vibrated through her cousin's corpse and punched her like fists. Under the shadow of her conical hat, she watched as the young, robust figure of her husband reeled backward, his face to the sky, and fell slowly to the ground, so slowly that in her mind's eye it seemed as if the air itself was made of water.

THAT NIGHT AFTER Harrison's visit, she raided the medicine cabinet looking for sleeping pills. She had been grinding her teeth all evening, and now a dull, nagging ache in her left jaw kept her from sleep. The cabinet was filled with vials—mostly prescribed drugs left over from when she was ill with pneumonia and then again with bronchitis. Some others belonged to Hoang, her last boyfriend, who was very handsome and young but who had, as he put it, "nerve problems." A few other vials, outdated and forgotten, belonged to her daughter, who took samples home from UCSF hospital when she was working there and simply left them behind when she moved to New York.

Somehow, a few strange pills ended up in her hand. She studied them. Effexor and Zoloft, Tylenol and Xanax, BuSpar and Benadril, Vicodin and Valium. Shiny and bright—red and blue and green and transparent with tiny colorful balls vibrating inside—they resembled semiprecious stones. She thought, "What if?"

In fish sauce with chopped garlic, crushed red pepper, brown sugar, and thinly sliced strings of pickled carrot, you would not be able to detect the medicine's bitterness, only the complex Vietnamese taste.

In the catfish soup, with tamarind base and mint leaves and fried basil and slices of succulent fish and minced green chili peppers and roasted garlic bits, who would notice the vaguely metallic taste of slow poison? Say, less than 1 mg?

With the taste of crushed and roasted rice and the sizzling fat of grilled pork, you can only appreciate the rich texture. In the special chicken curry simmering with coconut milk and lemongrass, what's a little Zoloft compared to cumin, coriander, and the thick, tender melt-in-your-mouth chicken?

Instruction to self: Don't add too much, just a little. Tease him. Please him. Harm slowly with kindness and kick-in-the-pants good food. Make him confess. Let him trust. Squeeze the past out of him.

Back home she had learned how to grow rice, how to fish, how to play dead so as to survive. So what if it took her half a world away and two decades later to bag that prized fish by serving him special dishes of rice?

Yes, yes, let's wait and see what will happen. All at once an intense love erupted and warmed her face as she thought of her estranged daughter, and somewhere right under that warm glow was a cold rage that ran in her veins, and she clenched the pills tightly in her fist, as if she could squeeze them into blood.

How would Mister Harrison, VP of Human Resources, take his coffee? Bitter, she hoped. She imagined him dying, slowly, saw him in agonizing pain. In the kitchen she ground the colorful pills into a fine gray-blue powder in her stone mortar as she schemed his death. Using green Post-it notes, she meticulously wrapped the powder into tiny squares, the shape of mock rice-cake offerings she used to burn back home during Tet to appease the insatiable hunger of the dead.

"Hoang?" she said absent-mindedly when Lien, her head waitress, told her who was on the phone. In the middle of putting chopped lemongrass into the blender with her special curry paste, she almost said, "Hoang who?" But she remembered. Hoang, who was thirteen years her junior; Hoang, who cried uninhibitedly when she broke up with him. That Hoang. "Oh God," she laughed, feeling a sense of relief. A knowledge made itself clear to her: he had no real power over her, never did, and she was at best indulgent. "*That* Hoang!"

"Pass The Kisser to me if you're done," said Lien, giggling.

"Oh, Lien, feel free," Kathy said, rolling her eyes. "I'm done. Kisser's all yours."

They laughed. It occurred to her as painfully funny: Wasn't it just a few weeks ago that she was still nursing a romantic wound, making a big fuss out of it, losing sleep, losing weight? It was his fine physique that she pined for, after his singing voice, his lush lips and kisses. He made her feel young. Was that all she could think about? But now, compared with Harrison—Harrison who limped a little as he walked, who stammered when he was nervous, who listened attentively to her every word—Hoang was like a skin abrasion to a hopeless case of internal bleeding.

On the phone, Hoang begged her to take him back. "Oh no, honey," she admonished him with the playfulness of a rich but weary aunt. "I can't baby-sit. Two years, a nice little BMW, not to mention settling your gambling debt, isn't that enough?"

"Lan, you sound different," Hoang said. "Are you all right?"

She tried to effect bitterness in her voice, but it came out non-committal. "Thank you for asking. I'm feeling super, actually."

"Lan, listen, I don't care about the car! I'll pay you back for the gambling debt. You know you love me. You know I love you. I *need* you."

Hoang never called her Kathy. In Vietnamese, her name means "orchid." Hoang was one of the very few she allowed that intimacy.

She giggled. "Oh no, honey. Don't be so theatrical. I don't know anything. Go back to your real mother, Hoang. I'm very, very busy now."

It was true. Even before she hung up on him, her mind was already somewhere else. On Pacific Heights. With Jay Harrison. His rueful smile. His drowning look when she asked him about Vietnam. The twinkle in his eyes.

She had been fretting. What if Harrison doesn't come back? What if she didn't see him again? Did he really like her cooking, or was he just being polite? So she lit incense and stood in front of the small altar in her living room and prayed each morning. To Buddha and Quan Yin. To her dead husband. To her dead parents. To her dead grandparents. To her dead cousin. To all the others, long dead. The dead floating in rain, sinking in mud, rotting among the ripened rice blades. Together, they willed him to her.

KATHY NGUYEN COULDN'T suppress her elation, her manners verged on the gleeful at Harrison's second visit. "I knew you'd show today."

"Wow, how intuitive. I was away on business, but I kept wanting to come back."

She asked about his business trip to Hong Kong, which he'd casually mentioned the last time he visited.

"Kathy, you remembered," he said, genuinely surprised and beaming from the attention. "Good memory!"

"How can I forget?" she said. She couldn't stop smiling. "So how's Hong Kong?"

"Good, very good," he said and looked into her eyes. "But nowhere as good as San Francisco, Kathy, I'll tell you that much." It occurred to her that it was not his eyes that she was looking at but the South China Sea. One morning on that crowded boat, when everyone else was still sleeping and exhausted, thirst-filled sleep, she woke alone and looked out. The sea was calm and seductive, and she had to close her eyes lest somehow she would yield to it.

"Yes, yes, of course," she agreed tentatively. "Very nice." She gave him the menu. "Now let me see, you want an Anchor Steam, correct?"

"Correct."

"Jay, we also have two special dishes today. I'll make both if you want."

"Yeah?" he said, winking. "Special is what I want. Surprise me."

She did. She hovered about him. She fussed. She told her regular chef that she'd take care of the VIP at table six personally, and managed to sprinkle into the catfish soup a tiny pinch of her special powder from one of the squares that she kept in her purse, and near the end of the meal, she thought he had a glazed look in his eyes. Harrison seemed more at ease. "Kathy," he said, his face red, voice slurring a bit, his Southern twang a little more pronounced, "your soup's damn good and hot! Christ, I'm tingling from it."

"Eat, eat," she said cheerfully, trying to ignore his remarks, though her stomach felt like it was filled with ice. Was she imagining it? Or was it just the alcohol? She didn't put too much in, did she? She wasn't aiming to kill right away. But who knows? "Your Vietnamese will improve if you eat," she said.

He laughed. "Say, I feel like I'm somewhere else. Back in Bangkok on R&R, maybe, eating this stuff. Damn spicy-hot. Good, though." Then he said, with a drawl, "Hey, Kat, *moi ngoi*. Sit. Sit. Why don't you sit with me?"

She did not sit. She stared at him, half waiting to see if he'd keel forward, half waiting to see another Harrison, a younger version, emerge. But Harrison just sat back on his chair and blushed, seemingly embarrassed with what he'd just said. "Sorry! I mean . . . ," he mumbled something that was constricted in his throat then, like a student caught cheating, looked down at his hands on his lap. "I'm sorry," he said through a sigh. "I hope that wasn't too forward."

"Never mind," she said. "You are still jet-lagged." The man's nervous demeanor made her feel oddly powerful and young. She placed her hand on his back and felt his heart, which now beat excitedly, his body heat warm and sweaty against her palm.

"I guess so," he said and wiped his forehead with his napkin.

"Still hungry, Jay?" she said tenderly. "Have some dessert? Banana flambé'? How 'bout some coffee? On the house, OK, no problem?"

Kathy, you remembered!

Pop! Pop! Pop! Pop!

She should be sad. She should scream and weep. But by the time her husband hit the ground, she was no longer in her own body. She had evaporated into a bright mist and hovered above them all. Below her: a bloody theatre. Soldiers with rifles and radios and helmets and rucksacks against a sea of golden rice, dead bodies strewn about, her own included. They seemed to her like discarded dolls in little square paddies. Yet she was disinterested. Her gaze was elsewhere—the horizon, where a bright light wavered and beckoned.

Then she was there, merging into that light.

What she felt next was for years impossible to describe, until one of her lovers, an American who avoided the war smoking dope in Canada, explained it to her: "Yeah, Kat. Absolute bliss. Nirvana. Yeah, that's what it was," he said and kissed her. "I had an out-of-body experience, too, but it was LSD and, thank God, not a bullet."

It sounded about right, but in truth, no words could ever capture what she experienced. Perhaps she had died then. How else to explain that intense sense of well-being and yet, not being? Perhaps that was what it was like not to have a body any longer, to be free. In retrospect, she could have willed herself to remain there, in that sea of light, never to return to mud and rice and harsh sunshine and buzzing insects and oxen dung and blood and grief—were it not for a kick from inside her stomach: her unborn child, wanting life, wanting the world, and somehow that kick created a field of gravity that defined the limit of her body.

Back on the ground with the flies buzzing above her, she experienced agony. It took all her strength not to scream, not to move. On her left breast the wound seared and throbbed; blood oozed down her skin. She was intensely alert. Through her conical hat she noted the fragment of the sky. How blue it was, the blue of the finest china, the blue of eternity!

Lying still, she was going mad. She wanted to scream and thrash. She was dying of thirst. Anguish engulfed her. To stay inert she kept an accounting of her losses. She recited them like a mantra: a dead husband, a dead cousin, a few dead neighbors from the adjoining paddies; the rice, ripened, unharvested.

Above her, the soldiers, their voices solemn and tempered now, walked about while smoking their cigarettes. The young officer was within her sight. He stood scratching his neck while he stared down at her husband's corpse, his eyes squinting in the sunlight. He took off his helmet and wiped the sweat off his forehead with a handkerchief. It was then that she saw his eyes, so startling, so clear, they twinkled. He lit another cigarette. He took his time as he studied her husband's body, his face contemplative, smoke rising from his nostrils.

Far away, on the flame trees, among the blinding red clumps of flowers, the cicadas hummed.

She swallowed him with her eyes.

JAY HARRISON ON OCCASION had an ominous look, hungry, perhaps, especially after she fed him her special entrees—or wild, maybe—she couldn't decide. At those moments his eyes belonged to another man, one not so kind, not so polite, but with the hunger of an alley cat. Those moments would only last for a few seconds and then a veil would fall over them, a solemnity, a will to suppress desire, and it re-enshrouded Harrison in a pallid mask. Kathy couldn't tell which was the real Harrison, perhaps both, but she did decide on one thing: he looked good.

"Kathy, I'm a new man," he told her one afternoon, dressed in shorts and an Adidas shirt. It was his day off. He was drinking much less, he told her. Had started going back to the gym for the first time since his divorce four years ago. At his office, he told her, his secretary referred to him as Mr. Extra Nice. He thought it was funny. He thought it was flattering.

Kathy Nguyen stopped him in the middle of the story. "Why, Jay?" she asked sharply.

"Why what? What's the matter?"

"Oh, nothing's the matter. I mean why Mr. Extra Nice?"

"Oh, that. It's just my office. They all think I'm really nice to them, that's all. And now the girls think I'm looking good to boot. Don't you think I look good, Kat?"

"Oh sure, good, very good. But nice? How nice? You buying them donuts?"

He started to laugh, but his face turned serious when he saw her eyes. He cleared his throat. "More than that. I buy them gifts. I give them half days off. I give them bonuses. I take them to lunch. Hell, I drove one girl to the emergency room when her water broke." Then he paused, his voice a little choked. "I work them hard. Sometimes their feelings get hurt. I make it up. Kathy, I don't want them to feel bad on my account."

She trembled slightly with an unexpected rage. "On your account," she whispered.

"Yes, it's a tough business, lots of stress, but I try as much as I can not to hurt anybody's feelings. So I do nice things."

"Of course not." She nodded. "Nobody should get hurt."

She had to sit down. Twice a week as her regular for almost three months now, and Kathy Nguyen never sat at his table. "Yes. Sit. Sit." She said nothing. "I started jogging again," he volunteered, smiling nervously. "Feel like a million bucks, Kathy."

"Well, if my food is part of why you feel so rich, I am very, very happy," she said, her voice grave. He stared at her. She was about to say something else when Lien appeared and placed between them a steaming bowl of stuffed bitter melon and minced prawns and laid a pair of chopsticks on it, then conspiratorially winked at her. Kathy pushed the bowl a few inches toward Harrison and gave her trademark proprietress smile. "Here you go! Eat, Mr. Extra Nice."

Harrison reached out quickly, not for the food, but to cover her hands in his. "Nice," he said nervously. "Something is. Something sure is."

She wanted to pull her hands back but did not. Rather, her hands failed to follow her mental orders. Between the bowl and his palms, she felt as if imprisoned in walls made of fire. She looked helplessly at the pair of black lacquer chopsticks lying on top of the soup bowl and thought they looked like the treacherous monkey bridge made of bamboo back home, the one that she as a child was terrified to cross.

She opened her mouth trying to frame a word, but she was an actress on stage without a script. Words did not come out, only a sigh. What was she supposed to do next, anyway? She didn't really know. She looked up, into his eyes. She felt dizzy. It was very hot inside her restaurant. It was humid. Her gaze drifted downward, to the whiteness of his shirt.

White. White headbands.

Green. The green of the Mekong Delta's rice fields. Of palm trees and elephant grass.

The green of the South China Sea.

Yours were the first pair of green eyes I'd ever seen, Jay. The most cold. The most beautiful.

It all came welling up insider her then, a swarm of memories yearning for a narrative, for an outlet, and she clenched her jaw to stay the impulse to tell Jay Harrison everything—everything. Her losses, her gains—how she survived and escaped out to sea after the war ended and her family's land was confiscated by the communists, how she alone had raised a child in America, how she went from man to man but never found love again, and how much she, above all else, loved her strong-willed, independent daughter, who no longer needed her and found her love stifling, and how, without her only flesh and blood, she felt like she had lost everything again.

She looked at him and clenched her teeth, her jaw clenched shut.

Of all the people in the world, Kathy Nguyen noted, Mr. Extra Nice Jay Harrison alone would appreciate it now, her story, his masterpiece.

Four funerals in one day, Jay, can you imagine? Could have been six, you know. The entire village wore white headbands. Lots of Buddhist chanting. Children weeping, widows crying, aged mothers with white hair and wrinkles deep as ravines clutching at their grandchildren's arms under the sun, wailing, "Why? God, God. Oh, why?"

She alone acted stoic throughout. During funeral preparations she did not weep like the others, did not tear at her hair, could barely cry at all. She could not even pray to Buddha, not even silently. Had she opened her mouth, the sounds she would have made would have shattered her. She washed her husband's body with jasmine-scented water. Under a flickering oil lamp she trailed the gaping holes on his chest where her tongue had licked and tickled only a few nights earlier, the dark nipples that had hardened at the slightest touch; with her other hand, weakened and pained and limited by the wound on her breast, she cupped desperately at his groin.

A widow at twenty-one.

Boat person at twenty-five, mother of a beautiful, giggly little girl.

At Cafe Du Nord they listened to Latin jazz and drank cosmopolitans. Her third drink, his fourth, and they held hands. At the Caribbean Zone they danced past one in the morning. "It's way past my bedtime," he said, laughing, looking ten years younger, "but I don't care." She taught him, with some success, how to cha-cha. She'd learned it in the refugee camp in Pulau Bidong, Malaysia, from a young man with whom she had her first affair. He'd been a wealthy playboy in Saigon during the war, but in that camp was a nostalgic pauper. Harrison, despite his weak leg, was quick and limber when drunk. Mr. Extra Nice did not complain even when she stepped on his foot, twice, the first time intentionally. When the band's "La Cumparsita" ended, Harrison kissed her, and she, drunk and out of breath, cringed at first, then found herself kissing him back.

"Throw a spear, follow it," she told herself as his tongue probed the insides of her mouth. It was a proverb her mother taught her a long, long time ago. They were killing four chickens together for Tet, and she wept as she was told to slit the throat of the rooster she'd personally raised and called Ca. She was eight or nine. Her mother rapped her knuckles on her head when she first refused. "If you want to learn how to cook a chicken, you'd better learn how to kill one," her mother scolded her. "Throw a spear, follow it."

Follow the spear till the very end. She cried, but she slit Ca's throat. As its blood spurted out, Ca made a gargling sound, jerked a few times, then was still. Follow the spear. Besides, wasn't it better to carry out what she must at his house than at her restaurant? Perhaps. But did it require kissing him back so passionately? And did it require holding onto his neck with drowning desperation? She tried to imagine her husband's face, but it had faded. She tried to remember Harrison as a young man, short hair, thin, cigarette dangling from his lips, a malevolent gaze, a soldier who smoked while her husband breathed his last breath, but that memory, too, failed to guide her.

In his arms she felt alive, yet not herself. This man, his lips on her lips, his tongue probing inside her mouth, his arms holding her waist, his heartbeats echoing through her body—there was a reason that she had to kill him. But, in the thrall of the embrace, evaporating slowly into nothingness in his arms, she could not remember what it was.

In Harrison's king-sized bed, near dawn, she awoke with a start. Parched, she got up for water. On the mantel in the living room, there was a picture of him in his army uniform, young and cocky, standing with arms on two army buddies, the sun bright on their faces. Just like she remembered him.

Back in his bed, he drew her to him, showered her with sleepy, alcohol-breath kisses. "Just a bad dream, sweetie," he cooed into her neck. His fingers glided over her breast, over the slightly distended scar and lingered there. Her skin tingled where his lips alighted. She was disappearing in the heat of his body, lost in his affection. "It'll go away. You're all right now. Nothing bad will happen, I promise."

His whispers she found strangely reassuring. She could believe in what he said, because she was no longer afraid. Under him, making love, she had slowly faded. Now, in his arms, she felt as if she was someone new, a stranger. She was alive, alert, detached.

What woke her from her sleep, however, was a familiar voice, one she hadn't heard in years. And in that voice she saw a sturdy young man, someone so centered in himself that he grew to be, in memories, more than a husband but a way of life—chores and seasons, mud and rice fields and sweat—what she left far behind.

Live, I'll take revenge. Dead, as a ghost I'll haunt you.

At yoga, the instructor said quietly: "Lie as still as a corpse. Savasana, corpse pose. This pose is, in fact, the most important of all yoga postures."

She almost laughed out loud. *You want corpse pose, honey, I'll show you. I'm the expert with corpse poses.*

Afterward, in the locker room, still wrapped in a towel, the showers running, with women's voices rising, falling like a chorus, she listened to her cell phone messages. "Lan, I need you," Hoang said. "I won't gamble again. I miss you so much." Then his voice changed. "Sudafed and methamphetamine, a sure heart-stopper, with a bottle of whiskey, guaranteed. Lan, I swear, that's what I'll do this evening if you don't call me."

"Lan," she mumbled to herself as if trying to remember, "Nguyen Thi Thu Lan." In her mind she saw a young peasant woman in black pajamas lying still among the dead. But in remembering, it was someone else who rose, leaving a fading ghost-like corpse behind. It was Kathy who tried to save the young man by filling his bleeding wounds with mud. A couple of green bottle flies had lighted near the wounds. The blood hadn't congealed but his breath was long gone. She stood in the same spot where his killer stood, her bare feet sinking slowly in his boot prints. She tried to cry but only managed a hoarse, raspy cough. Her mouth and throat were so dry that her breath felt like fire. She squinted her eyes and tried but failed to understand what the GI saw when he stood staring down at her dead husband.

"*Lan, anh nho em qua,*" Hoang continued now in a teary voice. Vietnamese for "I really miss you." "Darling, my darling, don't you miss me?"

She wasn't sure. She looked at herself in the mirror. But from where she stood, amid the steam air, her face was a blur, indefinable.

"Lan," Hoang said. "I really want to see you again."

"The Kisser wants to kill himself with Sudafed and methamphetamine and whiskey," she told Lien the next day, and they both laughed.

"That would be a waste of whiskey," Lien said. "He'll only get drowsy and a headache. If The Kisser really wants to off himself, he should visit old Mrs. Linh on Eddy and Leavenworth. She's got the real deal: *ngai den*. Easy. Put that black grass in your tamarind soup. Tastes good. No American knows anything about it. Won't show up in any autopsy tests. Euthanasia soup."

"Hey," she said, laughing still. "What a good idea."

THE AIR IN HARRISON'S kitchen was redolent with the complex smells of fish sauce, fried garlic, and freshly chopped cilantro. At the table by the window he sat watching the sun setting over the hedges, a glass of single malt in his hand. She stood stirring the soup as they talked, shouting to one another about the monsoon over the whirls of the ventilation fan.

"Damn rain, you can drown in it," he said, remembering.

"Yeah," she agreed. Mrs. Linh's chopped *ngai den* was waiting in a little vial in her purse on the counter behind her. He was pouring them each another glass of single malt. His third drink, her second.

"I remember," she said and went to pick up her glass. "Hard rain. Super, heavy-duty rain. On your tin roof like horses running." They clinked glasses. She drummed her lacquered nails on the surface of the table, repeating the sounds of the past.

He looked at her. "You're so beautiful, Kat, you know that?" he said. "I wanted you the moment I saw you."

"What? This old meat?" she said as she raised her slender arm, but she was pleased. He bent forward to kiss the crook of her elbow.

She tingled all over. But she was thinking of the monsoon, heavy as the weight of the dead. "Sometimes it rained so hard your plastic slippers floated away, your bed turned into a boat by morning," she sighed. "My daughter would pretend she was rowing down river, and after, I'd find catfish in the closet, crabs in my kitchen." Now that was rain. Not like in California. A few showers and people get into car accidents. Amateurs!

"It was really hard," he agreed, laughing, and taking another sip of whiskey, "Damn rain. Wading in the mud when you humped. Hump. Hump. Hump. When it's your turn, you know, and your men are getting picked off one by one like little Indians."

"You said you didn't see much fighting," she said, scowling.

"Well, I saw some," he said, scowling back. "I wasn't always sitting in my bunker cleaning my M-16, you know."

She stared at him. She was about to say something else but changed her mind. "Never mind. Soup's ready soon." She was turning away to look for her purse. But Harrison grabbed her hand and pulled her back to him. "Listen, Kathy Nguyen, I got things to say to you. But first I need to tell you that I've fallen for you. Maybe one day, you and I, we can go together to see Vietnam properly."

She sat down on his lap, astonished. The very idea! He and her—traveling the length of her country in peacetime, down the rivers in the Mekong Delta, up the pine-covered hills of Dalat, frolicking on the white sandy beaches of Nha-Trang. A future. Returning home. An American couple.

He wrapped his arms around her. She was trembling. When she spoke, her voice was so breathless he had to lean forward to listen. "Sometimes," she said, trying to be as honest as she could, "you make me feel like a cloud."

"You mean I put you on cloud nine?" he said with a half smile. But she shook her head.

"Listen, Kat," he said, stammering now. "I know we've got a lot to discover about each other." Then he laughed nervously. "I know we've both got scars from that war, literally. I know we've still got a whole lot of things we need to tell each other and work them out. But, you know, I've really fallen for you."

"No, it's OK," she said, the air congested in her lungs. She wanted to hear more; she wanted him to stop talking.

"No," he said. "It's not OK. I'm in love with you."

The main effect of the whiskey was a thickness of the tongue. She wanted to say more. She opened her mouth but no sound came out.

"Kat, listen to me," he whispered into her ear, kissing her neck, her temple. "I know a damn good thing when I see it. The way you looked at me that first day, I swear, I felt something immediately. You changed me."

They kissed. Inside her head a silver nimbus bloomed. When she spoke again, her voice was calm. "When did you give up smoking?"

"What?" he said. "How'd you know I used to smoke? What's that got to do with anything?"

"I know," she said. "I saw you. I mean, I saw the picture in the living room. With your wife and kids. Cigarette in your mouth."

"Oh that," he said. "Hell, that was a long time ago." Then he paused. A look of pain came over his face suddenly. "I picked it up during the war. When I came home, Judy said it was bad for the kids, so I quit. I'm Mr. Extra Nice, remember? I gave it all up. Not that it saved my marriage. But why'd you want to know?"

She looked up at him with tears in her eyes. "I mean, Jay, what would you do, what would you give up for me?"

"Anything!" he said with a desperate voice. His lips were trembling. "Anything you want. Damn it. It's yours. All you have to do is ask. Kat, don't you believe me?"

The sun was almost gone. Harrison's kitchen was bathed in an orange glow.

Sitting on his lap, she wiped the tears at the corner of his eyes. The soup was almost ready. She steadied herself with her hand on his thigh where the shrapnel still lay.

"Yes," she sighed. "I do believe."

In the dining room Harrison started to sing as he set the dishes. She paused from stirring her soup and listened. There was a poetic twang in his voice as he sang Ned Miller's song:

From a Jack to a King.
From loneliness to a wedding ring.
I played an Ace and I won a Queen,
An' walked away with your heart.

She'd never heard him sing before. His voice was warm and sweet. It caused her to pause. She willed herself to think of Ca, the rooster she killed with her mother. Do it swiftly, her mother had said. As a ghost, I'll haunt you, her husband had said. She opened her purse and took out the vial, but her eyes focused instead on her ring finger. She could imagine the gold band, and her hand trembled as if she was having a seizure.

It came abruptly to her then, what Harrison was thinking years ago in that sun-drenched afternoon after he shot her husband in the chest and stood looking down at her husband's corpse. He was thinking of his wife and kids, and how he could ever explain to them what he had turned into under that hateful sun. She didn't know exactly how she knew, but she knew.

A sharp, jolting pain seared her breast. It was as if the old bullet wound was throbbing anew. Her heart ached. Her hand went up to protect her breast, and the ladle, caught in the gesture, tumbled out of the soup pot and onto the tile floor with a loud clatter.

"You OK, Kat?" Harrison asked from the dining room.

"Yeah," she said. "No problem." But she was not OK. She threw the little vial in her purse and let herself quietly out the side door, down the stairs and across the street into her Volvo.

Now what?

Now, inside her car, with the engine softly humming and the heater blowing a steady warm breeze, she listened to Billie Holiday sing the blues. Kathy Nguyen looked down at her open purse in which she kept her powder squares, a tidy package next to the vial of poison grass. She took the vial out and looked at it. It was going to be the grand finale. But now what?

Since they met, she'd imagined—nursed—the kind of conversation they would have tonight. It was fate, after all—how else could she explain their encounter? She'd played out over and over in her head the final act. "*Viet Cong o dau*; VC—Charlie—where?" She would repeat it to him, mocking his voice as he lay dying on the plush carpet looking up at her. Then, like her husband did, she would spit on his face, the final insult.

He would be shocked. Shocked. The shock should finish him off if the *ngai den* did not. He would beg her to forgive him with his dying breath. He would tell her that he wasn't evil, just young and dumb. But she would not forgive. She would say in a deliberate voice, "Did your men spare me, my cousin when we begged? No. You let your men shoot us. Then you shot my husband."

"*Viet Cong o dau*?" She said it out loud now, staring at Harrison's tall silhouette at the bay window. But her voice was not manly, nor was it chased with sarcasm or vehemence. It was plaintive, hoarse. "Damn you, stupid, stupid Jay Harrison, bastard," she said and pressed hard on both sides of her nose, under her eyes, so that she would stop crying. "Stupid," she said. "Stupid me! Stupid men!" She lowered her car window and the cold air rushed in. But whose death was she crying for? Her long dead husband's? Or Lan's?

Lan, the young widow, would have thrown the whole thing in the soup with glee and not trembled like cowardly, tongue-tied Kathy Nguyen. Lan, as she cleaned her husband's body for the funeral years ago, had envisioned Harrison's death. But how could that peasant girl, in her wildest imagination, conceive for herself this other life, this other possibility?

She looked up. She ached for him, even now when she was so close to finishing off the wounded beast with her spear. If she waved to him, maybe. If she turned on her headlights, honked her horn. Instead, she flung the little vial out the window and it hit the pavement with a clank and rolled away into the dark. Kathy Nguyen closed her eyes and hugged herself.

She should drive away, never go back. Forgive. Wasn't that the Buddhist thing to do in order to be free? But Harrison would pursue her surely, until the truth emerged.

She should go back inside then. But it would be like crossing yet another ocean—the stories they would have to tell each other, the things they must confess, the ghosts they must appease and confront together . . . and apart.

Up by the bay window, Harrison moved and faced her direction finally. Behind him lights gleamed. He was searching for her, she could tell, even from this impossible distance.

Close to the Bone

"RAIN DELAYED NAPOLEON. He wanted the ground to dry out a little before the attack. Wellington's army was over here, on St. Jean, but they withstood repeated attacks. By nightfall they counterattacked and drove the French from the field. . . . There were heavy losses on all sides."

I already knew the story. It struck me then that not once had my father told me a fairy tale; he probably didn't know any. But war stories he told too often, turning our dining room table into the battlefield, our spoons and chopsticks into battalions, bowls into bases and hills. The Duke of Wellington was drunk. Napoleon was not, but there was nothing he could do; he was there, against fate.

This was our European vacation: our last as a family, though my older sister had by then left home for college. I don't remember much about getting to Waterloo, except that the countryside was streaked and blurred, light over darker green under a dismal gray sky. Father drove; I had the map; Mother had a headache and complained about the cold. Why didn't we go to the hotel first to drop

159

off our luggage and what was the rush to see another battlefield, in Belgium, of all places, she asked?

I gave wrong directions. Father cursed, calling me names in French. I was rude, also in French, which surprised him since I rarely spoke the language. Everyone was tense. We'd turned into an American family, complete with sullen teenager and bickering parents.

It was still gray out when we reached Lion's Hillock, the windswept monument of the Battle of Waterloo, a rounded topographical knoll that overlooked the battlefield. Mother declined the climb, made a show of sniffling, and went to the souvenir shop for hot chocolate. Father was flailing by the time we reached the top, but I could tell he was excited, and all at once he was pointing wildly and talking and trying to catch his breath. "There, Napoleon's army stood. Over there stood Wellington. It is close, very close. The Imperial Guard, the crème de la France," he calls them, "assail the British line at great cost and victory is within his grasp, when, from there, the Prussians come." Father's favorite military tactician has lost and is exiled to Saint Helena, where he dies.

After so many years of hearing this story, it should have meant something to me to finally see the place, but that summer afternoon I was homesick and missed Tristan and was replaying over and over our first kiss by the ocean. It was why I misread the map, why it was not until Father stopped talking and looked out to the far-off distance in the direction of Napoleon's flight that I actually looked around me. There was no battlefield, there was just a mist drifting lazily over green pasture, the air faintly smelling of upturned earth.

I looked at Father, who, his story done, seemed so alone and a little lost. His sparse hair was tousled by the wind, his face contemplative. It came to me then that this was how he looked on that naval ship as they headed to Subic Bay from Vietnam at the end of the war. I imagined him staring at his gun for a long, long time before he tossed it into the sea.

A deep sadness welled up in me and lodged in my throat. I felt like I was suffocating, and had to turn away for fear that Father might see tears brimming in my eyes and think that I, too, was mourning Napoleon's defeat.

MY FATHER WAS a colonel in the Army of the Republic of Vietnam, the losing side, when decades of war ended with the fall of Saigon in 1975. Now, he's a retired bank executive and an American citizen, energetic in his late sixties, fond of weekend tennis, swimming in summer, and *tae kwon do* each afternoon out by the pool.

He also drives my mother crazy.

Father likes to fix things around the house. Sometimes I think American life is just like a sitcom, but where the laugh track should be there are mostly tears. Changing a washer leads to a burst pipe and a flood in the kitchen; repairing small cracks in the dining-room wall ends with broken glass and the destruction of a Marc Chagall poster, the one depicting the hectic atmosphere of a circus in swathes of turbulent red, blue, and orange.

In the garden, where Mother grows azaleas, hibiscus, daffodils and roses, he drove a shovel through the root ball of her favorite rose bush after deciding it needed to be in a sunnier spot.

"He is killing me," Mother said on the phone. "Come home. Do something!"

Mother wanted him out of her way, preferably confined to his study, where he was writing, on and on, his wartime memoir, or in his armchair with his Chivas Regal on the rocks watching CNN and intermittently cursing in French, his default language when angry, at the woeful state of the world.

One visit, over whiskey and dried squid, I tried the Vietnamese approach: "Ba, why don't you teach? Lots of high schools around here need teachers."

"Yes," Mother yelled from the kitchen. "That's good idea!" This she said in English, a language she dislikes, claiming it hurts her ears. "Your father, he is great, great teacher!"

CNN was playing up footage of a train wreck somewhere in India. As I talked, Father stared at the dead being removed from the mangled cars and grunted. Now, depending on the intonation,

I had learned that his "huh" has many meanings. It might mean "Let me think about it" or "Really?" or "India's train system is despicable." It could also mean "Back off, mister." This was the last of these.

"Why not?" Mother persisted. "You speak French. You are good, very good, in math. You got MBA. Can teach PE even, with your three-degree black belt."

"Third degree," Father corrected.

"Yes, why not? Extra income not so bad." Then she switched to French and said they could use the money to go to France again. Father raised an eyebrow and glanced sideways at her. My mother hated France, hated Europe. After their last trip to Paris, she swore that if she ever saw another rude Frenchman, it would be one too many, our relatives in Paris and Lyon be damned.

Father loved Paris. He loved France. Born into an upper-class Chinese-Vietnamese family in colonial Vietnam, he had French citizenship and as a student had spent a year in Paris. But, like his uncle, who fought in the Algerian war, Father was conscripted to serve in the French army to fight against Ho Chi Minh and left behind a blond girlfriend and his dream of becoming a lawyer. After the French were defeated in 1954, Vietnam was split in two. Father stayed in the south and in the army, and met and married Mother, a refugee from Hanoi. They had two children. By the time the American war got into full swing, he was a colonel. He was thirty-three. Ten years later, he was without his army and his country.

CNN had moved from carnage to chaos, a riot in some ancient, dusty city in the Middle East, with soldiers shooting tear gas at a fleeing crowd and clubbing those who didn't run fast enough.

Father muttered "*putain*," as if the protesters deserved worse.

THEIR LAUGHTER COULD be heard from the street when I stopped by and found Father, drunk midafternoon, boasting to Uncle Duy, his brother-in-law, about passing the exams to become a high-school teacher. He had his certificate and, within days, a part-time teaching position at a nearby school.

"The others taking the test, they said, 'Colonel, you're amazing!' but I said, 'Not really. You young men should have prepared. You probably played too hard or are just too lazy to study. Go back and study seriously this time and you'll do well.'" Then Father added, "Of course, they're right. I suppose, at my age, I am amazing."

"Watch that tongue!" Mother yelled from the kitchen where she was washing salad with her sister, Aunty Ly. Mother's lifelong occupation, it seems, was to keep everyone's tongues in check, especially Father's. Aunty Ly shook her head as she looked at Mother with sympathy, and said, "Sister is right. No one likes an indelicate man." Then, in a lower voice, as she watched Mother adjust the faucet to keep it from leaking, "Or an amateur plumber!"

"Huh!" Father said, and continued boasting to Uncle. Once a captain in the ARVN airborne division, Uncle Duy for years fixed refrigerators and heaters for a living until he, too, retired and took to repainting his past—how he was manager at his company, how he was a doctor in the ARVN.

I hugged Mother hello. She whispered: "Mama's saved!"

Aunty Ly then hugged me and whispered. "Now, Ethan, save Aunty. Get Uncle a job, too. Please!"

What "saved" my mother were the frequent visits of relatives and friends, and in part, the house itself—a four-bedroom suburban home on the northern edge of Silicon Valley at the foot of the mountains—plenty of room for them to find peace from each other.

Mr. Lopez, their chatty neighbor from the Philippines who owned a busy auto shop on Calaveras and Brentwood, confirmed their life to be the "Amerrican drrream!" He said it so often, over-trilling the *r* each time, that it became something as tangible as his black BMW or his wife's cherry-red Porsche. A burly man, Mr. Lopez always complimented my parents on their—and their children's—achievements whenever they chatted across the fence, which let him boast about his own, though he never mentioned his two obese kids who were still in high school and threw noisy and dangerous parties when their parents were away—the youngest was facing charges for dealing dope.

Behind his back, Mother called him "Mister Good-for-You," which was her usual response to his vainglory. If it weren't for his discount tuneups and the crunchy persimmons that grew in abundance on the tree that draped over our fence in the backyard, Mother wouldn't have bothered. Mother, who loved the fruit and always left the freshest as an ancestral offering at the family altar, gave Mrs. Lopez roses in return.

My parents believed family was private business and the past was best left alone. Not that they hid themselves or anything. Their biography of sorts was on display on the mantel for all to see: framed black-and-white photos we managed to take with us when we fled at the end of the war. Life in America was for my parents a big letdown, a reality defined by disappointment and loss. They would never have in America what had been taken from them in Vietnam.

In one photo, Father is emerging from his helicopter, silver baton in his left hand, his right reaching out to a young army officer who stands with hunched shoulders under the whirling rotor blades that push down on the elephant grass. In the distance are the silhouettes of bent-backed farmers in conical hats. Father's face is dark and somber.

In another, a little boy in suit with bow tie, an older girl in a red *ao dai* dress. I am the young boy: round face, cute, I suppose, in a gloomy way. I rarely smile in the old pictures. My sister holds our dog, Bisou, a Japanese poodle, which has shed on her dress. We stand on the landing of the stone steps of our little villa in Saigon.

Another. Mother and Father. A beautiful couple would be an understatement. She wears her multistranded gold-bead necklace outside her lavender brocade. She looks stunning and regal. Father, on the thin side, is dignified and suave in a gray silk suit, a cigarette in his hand. The picture is most definitely posed. It is the first day of Tet. Behind them, two Chinese brush paintings hang on the wall, one showing a gathering of Chinese fairies on clouds, the other a ferocious dragon descending from a misty mountain. I don't know why, but I have a flashback to when I am a little boy, hiding inside Mother's walk-in closet, the size of a small room with windows opened and the hundred or so painted and embroidered *ao dai* dresses and brocades swaying in the breeze. I can smell the camphor and Guerlain. I am lost in the fabric. From far away I hear my sister's voice calling out: "Father's home! Father's home!"

None of the pictures shows how it all ended. There are plenty of those online under "Fall of Saigon" or "April 30, 1975," "Vietnam evacuation," "Evacuation+Saigon." Tens of thousands of them. Tanks rolling into Saigon; helicopters flying out to waiting American ships; fear-stricken Vietnamese climbing over the razor wire of the American embassy. There are no pictures of my mother, my sister, and me crowded into a C-147 cargo plane two days before the end.

I remember a green sea below the plane's window, the wails of a woman, the smell of vomit, night turning into day then back into night, the throbbing of the engines, green tents flapping in the wind, a scorching sun, long lines for food.

Father left after us, on a warship with hundreds of well-placed others, for the U.S. Navy base at Subic Bay in the Philippines and asylum. He folded away his army uniform, changed into a pair of jeans and a T-shirt, and tossed his gun into the sea.

I was seven when I came to America, old enough to remember, young enough to change.

If I still remember playing soldier with Father, hiding behind the couch and taking imaginary shots at him, and if I still remember wanting to grow up and march in his soldierly footsteps, I also learned to quickly outgrow that childhood vision.

I grew up here, after all, reached puberty here, fell in love here. When my voice broke, it felt as if my new American self was being born inside me. My Vietnamese self receded, as the country had done from the C-147's window, into the stuff of dreams, a place that might haunt my parents nightly, but irretrievable just the same.

And yet ...

I WAS IN THE MIDDLE of a meeting when Mother called. My secretary slipped me a note: *It's Mama! Sounds frantic. Or is it the usual?*

"Can you believe it? He break bricks!"

"What? Is Dad all right?"

"With bare hands! At his age! Who your father think he is? Superman Teacher? Bruce Lee Teacher?"

Father had a troublemaker in one of his classes. A sixteen-year-old Chinese-Vietnamese named David Huan. Tigers pranced on his biceps, snakes slithered. Mother has the gift of storytelling and can make an entire epic from very little information. This story relied on a classic scenario, in which the novice teacher is tested by the headstrong student. But the story is about Father, so there will be a twist in its tail. I signal that I'll be awhile, and my secretary closes the door.

Father enters the classroom. A boy is sitting on his desk, talking with a few heavily made-up girls who giggle as they comb through their hair or repaint their lips. Neither he nor the girls pay any attention to the new teacher. Father loses it. "All of you, shut up! You . . . sit down! Sit, or I will break your neck! I have a third-degree black belt in *tae kwon do*."

Silence, for a moment, then a flurry of questions.

"Serious? How'd you learn it?"

"You're like Mr. Miyagi in *Karate Kid*, right?"

Laughter.

"But aren't you, kinda, like, too old to break our necks?" This is from the tattooed boy, David Huan, who still sits on Father's desk. "Why don't you break Tony's neck? He's skinny. It shouldn't be too hard."

More laughter. "Ha ha," says Tony.

"Yeah, show us!" someone yells.

"Show us!" echoes the class. "Show us!"

Father orders silence and to maintain it tells them how he was a soldier, an officer, in South Vietnam fighting the communists. He is still within their knowledge zone, and they are still silent, so he continues. Father learned martial arts from the Korean soldiers at his military academy. He came to America many years ago and thought about teaching *tae kwon do*—he takes a dramatic defensive stance here and wins them back. Instead, he became a banker, but he practices every day. He has told a room full of teenagers in ten minutes more than he has Mr. Lopez in fifteen years.

"What rank were you, mister? My dad was a sergeant. He knew some *kung fu*, too."

"Did you kill commies with your bare hands?"

All of them are talking. Few remain at their desks. Some mimic *kung fu* moves. It is mayhem, until David Huan gets up finally and lets out a piercing whistle. The class falls silent. He turns to Father: "OK, Mister I-Break-Your-Neck. We'll give you the benefit of the doubt. Today. Tomorrow, you have to prove it."

The next day, Father finds three orange bricks on his desk and David Huan sitting up front, chin on knuckles. "Judgment day, teach," he says, a green dragon dancing to the flex of a bicep. "I'll be satisfied with one brick."

Father hasn't broken a brick in maybe a couple of decades. And even three at a time wasn't a problem back then. These days he practices his *hyeong*—a sequence of martial arts movements—but he hasn't seriously sparred with anyone for many years, or broken anything, Marc Chagall and water pipes notwithstanding.

"I accept your challenge," he says, then puts down his briefcase, sets the bricks on the floor, two edgeways, the third across the top. "In return, I expect you all to behave in my class." He takes off his suit jacket and tie, rolls up his shirtsleeves, and takes his brick-breaking stance. He makes a few air chops, slowly at first, then more focused. Even so, he still looks like a gray-haired, dark-skinned Asian man in his sixties.

The students form a semicircle behind him, jostling for view. He shouts his *K'ihap* to help concentrate his fighting spirit as he chops down on the brick. It doesn't break. His hand goes numb. Jeers. Father shouts again and chops. Still no effect. He closes his eyes. There is laughter. Perhaps he's thinking of the war, of the necks that he actually did break.

He breathes calmly, then releases a deafening "Harhhhh!" as his hand descends a third time and the brick breaks neatly in half. The kids cheer. David Huan gives Father the thumbs up and a boyish, crooked grin.

Word spreads quickly. In the corridors, it's "Hi Mister I-Break-Your-Neck" for the rest of the day as Father's hand swells and throbs and turns blue. Writing on the blackboard is agony. In the teachers' lounge at lunch he soaks his hand in ice water. The school nurse says she doesn't think it is broken but makes him go for an X-ray to check for a possible fracture. She calls him, not unkindly, "an old fool."

"I said to him 'Are you crazy?' " Mother said on the phone. "'At your age? What you going to do next? Kickboxing? Join the 49ers? Your father, he is killing me!"

If David Huan was passionate about anything, it was martial arts. Though his juvenile record was rumored to be extensive, it wasn't. I checked. He was arrested only once for breaking and entering. He stole from his neighbor, who, charmed by the offer to mow his lawn and clean his yard for a year, dropped the charges.

Sometimes he would call my father "Mister I-Break-Your-Neck," but mostly it was "*Siu Phu*," Chinese for "teacher," or in Vietnamese the most intimate "*Thay*."

He first showed up at my parents' house not long after the brick incident. He was there for extra math and English lessons, but I think mostly he came for the war stories and martial arts. He got a lesson after schoolwork was done for the evening. Mother, normally highly suspicious of strangers, and one with tattoos no less, turned into a doting "*Siu Mau*"—"wife of teacher." Father never had any classroom problems when David Huan was in the room.

I was barely acknowledged when, late one afternoon, I dropped by and found the three of them engrossed in a Hong Kong *kung fu* movie, early Jackie Chan—it could have been any of them. Vicious assailant murders protagonist's beloved *kung fu* teacher. Hero confronts villain but is badly defeated and barely survives. Rescued by an eccentric beggar drunk, who, after pleading and supplication, agrees to teach Hero amazing fighting technique, which for some reason requires being very drunk. Hero struggles with steely determination and, though bloodied and terribly wounded, kills powerful villain. The End.

"That's what heroes are made of," Father said.

David saw me roll my eyes, and giggled. I liked him immediately.

At dinner, David was a perfect guest, sincere in his compliments for Mother's cooking—"Wow, this tastes like at an expensive restaurant. *Siu Mau*, I want to move in!"—and earnest as he asked Father to tell his war stories—"*Siu Phu*, you never finished that story about how you kicked VC ass in hand-to-hand combat."

It was one of Father's more famous stories. He needed to take a leak and ordered his pilot to land their helicopter. There were a couple of Viet Cong hiding in nearby bush, but they were too terrified to shoot him, or didn't want to give away their position—either works. Father had already spotted them, but took his time doing his business and, after slowly buttoning up, launched himself into a dive, grabbed one and shot the other with his service pistol at close range in the chest. He knocked the live one out with a chop to the neck, dumped him in the helicopter, and brought him back to base to be interrogated. The story is true. It is told and retold by soldiers on both sides because hand-to-hand combat is pretty rare in any war, and for a colonel to be involved is rarer still.

In the middle of Father's story, David looked at me with that smirk. Then he eyed his water glass. I looked at mine. At first I thought it was a mild earthquake. The water rippled. But Huan subtly gestured his chin toward Father. As he told the story, Father was absent-mindedly chopping the edge of his right hand against the edge of the dining table. No doubt he was honing his brick-breaking skill for the next year. I could hear the utensils subtly rattle against each other and against the china at his every chop.

"SO, ETHAN, WHAT'S your story?" Huan asked me later outside, where I'd gone to have a cigarette. He was jumping up and down to keep warm. We were in the backyard. It was windy and he didn't have a jacket.

"Don't have one," I said and offered him a cigarette, our hands cupping together as I lit it for him. It was a clear sky, and the moon, almost perfect, was exceptionally bright.

"Dude. Everybody's got one."

"OK," I said, fairly sure he was smarter than he let on. "Remember, you asked for it. I'm gay and liberal. He's conservative and gloomy. My mother's manic and hysterical. They're ashamed of who I am. My sister avoids it all by marrying someone in another state. It sucks, but I play the dutiful Vietnamese son and come when they call. We're like total strangers. They don't acknowledge my partner. I can go on . . ."

"Whoa, dude!" He dragged on his cigarette and looked at me sideways. I half expected him to go back inside or say something crude. But after a full exhale, he said, "Yup, that's a story. I'm cool with that. I don't care. The gay thing, I mean. I like pussy myself, but you do what you gotta do."

I laughed.

He giggled.

Huan was a lot more charismatic than I had imagined from my parents' reports, more cocky and, when he laughed, very young.

"Your parents are proud of you, though," he said. "They brag to me about your accomplishments. Your dad's cool. I wish I had him for a father. Mine was a prick, always in debt. He'd get drunk and beat my Ma, brother, and me. When I got old enough I kicked his ass out of the house." He paused then and looked up at the sky. "Some dude in Reno stabbed him in the heart." The last bit sounded like an afterthought.

"Sorry to hear that."

"Don't be." He twisted the hot ember out of the cigarette stub and scattered it out in the grass, pocketing the spent butt. "I hate that American phrase. Always apologizing for things they got nothing to do with, never apologizing for things they did." Before I managed a reply to say that it's not they but we, he changed the topic. "*Siu Phu* is cool. He never goes back on his word. Proud old guy. Showed me some good moves today, man. Harmony. Fluidity. All that stuff."

"He showed me some, too," I offered. "But harmony is probably overrated—it works only for some and not others."

"Huh?"

"When I was young, younger than you, he taught me. He was always yelling, cursing me out, how I lacked attention and motivation. When he caught me kissing my best friend, the lessons ended. I was sixteen. We barely talked after. Harmony means holding your tongue, accepting your role, and not speaking up. And I never learned to break any bricks. You can probably kick my ass with one hand tied behind your back."

"You're still in good shape," Huan offered, then endeared himself more to me by adding: "For an old guy."

"Thanks, I think. Since I can't kick ass, I run. But I do who I wanna do."

He laughed. "Yeah, besides, if I kick your ass, you being a lawyer, you'll sue mine." He lit another cigarette and took a long drag. "You guys are so lucky." His voice was different, quieter. "Seriously. All success. I saw the photos and trophies under the altar. And all those awards. We're poor as dirt, dumb as oxen."

"Don't underestimate dirt," I said. "It keeps this garden lush."

"Yeah, right."

We were both quiet for a minute or so, just breathing in the cold air and making clouds of our breath. We had another cigarette.

"Look, David, you're way smarter than me when I was at your age. You could have given the old man two bricks to break, but you didn't. The outcome would be different. And honestly, do you really like my mother's cooking? She's lost her taste buds. She puts too much fish sauce in everything."

He was about to defend himself, but Mother opened the sliding door, scolded us to come in out of the cold, and announced that there was tapioca and banana in coconut milk dessert, before declaring to the neighborhood that we had both been smoking.

"Nasty habit!"

Huan was politely contrite and swore he'd try his best to give it up and, to prove his sincerity, snubbed out his cigarette. Mother seemed satisfied and gave me a dirty look as I continued to smoke mine.

The moment she disappeared back inside, Huan, giggling, asked me for another cigarette. I gave him the pack, and the disposable lighter, too, a reward of sorts. I went in first, to eat Mother's coconut pudding, and to buy him some time to just stare at the moon and the starry sky.

MY MOTHER LOVES to clean. As far back as I can remember, cleanliness for her was, if not godly, then something akin to religious devotion. Memories of servants cutting grass, waxing floors, rinsing fresh vegetables in purple iodine, and boiling water for drinking are still vivid in my mind. So is the sting of the hot washcloth scrubbing against my skin and that painful way she cut my fingernails, always too close to the quick—sometimes drawing blood. Even the two poodles suffered her attentions when they appeared to be mildly morose. Mother, who was trained as a nurse before her parents made her marry Father against her will, seemed to think that vigilance was enough to keep the dirty world in its place.

A childhood memory: I am sitting with Mother in a slow-moving jeep in Saigon. It is night. Under a thatched roof lit with blinking Christmas lights, a girl in a miniskirt is bargaining with an American GI. The deal is struck. The GI, sweaty, drunk, reaches for her. "Don't you dare look!" Mother says as her hand goes up to cover my eyes. "How dirty!" I hear her say and the chauffeur agrees, "Yes, Madame! They are." But through the cracks between her fingers I peek and see the GI's hand going up under the miniskirt.

In America, whenever actors kissed and made love and showed skin on TV, Mother would tell me to change the channel if I was alone, or cover my eyes if she was sitting next to me on the couch. Until I was ten or eleven, I didn't know that I could pull away. Mother sometimes called sex "*la cochonnerie,*" or, in Vietnamese, "playing the game of pigs." Women who betrayed or lied or stole another's husband were "odious" or "stinking, dirty whores," and once, "bloodsucking vampires."

But without servants and with a full-time job, Mother found it impossible to keep our home as clean as she would have liked, and dust gathered, even at the most sacred area, the ancestral altar on top of the bookshelf in the living room, where she prayed and lit incense and talked to the dead each night.

None of which makes for a particularly healthy environment in which to undergo puberty because, in the dark of night, with my hand gripping my insatiable erection and my mind on Johnny Moore's round smooth ass—the way he stood under the shower in the PE room with soapy water running down his crack—I also thought of dirt. Later, I'd be able to identify it as the classic war between humiliating shame and overwhelming desire, but then it was something I didn't understand or dare to name even at that moment of orgasm when we are at our most honest with ourselves, if nobody else.

Unable to put words to my feelings, I stopped talking altogether and, though the old, insular world was gone, did nothing to break away from its parochial powers. There were a few shouting matches, of course—apparently when self-enforced mutes speak they tend to scream—but even then I lacked the courage and the self-knowledge and, therefore, the words to say what I wanted to say.

My America, as far as I could remember, was always compartmentalized. There was my parents' world and there was the rest. In the former, nostalgia ruled. It was defined by the altar that housed the photos of the dead, and the stacks of videotapes of Hong Kong soap opera and martial art films—dubbed into Vietnamese, of course. It was reinforced by the streams of relatives and old friends—many from Father's ruling class—from the San Jose community that has become its own little world of exiles. I accepted its smallness and unchanging values, its old ways. It was to that world my parents retreated in retirement and into which none of their American friends—people with whom they ate lunch and went to the company picnic, people to whom they generously gave birthday and baby shower cards and gifts—were allowed to trespass.

Each time I re-entered that world, I became less than I was, all small-talk and shared nostalgia—a tongue-tied Vietnamese son with limited vocabulary. I played the role the way one drives on an empty highway, with part of the brain shut off.

In my world, I thought of myself as free, but it was a foreign land my parents had no wish to visit.

I TOLD MYSELF it was out of love, out of respect, that I didn't push for William to be included in their world, and except for one occasion when my car broke down at my parents' home and he came by to pick me up, he never formally met them. He sometimes answered the phone when they called for me, but they remained consistently cold if infallibly polite. William, a cool and calm Englishman, a professor of the eighteenth-century novel, shrugged it off with wry humor: "Why, they're just like my parents. Are you sure they're not, by chance, from Hampstead?"

I apologized. He joked. "Mark my words, Ethan, I'll have them wearing pink and giving you away at our wedding."

If it was love at first sight for William, or something close to it, for me, he was my port in a storm, my safe harbor. M had been gone for some years, but in dreams, in reveries, vivid scenes of unspeakable tenderness kept surging from the deep. M was, for a long time, my own lost country, my own Waterloo. My best friend and lover moved far away and got married, had children, while I, in time, withdrew deep within. For way too many years I had felt like an exile and a somnambulist. I hadn't noticed William because I barely noticed anyone, lost in my own abstraction, and in my work.

William is a firm believer in persistence—dinner in Half Moon Bay, brunch at the Ritz, *A Midsummer Night's Dream* at the American Conservatory, a surprise office visit with a bento box and roses—and that it pays off, because when I emerged from what can only be described as a mist, there was this genuine and nice man who was, in his own way, very beautiful.

William, even if I wasn't aware that I was in need of it, decided to rescue me.

"I KNOW, I KNOW, I know you're not gay. Trust me, I know. But, David, if you were to pick one of us, hypothetically, hy-po-thetical-ly, which one of us would you do?"

Sanjay, William's best friend and colleague, is handsome and knows it; he has a tendency to be pushy, particularly when he is more than a little smitten.

"Dude!" David said.

"Yes, dude, if you qualify as one, I mean," William said. "Leave the kid alone or I'll tell your sweet Brahmin mother in Calcutta that you've been buggering seminary boys."

Sanjay ignored him. "Come on, David. I'll stake you a carton of Marlboro for your answer."

"Make it two."

"Fine. Two."

"William."

William blushed. I blushed. Sanjay glared. Silence ensued.

"Marlboro Lights, please."

"Why?" Sanjay asked.

"I'm trying to cut down on nicotine."

"Dumbass!"

"OK! 'Cuz the way he loves and takes care of Ethan."

My heart skipped a beat. I felt William's hand on mine. I leaned over and tongued him. David laughed.

"I'm sooo . . . not happy," sighed Sanjay.

MY SISTER WAS VISITING with her husband and their baby. David dropped by in the middle of dinner, so we made room for him and he went to the kitchen and collected a bowl and chopsticks.

Mother, excited to have her daughter home and to hold her grandchild, was a little drunk on her Chardonnay and began talk-ing. She and Father had been to dinner at Mr. and Mrs. Thu's last week, she said. "Their son, François, is marrying a man in Europe, another Vietnamese man, can you imagine? I knew he was sick, but that was going overboard," she said in Vietnamese. "Can you possibly imagine? Both of them wore *ao dai* dresses! Oh, they said they wept like they were at a funeral and not a wedding.'"

Vietnamese often use the word "sick" to mean "gay." It was a word I rarely heard Mother use in that particular context as the topic rarely came up.

David was eating, but he stopped, chopsticks in mid-air, and in an even tone, with his mouth full, he said, "Gay people are not sick, *Siu Mau*. It's unfair to Ethan."

Mother blanched. I could hear my sister next to me suck in her breath.

"Huh," Father grunted. "Huh! Huh!"

It hadn't occurred to me to protest. The word had always been used without a second thought, and after a while I had learned to tune out.

Not David. David was angry, even if his voice was calm and his demeanor respectful. "*Siu Mau*. If William and Ethan are sick, there are not too many healthy people around either. I hope I am invited to their wedding next year."

Mother sucked in her breath.

I glared at David; there was no wedding planned.

"I agree with David," my sister muttered. "And thank you for saying that. Sick people are people who need medicine. Gay people are just gay people." She turned to me, put her hand on mine. "We never talk about this, but listen, Ethan. Congratulations. I would totally let William borrow my *ao dai* dress, by the way, if you guys decide to tie the knot."

My brother-in-law, a gentle Vietnamese man who never shared his opinion on much of anything, said, "The baby's crying. Excuse me."

"I feel a little sick," I said, aiming for levity.

"Huh! Huh!"

"Fine," Mother said. "I am just an unsophisticated woman. I didn't mean to be . . . Never mind, let's not talk about it."

"Well," David said. "I think . . ."

"Huh!"

"It's fine, David," I said. He risked banishment if he said anything more. "Let's talk about something else. But thank you."

David looked at me and winked. He still had food in his mouth.

DAVID GRADUATED HIGH SCHOOL, which came as a surprise to more than a few of his detractors who didn't know the influence Father had on his life (nor, for that matter, he had on ours), and with high enough grades to attend San Jose City College, something William literally begged him to do and for which we were prepared to pay. But his mind was set, and he joined the army. He believed it was his duty.

In the middle of his second tour, three weeks short of his twenty-first birthday, Specialist David Huan was killed in Basra. From what his younger brother and mother told us and what was reported in the local papers, his Humvee was hit by a roadside bomb. He and two other soldiers were killed. Shrapnel took out part of his jaw and his throat.

Father went into his study and slammed the door. Mother wept, then proceeded to call everyone in the community to raise money for his funeral; David's mother didn't want the military anywhere near her boy.

My sister called and cried. She said she'd name her second baby David, if she had another one and he were a boy. "He was something else," she said. She had only met him twice. "Brave. I mean, fearless. He did things his way, you know."

My mother did something I never thought I would ever see. She set up a little table with David's photo in the middle, made his favorite dishes, then lit incense. She even went over to the Good-for-Yous and, with a bundle of roses, sweet-talked them for a basket of persimmons, which were in season.

William wept in my arms.

The night before the funeral I watched a Jackie Chan movie with Father.

In the middle, all flying kicks and lightning punches, I looked over and saw tears streaming from his eyes, which remained fixed on the TV. I gave him a box of Kleenex. "Huh!" he rasped and went to his study.

Sanjay and William were already at the funeral parlor, sitting at the back, when I brought in my parents. William said hello to Mother. She nodded politely.

Father's old students surrounded him. A few even said, "Hi Mister I-Break-Your-Neck," but if it was meant to be funny, no one laughed. Instead, two young women hugged Father and sobbed as if David had been his son.

There were dozens of older Vietnamese from the community in San Jose, three of them were from the old ARVN airborne division. Despite their bulging stomachs and gray hair, the men wore newly tailored and perfectly detailed uniforms, replete with red berets, and they saluted Father in unison. There were a handful of American vets from Iraq, too, and, not completely unexpected, a few Chinese-Vietnamese gang members, David's old posse.

Too distraught to speak, David's mother, in a white *ao dai* dress and white mourning headband, huddled between a few Vietnamese women and wept. Tom, his younger brother, spoke only briefly before he, too, succumbed to grief and left the lectern. There were a few letters from David's comrades and his commander, all expressing their gratitude for his sacrifice and their admiration of his bravery.

Several young people spoke about David, too, most notably one with a Chinese character *Zhong*—"Loyalty"—tattooed on the nape of his neck, who possessed a poet's eloquence.

"I want to say something about Dave, but I don't have the words. I don't think words can ever tell my sadness, and how much, how very much, I miss Dave. I think of the years—stretching now before me, and Dave not being in them—part of me has died."

Apart from a stifled sniffle, a small cough or two, everyone was silent.

"Every haunt I drive by—the old basketball court, the coffee shop on First and Santa Clara, that playground, even in my uneasy dreams—I can't help but see his shadow everywhere," he said and gathered himself, his hands gripping the sides of the lectern. "I don't know how I feel about this war, but I know this much: I would gladly have shielded him, so that, dying, I could have the comfort of knowing the years ahead would be filled with Dave's laughter."

People wept. William sobbed.

David was awarded the Purple Heart, which now draped the large picture frame that housed his portrait. It had caught him in half smile, eyes sparkling, mischievous, as if trying hard not to laugh. Nothing about the face suggested death. But its vivaciousness stood in stark contrast to the closed casket enshrouded by the American flag behind it.

Father had been asked to give the formal eulogy. He began with the brick story, his warm and dignified voice tinged with a dark Vietnamese accent. He called David "a patriot," referred to him as "like my own son," then observed, "David Huan died a soldier and a warrior." He talked of how David turned his life around and how he had made everyone very proud.

"As a student, David Huan loved to tease, but he was also quick to defend . . ." Father stopped, closed his eyes, his hands went up to his face, his shoulders shook. For a brief moment, I thought he would weep, but he quickly recovered. He went on to talk about how David protected weaker students from bullies and how he pulled himself out of being near the bottom of the class to becoming one of his more exceptional students by the time he graduated.

"David was a shining example of how young people are still idealistic and patriotic, and how Vietnamese in America prove their patriotism," Father said near the end. "We are willing to defend America against the threat of terrorism. Those young people in the audience should consider his fine example and think of what you can do for your country."

That statement echoed in my head until it seeped into my blood and I felt hot and angry. Barely conscious of what I was doing, I rose from my seat. Mother said, "You don't have to. Father already spoke for us." I ignored her.

"I wasn't planning to speak today," I said, catching my breath at the lectern. "But here's what David Huan taught me: To be honest with yourself, and, therefore, true to others. He was thirteen years younger than me, but he was far wiser and braver in so many respects.

"He and I disagreed on the war, sometimes vehemently. I was against it from the start. I marched in protest. But I never doubted David's patriotism. His need to protect and defend America seemed to me a natural extension of his need to protect his family and friends. So I deeply respect that.

"But my Father, his former teacher, who taught him many good things, just now asked young people in the audience today to consider following his footsteps, and I'm sorry, I can't hold my tongue. I am asking young people here to think twice. Does patriotism always mean going to war? I mean, maybe patriotism is not always about absolute obedience and loyalty. Maybe it means to seriously examine what's right and wrong, whether a war is just or not. Some of the most patriotic people I know, some of the bravest souls, speak for peace even at the risk of their jobs, their own safety."

Some older Vietnamese started whispering to each other, and a couple of young people hissed. But I felt energized by their disapproval. "And here's another thing on speaking up. David never hesitated to speak up, often in my defense. So I'm speaking up now." I stopped to breathe. My heart was racing. "I was always taught that if you betray your family, you have no honor. But there's no honor in staying silent when you need to speak up. And there's no honor in waging unjust wars based on lies either."

Someone gasped, and the audience began to talk at once in whispers. I went on.

"Well. I'm gay and I'm anti-war. And David and I may not have seen eye to eye on everything, but I loved him like a brother. And I know he would be proud of me for speaking up, even if to disagree. He taught me that the world is what you make of it. He never let anything or anyone silence his tongue. He taught me that much."

When I was done, I went to William and sat next to him. His eyes were red, but he was grinning. I held his hand. "I love you," he whispered.

"Remind me to come out at the next funeral," quipped Sanjay though he, too, was crying.

There was nothing left to say after my performance, and the little crowd broke up with hugs and handshakes, and gossip—some watched me as I went through the crowd, but none would meet my eyes.

I DROVE MY PARENTS home. Father grunted. Mother sat in the back and sighed, her eyes hidden behind dark glasses.

"You made us lose face . . . " Father began.

"You mean I shamed you by being honest?"

"Honest? Save your radical ideas. Why did you say that you are against the war? And that . . ." He couldn't bring himself to say it.

"That what?"

"Huh, huh . . ."

"Madame Khai was there," Mother said almost to herself in English. "Tomorrow everyone, they know we are hippies!"

I looked into the rearview mirror and snapped. "You are as much a hippy as I am a straight Republican, Mother."

"Huh! Huh!"

Mother started crying. It wasn't clear whether it was because I was rude or because of what Madame Khai, Little Saigon's biggest "*haut-parleur*"—"loud speaker, gossip"—would be saying to her friends. No one spoke for the rest of the ride.

I SHOULD HAVE JUST dropped them off, driven home. I don't know why I stayed. Perhaps I was hoping to have it out with them, to revisit the old battlefields. Perhaps I wanted them to acknowledge that they had at least heard what I had said. Perhaps I wanted them to see me as who I was in the larger world, to understand me, and see my wounds the way I had always seen theirs.

But now, in my parents' living room, CNN a prattle of empty heads and Father outside by the pool practicing his *hyeong* and Mother chopping vegetables for dinner in the kitchen, I lost the will to fight. Instead, guilt plagued me and I felt sorry for changing my parents' status in their small world.

A text message from William asked if I'd be home for dinner, and I replied yes. But I sat and drank more of Father's Chivas Regal and nibbled on dried squid and shrimp chips. Should I apologize? Or should I lecture them on the price of silence? I did neither, and kept on drinking instead.

On CNN, a young Iraqi hugged himself as he wailed, eyes tight shut. It was something about a suicide bomber, twenty-four people killed in a Baghdad market, an unspecified number wounded.

I grabbed the remote and turned it off and went outside for some fresh air. Father was nearing the end of his exercise—arms blocking, knife-edged hand striking, elbow aiming for the face of his invisible opponent—"Arggh! Arggh!"

I hadn't bothered to really look at him for some time. His remaining hair had turned mostly gray. Age spots marked his dark, thin face. And his bony body seemed a minor version of the robust man I knew as a child. Father's movements were restricted, lacking power—they seemed now a parody, or at best, a gingerly effort to relive once more the vigorous past. When did he age so much?

A few more minutes and Father was done. He bowed and came back inside, passing me without a word.

It was near dusk. The sun had gone behind the neighbor's roof and the air was cool and the breeze gentle. I leaned against the house and lit a cigarette. David, wherever he was, must have gotten a kick out of Ethan's coming out at his goodbye party, stealing a bit of his thunder. I laughed.

It was then that I saw it. Out of the corner of my eye, a movement, a flash of . . . something. I turned. A mangy fox stood staring at me, its tongue hanging out. It was neither afraid nor surprised. If anything, it had an expression of (and I surely must have been imagining this) bemusement.

Then it was gone, behind a pile of bricks and through the space under the fence and into the Good-for-Yous' garden.

I'd never sighted a fox in the area before, and by the time I reached the fence it was nowhere to be seen. At my feet, however, were the bricks, some broken, some intact, and yellow daffodils had grown between and around them. It took me a few seconds before I realized the bricks had belonged to David. Father had taught him how to break them—and before he enlisted, David had broken two at a time.

Over the bricks hung a branch of the persimmon tree. With the fallen fruit scattered about, the whole thing looked oddly like a little shrine.

I gathered some of the least damaged fruit and piled it on top of the bricks and, after taking a few drags, wedged my cigarette between them. I sat down cross-legged and watched the smoke waft in the wind. I thought then of the sadness in William's eyes even as he laughed, and David's smirk and Mother's obsessive cleaning and Father's look of betrayal when he saw me and Tristan kissing, betrayal that followed from the disappointment and shock. And Tristan's silent eyes, the last time we made love, before he drove away and out of my life.

I was barely aware of what I was doing. I placed two bricks side by side and a third across the top. In the twilight, the breeze turned colder and the air smelled of petals and cut grass. I did not focus on breaking the brick. I did not take a stance. But before my hand descended I heard wry William admonishing me: "Empathy should only go so far, Ethan. Please, for God's sake, don't drink and drive your hand into bricks." I could see blood drip onto grass. I could hear bones breaking. I resisted the urge to hurt myself and instead covered my face and wept.

Part of me was rushing forward. Part of me needed to laugh at my own stupidity. I could break all my bones and there would be no full concord between my father and me. But when I opened my mouth, perhaps to respond to William's imagined admonishment, I retched instead. And amid mother's rose bushes, I began to throw up bits and pieces of my inheritance.

Step Up and Whistle

H OW MY UNCLE ended up almost exactly where he was three decades ago, repeating the same gestures that turned his life upside down, would be too bizarre to imagine, let alone make up. But since "The Staircase Incident" was written up in the local papers, and he was called "mentally disturbed" on the evening news, it demands explanation.

First, given his profound losses, Uncle Bay is far from being "disturbed" and is one of the most caring human beings I know. Since he is a devout Buddhist and a vegetarian who volunteers weekends to teach kids math and Vietnamese at the Vinh-Nghiem Buddhist temple in San Jose, the idea that he assaulted someone is absolutely absurd. The security guard fell off the stairs. The guard was not pushed. We have witnesses who can testify on Uncle Bay's behalf.

Second, my wife, our daughter, and I were with him when the whole thing happened. As a matter of fact, we were witnesses *and* participants, especially my daughter, who, if you come down to it, was his accomplice, if not the instigator of the whole thing. It was Kim-Ninh who skipped up and down those stairs and cussed like a sailor, which caused Uncle Bay to immediately give chase. She was the main reason he'd come up to visit every six months or so, to see his "precious," as he would often say. And going back a little bit, it was Dianne's idea to visit the museum. She thought it would be good to show Kim-Ninh what Vietnamese went through during the war. And, without a second thought, I said, "OK, honey, why not?"

Uncle Bay didn't know what to expect, but why should he? He was visiting us from San Jose, California. He visits because it's us he loves, not the Midwest weather.

Third—and this is very, *very* important—Uncle Bay has Tourette's Syndrome. I informed the police that he had TS when they arrested him, and, for that matter, so does my daughter, Kim-Ninh. That's something the newspaper didn't bother to mention, and neither did the anchorwoman on Channel Five. If his case goes to trial, and I sincerely hope it doesn't, people need to be informed about TS. It'd help make a whole lot of sense of why he and my daughter were seemingly acting out of the norm.

Here's a definition of TS from a medical journal:

> An inherited neurological disorder with onset in childhood, characterized by the presence of multiple physical (motor) tics and at least one vocal (phonic) tic; these tics characteristically wax and wane. Tourette's was once considered a rare and bizarre syndrome, most often associated with the exclamation of obscene words or socially inappropriate and derogatory remarks (coprolalia). Tourette's is defined as part of a spectrum of tic disorders, which includes transient and chronic tics.

Of my mother's many siblings, he was loved the most by her. He lived with us and helped us out in America until my little brother went to college. Since our father was long dead—killed near the end of the war in the DMZ—Uncle Bay helped my mother raise us in America. She, who regularly yelled and screamed at her two boys, would automatically soften her tone when addressing her Bay.

Yet even among folks with TS, Uncle Bay's symptoms are considered a rarity. He indeed has a phonic tic, and it's quite a talent. He doesn't cuss, and there's none of those repetitive movements like hand gestures or frequent jerks of the head to one side. Nor does he utter weird phrases or derogatory remarks. No, he whistles. His lips, when pursed, become a bona fide musical instrument. With a few bars of his clear, pitch-perfect notes, you can easily "name that tune."

But here's the thing: he whistles *all* the time and especially when it's inappropriate, and it's almost always something jarring and ironic. A series of loud wolf whistles, say, when someone's kissing a baby at the park, or "Take Me Out to the Ball Game" when two men are having a row on the street. Heads turned in church at his rendition of "La Vie en Rose" as a wailing widow fell on her husband's coffin. Uncle Bay is prone to making an awkward or stressful situation disastrous. Which explains his general nervous disposition. I mean, who wouldn't live in trepidation if his lips possessed an uncontrollable, wicked humor of their own?

Yet as disconcerting as his spontaneous whistling can be, it wasn't the cause of his troubles. What ruined his life was that accursed motor tic. Since it's not so frequent, it manages to surprise, or even shock, when it rears its ugly head.

Simply put, my uncle is vulnerable to language. To be precise: he is susceptible to a few action commands—*kick, slap,* and, alas, *let go* being the worst.

If he were carrying Mother's favorite vase, say, and weren't on guard, and you really wanted to screw him over, you could say with authority in your voice, "*Tha!*" or "*Tha ra!*" which in Vietnamese means "Let go!" and the vase would drop, guaranteed. In the aftermath, Uncle Bay would look down in horror and shame at the broken mess at his feet while whistling a refrain from "La Marseillaise."

And you? After you giggled in triumph for having power over a doofus and a loser of an adult, fear and guilt would start bubbling within. You'd also feel like a major asshole as you watched a grown man cry. Then you'd get scared—no, *horrified* is more like it. "*Tha!*" or "*Tha ra!*" was the command that destroyed his life, and you would not believe that you used it, and you'd stop being mad at him for acting like such a weirdo.

Watching him kneeling on the floor to gather the shards of what was once a tableau of Chinese gods and spirits lounging on the clouds would be like being splashed with hot water, then cold—hot for shame and cold for fear. Eventually you'd realize the enormity of your action, what it meant: that your mother would tan your hide when she got home and you were done for.

WHEN I WAS YOUNGER, I couldn't tell whether I hated him or his disease. To be honest, I didn't make that distinction until a few years ago, when I joined a support group. That was when Kim-Ninh began showing *her* symptoms and I, plagued by nightmares and suicidal thoughts, had to deal with it head-on.

All I knew back then was that I hated feeling ashamed of him when we were in public. When he kicked awkwardly at an invisible ghost simply because someone said, "Kick!" I would close my eyes and drop my head and pretend we weren't related. Once, on a bus, he spat repeatedly simply because a mother nearby commanded her little boy to spit out a cherry pit, and everyone laughed. And me? I got up and sat far away from him as he whistled. I remember wanting to hit my own uncle because some of the passengers were watching me to see if I would also do something bizarre.

Yet Uncle Bay has always been nothing but kind. He might get mad at you for yelling "*Tha!*" but he would recover quickly. He'd rarely stay angry. He would just ask in a somber voice, "Son, why did you do that?"

But what answer could I offer that would make sense? That if most of me was horrified at what I'd done, a small thrill washed over me? That there was satisfaction in knowing I was nothing like him, even if my mother kept saying I looked just like him? That, despite my horrid reaction, I could do something as nasty as bully my own uncle? That secretly I reveled in possessing magic words that could make a grown man jump?

So I'd start to cry, and he'd just shake his head in disappointment. Then he'd say, "Son, you don't have to answer, but you need to think about why you did what you just did, all right?" He would walk away, muttering to himself, "Bad karma! Bad karma!"

By the way, that's his favorite phrase, handed down from my grandmother, who, near the end of her life, lived as a nun in a temple on the outskirts of Saigon. But bad karma or not, he'd take full responsibility for the vase. Which made it worse for me. I mumbled my apologies, of course, when I mustered up the courage. He patted me on the head. Then I spent several nights crying into my pillow so I wouldn't wake my little brother.

Since no one kicked my ass, I guess I kicked it myself. It didn't happen right away, but my sophomore year, I started cutting class. I started smoking weed. I ran with a new posse whose ringleader was popular Al Paterson, a jock and something of a class clown.

Then one morning my uncle drove me to school because I was late for the bus. We were in a rush, and I left my lunch in his car. But instead of driving away, my uncle went looking for me, calling out my name in the hallways, yelling out in Vietnamese that I'd forgotten my rice and fish.

I don't know why, but my native tongue sounded so loud and ugly and visceral in the school setting. And worse, to have him chase after me was mortifying, especially when I was saying hello to Paterson, who was standing there by my locker with Frank and Mike, his sidekicks.

Anger rushed to my face. I snatched the bag from my uncle, and as the guys were watching me, I said, "Hey guys, wanna see something funny?"

"Sure," Paterson said.

I turned and yelled, "*Sua! Sua!*"—"Bark! Bark!"—and my uncle, who had already walked away, stopped, and as if shocked by electricity, let out a few quick, helpless yelps. "*Whau! Whau! Whau!*" he said, followed by a very human whimper. It lasted all of two seconds. But it was enough. Al Paterson's eyes widened, and the class clown roared with laughter, along with his two buddies.

I stood petrified. What possessed me to do it? I didn't know. Uncle turned and looked at me. What did I see: hatred? anger? humiliation? Or was it a man trying very hard to overcome anger and disappointment? Or was it pity that I saw in those eyes? I felt as if it were me, and not him, who was afflicted.

Uncle studied me, and I stood trembling and shocked at my own behavior. I couldn't look into his eyes, and I fully expected him to walk back and slap me. I wanted him to slap me. But he didn't do anything, and he didn't say anything. Yet I heard it all the same: *Bad karma! Bad karma!*

My uncle disappeared around the corner. But his whistling of Elvis's "Love Me Tender" echoed through the corridors, sounding so sweet and sad that it even sobered up Paterson. "Your dad's a freak," he said when he recovered. "Tell him to go fetch next time."

We parted ways after that, Paterson and I, by which I mean I decked him. I got a black eye, a bloody nose, three bruised ribs, and a two-day suspension in the process. I also got a reputation for being unhinged and having a crazy dad. Inside, though, I was grateful. At least my ass was kicked finally.

Yet it was just a week or so after that, seeing I was late for school, Uncle again offered to give me a ride. I could tell it took him some effort to offer, and I mumbled something unintelligible and fled. That was the day I ran weeping all the way to school, hating myself, horrified at myself, and terrified of his capacity for forgiveness and love.

I never rode with Uncle Bay again after that incident, at least not to school. But I washed his car without being asked. I did the laundry without being asked. I even polished his shoes unprompted. I got up very early in the morning to join track and field. And each night, I studied hard. I mean really hard. I kept seeing my uncle in that corridor of the school, looking at me with those eyes, and that image spurred me on to be extra nice to my little brother, to my mother, to be as kind and forgiving as he was. On many weekends, I even went to the temple with Uncle and Mother to meditate and pray.

My family might have been curious about the transformation, but no one ever asked what happened. Everyone was happy. By the time I graduated from high school, I was salutatorian and had merit badges, medals for swimming and track and field, and scholarships. And guess who spent a little fortune taking the family and friends to dinner to celebrate my being accepted to engineering school at both Yale and MIT?

BEFORE HE WAS BARRY he was *Bay*, which means "Seven." It is not his name but his ranking in the family. Sixth of eleven siblings—two died in the war, two as babies, and one in the war's aftermath. That made him seventh instead of sixth because Vietnamese never refer to the first-born child as "One." Something to do with fears that jealous spirits and angry gods will steal the firstborns. And in a household with so many kids, numbers are far easier to remember than names.

Back in Vietnam, folks called his affliction lieu. *"Bay no bi lieu"*—"Seven, he's got that tic"—that was what Grandma used to say to visitors. Their jaws would drop when, for example, they saw Uncle Bay smack himself in response to hearing, "Tat," which meant "Slap," or yell when hearing *"La!"*

And here's a classic story my mother was fond of telling. Once as a teenager in Saigon, Uncle watched a soccer match on TV with his siblings and my father, who had come courting my mother. Someone yelled *"Da! Da!"* meaning "Kick! Kick!" Next thing you know, the coffee table is lying on its side, all the beer bottles and shrimp chips and dried squid are scattered on the tile floor, and the TV screen is splattered with dipping sauce. "He sure made an impression on your dad," Mother said, laughing. "He tried to apologize but, with all eyes on him, ended up whistling birdcalls instead." But guess why she married my father? "Your father helped clean up and never once worried if it was something that ran in the family. Never once asked. He just accepted it. He was kind to your uncle."

After a serious flu that nearly killed him when he was seven, TS plagued my uncle's life. The Cold War had just begun, pitting the U.S. against China and the Soviet Union. Unfortunately, Vietnam was divided in two and became the superpowers' chessboard. Grandma thought that since so many people were killed, jealous spirits had possessed my uncle. She thought the symptoms were caused by "the unfinished business of the dead." Why else would her most handsome and pious child act in bizarre and outrageous ways? The family invited a shaman, who drank rice wine and spritzed it all on Uncle's face, then mumbled spells and gestured fiercely with an ancient sword. But if there was a malicious spirit in Uncle Bay, it may have enjoyed the sacred sword dance and alcohol too much to leave. Grandma tried expelling the spirit a few more times, then bit the bullet and sent Uncle to the best hospital in Saigon, but the French-educated doctor didn't diagnose him correctly. The medicine Uncle received only made him listless and depressed. He was still responding to command words and whistling romantic tunes.

He tried to make friends after that, but despite having good looks and being an honor student, he was shunned. A few bullies would yell their commands and laugh when he acted on them, kicking the air or meowing like a cat. He became a loner. Except for a handful of friends in high school, he kept to himself. One of them was a girl who was always kind and protective of him. Naturally, they fell in love, and because TS saved him from being drafted, they married two years after graduation.

"The year Bay got married and the following year when little Thao was born were his two best years," my mother always said. "Bay, he barely had any symptoms then: you could tell him to jump or kick or drop, and he just smiled at you." Bay, Aunty, and the newly born daughter were a beautiful family. Love cured his problems. "Those precious few years," Mother said with a sigh, "he glowed."

But as in Vietnamese fairy tales, happiness occurs in the middle and sadness at the end. Those years when Uncle glowed with happiness didn't last.

MOST FOLKS OLD ENOUGH to remember the war will recall those famous photos of helicopters flying out of Saigon on the war's last day; Communist tanks rolling in, crashing through the iron gates of the presidential palace; and refugees on a big ship with helicopters landing, depositing more people, and then being pushed into the sea after the pilots bailed out. These photos, in time, came to symbolize America's shameful misadventures in Southeast Asia.

But of all of them, arguably the most famous was the photograph of a helicopter perching precariously on a small landing pad atop a building as Vietnamese climbed up to it and tried to get inside.

Well, I was there, was one of those on the stairs waiting to get rescued. And so were my mother and little brother. And so were Uncle Bay and his wife and baby. Of all my memories of Vietnam, that day remains by far the most vivid. It was the end of my Vietnamese childhood and the beginning of my American one. But for Uncle Bay, it was the end of his marriage and fatherhood and the beginning of his profound tragedy.

These stairs—they're just your ordinary industrial metal stairs found on top of many apartment buildings, with rusty railings and thin, perforated steps. Still, they are famous. Why? Because people jostled on these stairs to get to the helicopter that was perching on top of the elevator shaft of a building that was misidentified by the media as the U.S. embassy—and later correctly identified as the residence of CIA operatives and their families—and became immortalized in a photograph.

A curator had located and acquired the stairs, shipped them to the States, and installed them at the Gerald Ford Presidential Museum and Library. It all came back in a flash when I saw the stairs once more. People crowding around. Helicopters hovering overhead. People jostling for better space, cursing, crying. A woman praying to Buddha loudly. Black smoke veiling part of the sky. The *rat-tat-tat-rat-tat-tat* of M-16s going off nearby.

Under a scorching sun and around the stairs we waited. A few grenades exploded on the streets, and a baby shrieked. Outside the compound, more people were screaming, swarming at the locked metal gates, jostling to get in. Then someone said, "No more helicopters. It's the end!" which created hysteria. Uncle Bay held his wife's hand tightly while she hugged her baby with her other hand. My mother, my little brother, and I were ahead of him by a few people. We held on to each other, waiting for a helicopter that we hoped would come.

Then, there they were: two specks in the sky, making *chop-chop-chop* sounds. People waved and screamed in English: "Americans, we are friends!" "Help us!" "SOS!" And the first landed. What followed was a blur—who got in, who didn't. People who got in refused to let go of their loved ones who didn't, unless it was beyond their control. The copter took off without us, but we moved up the stairs slowly, and then the second copter landed.

My mom held my hand in such a death grip that I cried out in pain, not that it mattered since she wouldn't have let go in any case, and no one could have heard me in that chaos. My baby brother was tied to her back. There was no way we could separate. "Live and die together!" was how she described it later, when we got to America.

It was the same for Uncle Bay. He would die before he'd let go. But here's the thing: he got in and was pulling Aunty in with him, when a woman next to him yelled in a desperate, high-pitched voice, "*Tha! Tha ra!*"—"Let go!" Perhaps a stranger was grabbing her leg, hoping to get pulled along. We will never know what happened. But the person who obeyed that directive was, unfortunately, my uncle.

This is what I saw next: Aunty Bay falling backward into the shuffling crowd, her eyes looking at her husband, astonished. She and the baby weren't harmed as far as we could tell, but it was too late. We had already lifted high in the air. Uncle screamed and lurched forward, but people held on to his waist and shoulders and arms, and after the struggle, someone slid the door shut with a loud thud.

I remember looking down one last time through the glass window. I could see my aunt, crying and looking up and screaming, raising one arm toward us, waving. *Come back! Come back, Bay! Come back!*

I don't remember looking at my uncle's face. I couldn't bear to. His whistling, which had become nonstop, sent ice down my veins: "End of a Romance" by Trinh Cong Son. It was no longer a Tourette's tic but the soul itself trilling in despair. The whistling accompanied us as we flew away, out to sea.

On the ship, crowded with people, two more helicopters landed to deposit a dozen or so evacuees from elsewhere before we set sail.

But Aunty and baby were not among them. Uncle went mad. He beat his head against the rail until he bled and had to be restrained. In the refugee camps, in the subsequent years in America, even when reports from Vietnam were few and far between, he searched for her.

Two years after getting to America, after sending telexes and letters to our relatives back home, after trying and failing to make phone calls via France and Canada to Vietnam, Uncle received news from Aunty. It turned out that with Saigon in chaos and property confiscated and many people driven out of the city, Aunty had gone back with the baby to her hometown in the Mekong Delta.

They were alive! His wife and daughter were OK! He exchanged photos with them. He sent money and gifts. He worked hard. He promised to bring them over as soon as possible. He prayed to Buddha nightly, burning incense and offering fruit. He did all he could. His whistles were mostly happy, upbeat ditties.

But Uncle's happiness was again short-lived. In our fifth year in America, a flimsy letter came from Aunty that shattered his hope of reunion. Aunty couldn't wait. Rather, life was tough under the new regime, really tough. And despite Uncle Bay's support, she was pressured by her parents to marry a local Communist official who had been, over the years, kind and protective toward her family. Without him, their farmland would have been confiscated and her younger brother sent to fight a war in Cambodia. She had no other option. As much as she wanted to come to Beautiful Country, which is what Vietnamese called the United States of America, Aunty was already pregnant with another child and joining Uncle was no longer in the cards.

To say he was heartbroken is to call a leg amputation a superficial wound. He continued to send money home to his daughter, who became his *raison d'être*. He sent gifts and even videotapes of our family on Christmas and Thanksgiving so she could pretend that we were altogether. All that time, he helped my mother raise us two boys. The year my little brother, Binh, was born, my father, a soldier for the South Vietnamese army, was killed in the DMZ. I have very few memories of him.

Barry Le dated, but given his condition, the dates never lasted long. Those years that followed Aunty's "Dear Bay" letter, dishes and vases fell at regular intervals, windows got broken, and even a TV command from Tom Selleck in Magnum, P.I. could send a glass of water out of Uncle's hand. For by then, a few English commands began to burrow into his subconscious to share the space with certain Vietnamese words. It got so bad that he had to wear headphones or earmuffs when he was around crowds, and he avoided big gatherings like the plague. He loved sports—football and basketball and, above all, soccer—but restricted himself to watching them alone in his room.

The news of Grandma's death, followed by the disappearance of his next oldest sister, Aunty Nam, and her family, whose boat sank somewhere in the South China Sea near the Philippines, didn't help. Gone—an entire family of six, somewhere at the bottom of the sea.

Run! Kick! Spit! Spill!—these monosyllabic command words tended to reach him more easily. Uncle was a pariah, isolated by language. It got so bad that he avoided movies, parties, and even the park. On the weekends, he feared running into people with a penchant for disciplining their dogs.

How many jobs did he lose over the last three decades? Fifteen? Maybe more. Now that he works in a flower shop while wearing mufflers, he seems to have regained some control, and it's the longest he's ever held a job. Ten years back, he almost lost an arm when he worked in an assembly plant. The foreman yelled "Hold!" to someone else, and Uncle held out his arm to a passing forklift.

MAN ARRESTED at GERALD FORD PRESIDENTIAL LIBRARY AND MUSEUM

GRAND RAPIDS, MI—A 54-year-old San Jose, Calif., man named Barry Le was arrested after he allegedly accosted a security guard who ordered him off a set of stairs, which was part of a Vietnam War exhibit at the Gerald R. Ford Presidential Library and Museum, police spokesman Carl Olmstead said. According to museum officials, Le, a Vietnamese immigrant, climbed up the stairs and took his six-year-old grandniece with him. When ordered to step down, he refused.

John Spindler, 43, a museum security guard, climbed up after them. Instead of stepping down, said Spindler, Le "acted really bizarre and crazy" and pushed him down the steps. Spindler injured his back and required hospitalization. Police were called in, and Le was arrested without incident. A few witnesses at the museum said that Le did not push Spindler but did whistle during the struggle and afterward.

Accompanying Le were his relatives, Randy Tran and Dianne Stewart Tran, the parents of the six-year-old girl. They posted bail for Le, who was cited for disorderly conduct, vandalism, and accosting a security guard. He was given a court date.

Now that we have established who Barry Le is, his alleged crime, and his afflictions, let me say that the reporter got it all wrong. What happened was quite the opposite. My daughter, ruled by her compulsion with steps, was the one who climbed the stairs first. My uncle simply followed. Mr. Spindler was never pushed. He was *grabbed*. And *pulled*.

Here's what Mr. Spindler said: "Sir, I need you to step down!" And when my uncle didn't respond, he yelled, "Step down! Now!" Upon hearing it the second time, my uncle went one step higher, reacting to the command Step and not the secondary word, *down*. It was then that Mr. Spindler grabbed Uncle's hand, and Uncle gripped his and held on.

Sure, it freaked out Mr. Spindler. That grip, no doubt, was a vise. Mr. Spindler, who was overweight—rotund, actually, an odd yet common physique for museum security work, if I may add— yelled and yanked his hand out of my uncle's grip, tripping and falling backward, down the steps. That jolted Uncle Bay out of his trance. Uncle did not resist arrest, and as reported in police records, he tended Mr. Spindler until police arrived and was "arrested without incident."

But why did he hold on to Mr. Spindler's hand so hard? Why was he holding on to Kim-Nihn's? And why did she run up a staircase on the exhibit?

The short answer is TS, of course. Kim-Ninh's TS symptom is an odd one: whenever she sees stairs, she needs to jump on or run up and down them. And her vocal tic is classic: cussing. When combined, they can be discombobulating and humiliating. She cries after. I often cry along. This is well documented; my wife has videos of some of these incidents. Worse, Kim-Ninh cusses some of the most horrid words in the English language and often in the sweetest, most angelic voice. As to why my uncle held on to both her hand and Mr. Spindler's, the short answer is that he didn't want to leave anyone behind this time around.

Put yourself in Barry Le's shoes. If you suddenly had to flee Kansas or Alabama—or if the helicopter came to rescue you from your rooftop in flooded New Orleans after Katrina hit and you let go of your pregnant wife's hand for whatever reason—TS or lack of strength or slippery hands—how would you feel? Looking down at her on a rooftop in a devastated neighborhood as she cried out for you, and you rode away in a helicopter—would you survive that memory and the guilt, the self-hatred that followed? And given all that, if decades later, you suddenly found yourself on the old staircase where the tragedy had taken place, what would you do?

My uncle was understandably in shock. Who would have expected a scene from an old tragedy replaying itself on a new continent, and in a presidential *museum*? It is reasonable, then, given his state of mind and his afflictions, that, reliving that tragedy, he would hold on. No, he wouldn't want to let go the second time around. For it wasn't Mr. Spindler's hand that he was holding, but his young wife's. And it wasn't my daughter he held on to so dearly, but his own.

I KNOW YOU want to ask, What the heck was *I* doing? I mean what kind of father was I who didn't react to something as dramatic as his child running up a museum's exhibit singing, "Fuck! Fuck! Cunt! Cunt!" as if it were some nursery rhyme?

When my wife and I heard my daughter cuss, we turned. But Uncle was nearest Kim-Ninh, and though he hesitated for a second, he climbed up the stairs after her. He grabbed her hand, then he paused. And instead of bringing her back down, something took hold of him, and he, in a trance, went up a few more steps, taking her along. The two of them, Uncle and grandniece, stood there, holding hands—the young one cussing like an old sailor, and the old one whistling like a swallow.

When they recovered, they looked at each other and giggled, as if caught doing something naughty. But they didn't come down. They stayed and became quiet as they stared at that empty shell of a helicopter hovering at the end of the stairs. For a moment before Mr. Spindler showed up, they were so still that it seemed as if they were part of the exhibit.

And in that moment, two things occurred to me. The first was the magic word, but I didn't dare say it. The second was that, in remembering it, my whole being shook as a strange desire took hold. It may sound unreasonable and absurd, but I wanted for my uncle to succeed this time around. And I wanted him to take my daughter to that "beautiful country," where children wouldn't make fun of her and people wouldn't laugh at his antics, and they would be unburdened by TS. So powerful was this desire that it blurred my eyes and weakened my knees, and, as Dianne tried to move toward them, it took all my strength to hold on to her. My wife struggled before giving up and looked at me quizzically, but what could I possibly tell her? She trusted my judgment, but she clearly didn't understand my thinking. What could I say, though: that I felt my uncle and daughter belonged up there on those old stairs, waiting for deliverance?

Up there, lit by the museum floodlight, they struck me as unearthly, and for a moment I thought I saw shadows darting about and streaming past them, and I recalled the unfinished business of the dead and the sadness that we, the living, must endure. I heard my uncle whistle Trinh Cong Son's "End of a Romance" again, and it pierced me. I hugged Dianne and wept.

FOR MANY YEARS now, I have gotten up at four o'clock every day, and five out of seven days a week, I make myself run. No matter how I feel, I run. In the snow, in the rain, in sheer darkness, with a head cold, a mild fever, a bothered back, a hangover, a swollen knee, a sore ankle, I run. It's clockwork. I have been running since my uncle barked like a dog in my school hallway, and I ran farther and harder, training for half and full marathons year round, when my daughter was born. I couldn't imagine not running.

In a period of a month, after my daughter's TS showed, my hair turned prematurely gray. There it is, the wheels of karma spinning, I would tell myself in the mirror each morning. You can run like clockwork, but you can't outrun karma. Yet I didn't stop. As if chased by ghosts, I ran harder.

The day we came back from the hospital with the doctor's diagnosis, I held her till she stopped crying and went to sleep. A few hours later, I got up and ran. Running, I can bear it, my guilt, my sadness, my child splitting in two: one kind and sweet and wise, and the other owned by her vocal tics and compulsions, sad, embarrassed, and angry. If they can't control their bodies, their curses, their strange tics, perhaps I, on their behalf, can control mine. It's illogical, but there it is. I would try to be a sturdy, reliable pillar for my loved ones.

Lining two walls in my garage are three long shelves, and on them sit a handful of marathon medals and trophies and, of course, my worn-out running shoes, maybe five or six dozen pairs, maybe more. They stink up the place, worn to the soles and frayed, but I can't throw them out. They are testaments to my resolve.

One night last year, as we were waiting to go to the airport to pick up Uncle Bay, who was again visiting his "precious," I watched football by myself, and my daughter suddenly climbed up on my lap and hugged me. "It's OK, Daddy," she whispered, almost embarrassed by what she was about to say. "Uncle Bay's got it. And he's amazing. So I'll be OK. I'll be amazing, too. OK?" I never told anyone this, but my daughter more or less saved my life. "OK," I said. After that, whenever I have the compulsion to throw myself in front of a passing bus on some of my runs, I think of her consoling me, and I keep on running.

To tell the truth, I haven't been OK for a long, long time. Yet at the moment Kim-Ninh and Uncle stood on the rusted stairs, holding hands and giggling, I, too, became gigglish. I was OK because they were more than OK up there; somehow, they were, as my daughter had promised, "amazing." Silently, I rooted for my daughter and uncle. I wanted to yell out, to cheer them on in the Ford Museum (but Dianne would have killed me!). And before Mr. Spindler showed up and literally brought everyone back down to earth, I, possessor of magic words, finally spoke that powerful command. But I didn't yell it out to my beloved uncle this time. No, I whispered it to myself. "*Tha! Tha ra!*" And, just as he did many years ago, I, too, let go.

Biographical Note

Andrew Lam is the author of *Perfume Dreams: Reflections on the Vietnamese Diaspora*, which won the 2006 PEN Open Book Award, and *East Eats West: Writing in Two Hemispheres*. Lam is an editor and cofounder of New American Media, an association of over two thousand ethnic media outlets in America. He was a regular commentator on NPR's *All Things Considered* for many years, and was the subject of a 2004 PBS documentary called "My Journey Home". His essays have appeared in newspapers and magazines such as the *New York Times*, *The LA Times*, *San Francisco Chronicle*, *The Baltimore Sun*, *The Atlanta Journal*, the *Chicago Tribune*, *Mother Jones*, and *The Nation*, among many others. His short stories have been widely taught and anthologized. *Birds of Paradise Lost* is his first story collection. He lives in San Francisco.

CPSIA information can be obtained
at www.ICGtesting.com
Printed in the USA
JSHW012058080920
7737JS00001B/94

9 781597 092685